Kalahari Passage

Also by Candi Miller

Salt and Honey

KALAHARI PASSAGE

Candi Miller

**Tindal
Street
Press**

First published in UK September 2011
by Tindal Street Press Ltd
217 The Custard Factory, Gibb Street,
Birmingham, B9 4AA
www.tindalstreet.co.uk

A CIP catalogue reference for this book is available
from the British Library

ISBN: 978 1 906994 23 5

Typeset by Tetragon
Printed and bound by
CPI Group (UK) Ltd, Croydon, CR0 4YY

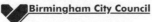
Birmingham City Council

*This book is dedicated
to the people of the Kalahari*

www.kalaharipeoples.net

I

The train had left the city at dusk. Three days and two nights across the subcontinent, through empty stretches of veld, past remote farms, on and on between dune and desert, carriages clicking along like a row of bright beads.

Now it sputtered towards the terminus, Onderwater, fragrant with orange blossom, last oasis before the Kalahari Desert.

Heavy-breathing, this train. Will it stop?

Koba longed to get away from the press of people, from the miasma of stale breath and unwashed bodies, from the rasp of the blue serge sleeve rucked up against her. She glanced down at her wrist, manacled to the policeman's broad, black one. The metal had rubbed a raw patch in her skin. She stole a look at his proud Zulu profile. Frightening, but not as frightening as what lay out there.

When he unlocks me . . . what . . . where must I go?

She felt again the frustration of all her dealings with authority. Always-always the same, even when they get a blue baboon like this to do their dirty for them, she thought. This policeman didn't care that his kind had left her parents' murders unpunished, had allowed her to be abducted, had raped her. She felt the burn of tears and refused to let them fall. She blinked at the filthy window.

Stained by the desert's red breath.

When she turned back, the policeman's fist was coming towards her. She ducked . . . but instead of a blow, a gentle dab on her face.

She started as he blotted her tear with a white handkerchief. He was saying something. She closed her eyes. She needed to think.

He excuses himself for leaning across me. He wipes the window with that white-white cloth a woman ironed for him . . . so *I* can see out. Maybe he's *not* a tame baboon for the Boere? But he does have South African Police badged over his heart.

She visualized the silver SAP insignia sitting like a chip on his shoulder, too. She sighed; she understood survival. She opened her eyes, but couldn't meet his questioning look. She turned back to the window. Through the cleared porthole she saw heat shimmer off the tin roof of the station building; flowers she now knew were called zinnias wilted in a bed under the signpost. 'Underwater,' she translated for herself. She decided to repay her guard's unexpected kindness.

'The water must be far under,' she observed, straight-faced, in Afrikaans.

'Ja,' the Zulu replied in the same language, 'but for-suh the Boer has taken the sweetest parts for himself.'

They shared a bitter-orange smile.

A shame I never knew his heart while our shoulders pressed, she thought.

It was unlikely they would have spoken. Even in her carefree days when she sat with the Marais family around their dining-room table and felt their love settle like a soft skin mantle across her shoulders; even then, she hadn't chattered. Chat was for the carefree and Koba had seldom been that.

The train stopped. She saw a station bench – on it, in wavering letters, a sign: WHITES ONLY. She and her guard remained seated while around them passengers of every shade of black and brown, except her own, scrambled to retrieve their baggage or gather their children and chickens. Women hitched their toddlers onto their hips or bound them to their backs with colourful wraps. They instructed their older charges to bring the bounty: shopping bags stuffed with starch, tea, coffee, tins of condensed milk; Rose skin lightening cream; Nivea body lotion; cobs of corn; mangoes, pineapples, avocados; cuts of meat beginning to pong after days in the heat.

The prepubescent girls lifted the bags onto their braided heads with practised ease, leaving a hand free to lead younger siblings. Boys swung squawking chickens in home-made cages. One grappled with a goose, trying to bind its beak as it attacked him.

Koba didn't notice. She was far, far away, remembering the quiet of Impalala with its frangipani trees and cool, clear tap water, remembering Mannie, friend of her youth, love of her life.

She wasn't sure how old she'd been when she first arrived at Impalala, the bushveld farm in South Africa. Ten, perhaps twelve? Her race were small, slim-limbed people to whom puberty came late. Survival was not counted in years, but in seasons of feast or famine; a child's fate was linked to the prevailing climatic conditions at the time of its birth. Koba felt she must have been that most unlucky of children – one born in a harrowing drought. She had no one to confirm this; her close family were long dead and she'd spent her childhood thousands of miles from her Kalahari Desert home. She'd grown fond of the white family who'd abducted her.

I did not want them, but they took root in my heart. And now the government wants to reverse me, send me back to my birth n!ore like I am still that Jul'hoan child who knows nothing of |Ton ways. Now I must go back to squat in the sand with my people; I must get my water from roots and my meat with a bow and arrow. But I am toothpaste now; I have been squeezed out.

The policeman's cuff brushed against her as he undid the handcuff. She couldn't help flinching. She became aware that people were staring, the bolder among them calling out, asking the constable what she had done.

'I am not permitted to talk about a prisoner,' he said, arms akimbo to block her from public view.

Koba heard speculation build among the waiting crowd.

'Passbook offence?'

'No, brother, you don't get your own police escort for that.'

'Political? Is she the one who shoot Verwoerd?'

'Huw, if she is, we should sing praise poems to her.' The group laughed.

9

'It say *here*,' a man with glasses spoke, holding his newspaper conspicuously high. 'It say in this *English* newspaper that Verwoerd was shot with a gun, not a bow and arrow.' His illiterate neighbours seemed to wither under his magnified glare. Except for one matron.

'Eish,' she countered, balancing a sack of flour on her head, 'better Verwoerd had suffered Masarwa poison; it brings a slow, painful death.' She patted the sack into place, raising a cloud of flour dust that immediately settled white on the black faces around her. 'A long death gives a man time to think about his evil.'

'You speak of apartheid, Mma?'

'Yebo.'

'You speak the truth. Let me read you from this *English* newspaper . . .' He rapped the pages with his knuckles, but his glasses were filmed with flour dust and he had to pause and wipe them. A younger man draped in a boldly patterned Basuto blanket stepped forward.

'What, uncle, is a Masarwa?'

'Must be you are not from here, nephew; you do not know our animals,' said Glasses. 'The whites call them Bushmen.'

'Eish, beware of those,' said the matron, jerking her thumb in Koba's direction. 'They look like children but they steal cattle like tsotsis steal pay packets.'

Basuto Blanket looked alarmed; he'd never had a pay packet, but he had been a cattle herder in the Drakensberg mountains.

Koba bit her tongue to stop from shouting out: 'You-people stole from my ancestors; stole our great meat animals, our freedom to follow the herds. You, Blindman, for all your four eyes, for all your reading in English, have surely not read how Khoisan people suffered from your coming. Even now, even still . . . I have read it with my own eyes. And in English.' Instead she ducked her chin against her shoulder as the conversation continued.

'I noted the Chinese eyes of the Masarwa girl; eyes like the Chinks who cheat you in shops,' Basuto Blanket was saying, not bothering to lower his voice.

Koba prickled with humiliation.

Your Ju/'hoan skin has grown thin, Bushgirl, a voice reminded her.

She heard this pest in her head quite distinctly when she was debating something with herself. It buzzed her like a mosquito, whining when she was less than honest with herself. I wish I could make decisions without having to look through an insect's eye, she'd said to Mannie Marais, the only person she'd ever told about her other voice. He'd called her pest a cricket.

'You know that fillum we saw – *Pinocchio*?'

Mannie's parents, Marta and Deon Marais, owned Impalala, a guest lodge catering for tourists to the nearby Kruger National Park. Deon had planned to build an open-air cinema there but, in the seven years Koba lived on Impalala, neither screen nor projector ever materialized. There were always more pressing needs around the lodge, like repairs to the exhausted Lister generator, their only power source on pitch-black nights when the roar of lion in the nearby reserve seemed closer.

Occasionally, Marta would raid what she called 'Koba's Train Home' fund. It existed largely in Marta's well-meaning mind, but the odd metal manifestation could be found in pennies dropped into jars in the empty pantry or in the storeroom where Marta kept her watercolour-painting paraphernalia. Random coins could also be found in her wardrobe, forgotten in scuffed handbags or in the toes of tramped-down shoes. Only the urgent need for a family treat in lieu of the holiday they could never afford would convince her to raid 'the fund'. Then she'd tear through cupboards with the urgency of an anteater in a termite nest. She'd emerge waving the fifty cents for the cinema fee. Wringing her hands, she'd assure her unofficial foster child that they'd soon replace the train fare money. The four of them would set off for the drive-in, stopping just before the paying booth with its glaring WHITES ONLY / BLANKES ALLEEN notice, to hide Koba under a blanket behind the car seat.

It was on one of these nights, with rows of cars balancing on the tarred waves like a pod of star-gazing whales, that Koba had seen her first Disney animation. She hadn't been impressed.

'You remember Pinocchio's friend, Jiminy Cricket?' Mannie had asked.

'Hnmpf, stupid gogga in a hat?'

'Okay, he's an insect, but it's only a fairy story . . . the thing is, the cricket's like Pinocchio's conscience . . .'

The way Koba was staring at him made him feel uncomfortable. Maybe he should fetch the big dictionary Ma kept in the kitchen in the place where Pa said most women kept recipe books. But then he'd have to know how to spell the word properly.

Koba had known she was staring, but she'd been struck by how soft she felt inside towards the worried boy.

She had never told even Mannie that she believed Insect had been sent to her by her deceased grandmother, Zuma. The old lady's lap had been her cradle; Zuma's spellbinding stories the distraction needed to keep a toddler entertained on long walks in the Kalahari sandveld as they foraged for roots and berries. The insect was one of several spiritual inheritances from her grandmother. When Koba was old enough to make a useful contribution to the family's store of veld food, Zuma had asked to be taken to her ancestral area to die. Koba had last seen her silhouetted on a ledge, her skin cloak billowing out like insect wings.

During her long, cave-dwelling years on Impalala, Koba had been lonely. She was used to being surrounded by people, to being parented by any and every adult in the group. She'd had dozens of playmates to sing and skip and dance with. Suddenly, she was surrounded by silence.

Then she began to hear Zuma. It was as if the garrulous old woman was seated on the other side of her small fire. This didn't frighten or surprise the girl. Her grandmother had been renowned in the band not just as a storyteller, but also for having powerful nlom. This gave Zuma the ability to move between supernatural realms and the everyday world of heat and hunger. As Koba became more integrated into the Marais family, Zuma stopped talking to her.

Or you just stopped listening, her internal cricket chirruped.

The cricket notion had become a private joke for Koba and Mannie. Once, sitting in her cave, he'd tried to stamp on an insect crawling across the rock floor. 'Don't kill my conscience,' she'd said, laughing.

Koba had fed several cockroaches in the prison cell she'd just been released from. She'd seen them as links to Mannie and her life on Impalala.

Impalala-Impalala, green and bushy with buck. Safe there until they discovered my love for a ǀTon man. Now white and black hate me.

Hush, Bushgirl. You have nothing to be ashamed of; in a wiser world what you have done would not be a crime.

She turned to stare out of the window and saw her reflection, blurred and red. She was no longer the quaking child of that first, terrible train journey. She was no longer dressed in animal skins. She wore western dress and shoes; she could read and write in English and Afrikaans. But what did it help? she thought.

I am speechless in the only language that matters now, my mother tongue.

Too light for in here, Bushgirl, too dark for out there; sticking out everywhere like a white lion cub.

She and Mannie had seen one once in the game reserve. When he'd brought news of the birth of an albino cub near by, she'd wanted to see it. Unconcerned about the danger, they'd slipped through the game fence separating Impalala from the Kruger Park and tracked the pride. Mannie said it was like seeing a snowball in the desert.

'Prey will spot it,' she'd whispered to Mannie. 'Unless that cub grows darker fur it will go hungry as an adult.'

'No-man, they'll put it in a zoo, or sell it to the circus.'

'Better it dies from hunger.'

2

On the platform, the crowd jostled towards the exit, laden with their treasures. Aside from shopping bags, they carried enormous sacks of ground maize meal, bolts of sturdy cloth, or transistor radios brash with buttons. Some turned the volume up and jive-walked to the kwela beat. Others readied themselves to meet relatives, donning the ill-fitting jackets their wider, whiter masters had cast off, or retying stiff new headscarves. Mothers moistened their fingertips to clean their toddlers' cheeks before Grandma came to pinch them; young men slicked their straightened hair. One jammed his comb into his defiant cornrows and left it there, waggling like a pink, plastic coxcomb as he minced to the music. His friends crowed with laughter as they pushed towards the non-white exit.

'Marais. Hi, André!' the sleek-headed police officer shouted to attract the attention of the only other white person standing near the exit.

André Marais stood head and beefy shoulders above the crowd. He lifted his bush hat lazily to his old classmate. Sergeant Du Pree shoved through the crowd towards him, oblivious of the woman he pushed past, or the box he knocked from her arms.

Marais's showing more beer belly than the last time I saw him, Hendrik Du Pree was thinking. Too late he remembered the big man's handshake – a hot vice, then the bone-crushing pump. He tried not to wince. André's grin said he hadn't succeeded.

'Long time no see, Du Pree. You still playing wing for that bunch of fairies in . . .?'

'Ag-no.' With his unmolested hand Du Pree patted the highly polished holster that held his police revolver. 'Too much work, ou maat.'

André's eyes narrowed. 'Is that what you doing here?'

'Meeting a prisoner off the train; a ball-ache, man; gotta take her to Nyae Nyae.' He grimaced. 'But what can you do? Duty calls.' He slid his bruised fingers into the belt of his uniform jacket.

'Nyae Nyae, hey? Bushman homeland they say. That's four maybe five hours, dirt road all the way?'

'You said it. And more corrugations on that track than on all the tin roofs in Soweto.' His companion laughed on cue. 'I ask you, what kaffirgirl can be worth that?' Du Pree shook his head.

'This kaffir – is she a Bushman?'

Du Pree looked surprised 'You *know* her?'

'The family, kind of, does . . .' André skulked among his chins for a moment. 'Ja-well, anyway, my ma told me that troublemaker'd been sent back.'

Du Pree noted the lock-down look. He waited, letting the silence build. André cleared his throat, took his hat off his head and flicked at something on the leopardskin band. He shoved the hat back and shifted his considerable weight from foot to foot. Du Pree kept his gaze mild.

He'd made an unofficial study of all the papers relating to the mysterious death of André's father, Etienne Marais, a member of parliament at the time and, more importantly to Du Pree, his mother's 'gentleman caller'.

Miriam Du Pree was a widow and lived in near-isolation in a town where the white inhabitants still harboured Third Reich sympathies. These burghers were mostly from German stock, save for the few South African miners who'd come hoping to find diamonds along the Skeleton Coast. Instead they washed up in inland towns like Onderwater. Du Pree's father, strong and stocky, was one of these, but he'd ended up working as a farmhand until malaria reduced him to a yellowed bag of bones. He died, leaving his beautiful young wife to support herself and her child with her Singer sewing machine.

Miriam's elegantly hooked nose and long-lidded dark eyes attracted interest from the men and hostility from their wives. But the hausfrauen were happy to use her as a seamstress once Etienne Marais had set her up in business, buying a discreet little house for her on the outskirts of the town. Soon Miriam's order book was full, and Etienne had to reserve her for their afternoons behind her drawn curtains.

Once, coming home early from rugby practice, Hendrik Du Pree encountered the big man on his way out. Marais hadn't been embarrassed; rather he had seemed genuinely interested in the scabby-kneed boy. They'd tossed the ball back and forth between them, Marais remarking that the boy was much more adept than his own son, André. Young Du Pree had dreamed then of having a father like this – a giant, with the newest car in town and the knack for making his mother happy and him feel safe.

'You look like your father, son,' Etienne had said, tweaking the boy's snub nose. 'You'll go far.'

Miriam had been devastated by her lover's death. She'd braved the community's disapprobation to attend his funeral, burying her veiled face against her son's chest as Etienne's elaborate coffin was lowered into the earth.

Du Pree didn't think his brash classmate, André Marais, premature inheritor of the rich farm holdings aptly called Weltevrede, well-satisfied, had any idea of the resentment he bore him. The fool had it all – money, status, well-satisfied family – but he was frittering it away. He intended to teach him a lesson. One day.

Du Pree was sure the whole Marais clan knew why the coroner's report stated Etienne Johannes Marais' cause of death as snakebite, when rumour had it he'd been shot with a Bushman arrow while out on a hunting trip. The poison the Bushmen used on their arrowheads came from a highly toxic grub. The man must have died in agony.

Regret about that was one thing he and André did have in common, Du Pree thought. He'd like to establish the facts. Now seemed a natural time to ask exactly what had happened all those years ago, but chances were it would light Marais' famously short fuse. Best let that sleeping dog lie until he needed to rouse it, he decided, especially as the Maraises were held in high esteem while he was still seen as the Jewish Jezebel's son.

Du Pree kept his blank stare on André. The big oaf didn't look fit; he'd easily outpace him down the wing of a rugby field, he decided. What people said must be true: Marais didn't spend much time farming – too busy boozing and flying off to Gaborone in that plane of his to gamble and taste a bit of brown meat. Everyone knew kaffirgirls were his preference.

Must run in the family, Du Pree thought. Manfred Marais, André's cousin, had been caught with the Bushman girl he'd come to collect – she'd been detained under Act 23, an amendment to the Prohibition of Mixed Marriages Act. It covered extramarital relations across the colour bar. The case never came to court and even the arrest was hushed up once the minister for Bantu affairs got involved.

Ja-well, it wasn't often you saw a Bushman in a city; they still lived like cavemen. This one had, the papers said. Some do-gooder had been trying to keep her in her natural state in a cave on a bushveld game lodge. Planning to make her some kind of tourist attraction, he shouldn't wonder.

Bushmen just didn't fit into the modern world, Du Pree thought, but was it a kindness giving them a homeland in the Kalahari Desert? Not enough there to feed a mangy dog, never mind humans. People said Bushmen were good at finding veld food, but he'd never seen one grow fat on it. The whole repatriation exercise was stupid and, if you asked him, a waste of taxpayers' money and *his* fokken time. Now he'd have to devote a whole day to taking the girl back to her place. And who knew where that was? Nomads didn't have house numbers.

At the sight of the tawny man sprawled across the bench Koba stood rigid. She felt as though every hair on her head had uncurled from shock. Her saliva dried, she wanted to jump back on the train and hide behind a seat. Or run away down the track as fast as her legs would carry her, but she'd been handcuffed again.

She felt André look at her the way a lion would, feigning indifference to its prey. He yawned and said something to the policeman standing next to him. Koba tore her gaze from him to assess this new threat. She saw a honey badger in a police suit – snub nose, a vicious smile and bright buttons. Her anxiety increased. The bite of the badger could be fatal. The dangerous pair watched, unblinking, as she stumbled towards them.

'Prisoner three-four-nine deliver, suh,' the guard said, snapping her wrist to his side as he stood at attention.

Snared bird. Food for a |Ton badger or a fat lion?

She riffled her memories, searching for an image that might lessen her fear of these men. She saw the boy, Mannie, blond head just visible over the steering wheel of André's gleaming Chevy. Its paintwork had been less than gleaming once Mannie had driven it through thick thornscrub to get to her. She smiled inside.

A few years after his father's death, André had turned up at Impalala ostensibly to show off the Chevrolet Bel Air he'd just taken delivery of at Durban harbour. It was the first of many expensive toys that young André was using farm funds to buy. While other landowners bought Mercedes Benzes, André wanted the Hollywood dream. The Marais family watched as the car floated up the track to the guest lodge trailing a long scarf of diaphanous dust, looking every inch the film star. Mannie had been mesmerized.

Koba had been down near the riverbank that day, searching for honey to barter with. Leaving the car, André had sneaked off and tracked her down. Mannie had reached her by using André's car to bash his way through the bush. He'd disturbed an elephant, at loose on Impalala that day. The enraged jumbo had damaged the car further, leaving the cab concertinaed down onto the body. According to Mannie, a photo of the wreckage of the Bel Air plus a picture of the famous tusker, Mafuta, had become a popular exhibit at the insurance company headquarters.

While Du Pree was dismissing Koba's policeman escort, André rose and stretched his arms above his head, showing two sweat patches. Koba shrank from the stink. 'So,' André addressed the white policeman, 'did you-uh say she had to go to Nyae Nyae?' Du Pree nodded. 'Well, it's your lucky day, ou maat; I can take her for you. I need to see some land up that way so . . .'

'Thanks, man, but it's a national matter. With the minister involved I better . . .'

'The minister.' André snorted. 'And when d'you think you're ever going to hear from him again? He just wanted a *photo* opportunity with the girl – show the voters the Homeland Policy at work. He's not interested in the other side – the bits and bolts of getting her back to her tribe. He's never been here. He's got no blerry idea how hard it is to find a Bushman in the Kalahari.'

Du Pree nodded. 'Ja-no, makes finding a needle in a haystack piss-easy.'

'There you are, man. I'm telling you, you're not even gonna hear from that minister's undersecretary's *undersecretary's underpants*. Out of sight is out of mind for that lot. I know; my pa was the MP for Onderwater. Fifteen years. Best representative this place ever had . . .' – Du Pree hastily nodded his agreement – 'until his . . . er, passing.' André pressed his lips firmly together. His glance grazed Koba, then continued through her away to the red horizon. When he had control of his bottom lip, he turned back to Du Pree. 'Let's face it, ou maat, you couldn't find a place further away from things than Onderwater. It's the end of the fokken earth for those Pretoria pen-pushers. If you think babysitting the little kaffirgirl is going to earn you points with the bureaucrats, think again. She's not going to write and tell them what a good job you did, is she? And I don't see Opitz from the local paper here to write up the story of you doing your duty.'

This point rankled with Du Pree. He'd prepared for a picture, getting a close shave, Brylcreeming his hair on the way. His shoes and holster shone, his brass buttons gleamed. If the minister and the girl had made the front page of *Die Burger*, it wasn't unreasonable to expect the local paper to record him taking charge of Onderwater's first official homeland repatriate. But no, the stupid local hacks wouldn't know news if it jumped up and bit them on the backside.

'Ja-no,' André was saying, 'you'd be better off getting back to the station to do some important work. I've got you covered on this one.' He jerked his thumb towards Koba. 'Least I can do for a tjom.'

Koba felt her mouth go dry. The insistent tapping she felt inside when she was in danger became a pounding tattoo – dit-dit-dit, dah-dah-dah, dit-dit-dit – a distress signal in her viscera.

'Well . . .' murmured Du Pree as he weighed up the situation. Had André Marais deliberately come to the station to get the girl? Did it matter? His own job was only to take delivery of her. As long as he had papers saying he'd picked the prisoner up and deposited her somewhere in what was now regarded as her homeland, he had no further responsibility for her. The girl may well be the bait he needed to set a trap for Marais. Time would tell. It took patience to reel in a big fish, Du Pree thought.

And who'd know if she never made it home? There were no villages in Nyae Nyae; no boreholes where people gathered to gossip. The Bushmen lived in small groups spread over a vast area. They didn't read papers; no one was expecting her. If she didn't make it, so what? Lions or leopards killed those who wandered around out there; or people got lost and died of thirst.

Still, no point being too lackadaisical.

'Better she leaves with me, in the police van; just to be on the safe side. We could meet on the road outta town, at the turnoff to the old quarry. The place's deserted. That's where I'll hand her over, Marais.'

3

An hour later Koba lay in the back of André's truck, bound hand and foot, a gag in her mouth. She recalled her captor's haste when the ITon policeman handed her over.

'Wait a bit: the handcuffs,' the policeman had said. 'You can't take them – government property.'

But not me, not now the government has used me and no longer needs me, she thought as a rag was rammed into her mouth. André tied the ends tightly behind her head, so tightly her eyelids were dragged downwards. Through the slit she'd seen the honey badger policeman turn away.

She tried now to concentrate on physical sensations rather than the fear numbing her brain. It was a smooth ride, so there must be tar beneath the tyres. They were on the great road then, the only asphalted strip in the Kalahari Desert. She'd seen it once on a map Marta had shown her, a thin red line running straight down the shin of Africa like a trickle of blood. Either side of it was nothing but flat brown space. How could that nothingness be her home? she'd wondered.

Her Kalahari was a place of high anthills and low salt pans, of birds ruby and rust and turquoise and gold, of animals striped, spotted, horned and clawed, of towering baobab trees and close-clustered huts. Her mother had been there, raking mangetti nuts from the coals, scolding her for eating them before they cooled. And her father, leaning against a tree, sharpening his hunting knife against the skin on his heel. And people, many, many people to whom she was related by blood or name.

She'd stared and stared, boring into the page, trying to discern this detail until her eyeballs burned and the images liquefied like salt-pan mirages.

I tried to hold my history, fleshed in my mind, but now I see it only through thick smoke.

Stop it, Bushgirl, remember that map; down dirt tracks this lion will drag you. You must picture your escape.

I cannot leap, Cricket. These legs of mine can't outrun a lion. But I don't fear death; I go there to meet my relatives. Grandmother will greet me with her gums. Soon we will laugh at one of her jokes – she will laugh loudest. And if I put my memory into my nostril, I get the smell of Mother – wood smoke and herbs.

'Rock me in your arms, little mother,' she murmured as the steady vibration of the moving truck began to soothe her. In the heat her eyelids drooped. She wondered, dimly, why her tappings had deserted her. Over the years she'd come to accept them as an early-warning system.

Fool-Bushgirl, is your sense failing you? You face danger, now!

Hush, Insect. I don't want to wake . . . ever.

The bitumen had softened in the intense heat. She felt the tyres squelching across it. She hoped this increased the chance of a burst tyre. She wanted André to lose control of the bakkie and crash it into a tree – a quicker death than what she imagined he had in mind for her when they reached their remote destination. He'd told her years ago that she'd pay for his father's death.

But his murder of your parents goes unpunished.

Shoo, Insect. Why you think life for a Jul'hoan must be fair? Fair is white in this world.

She felt the truck slow, then swing off the road. It juddered along a track. The remote place, she thought. Her equanimity vanished; she felt her pulse race. She barely registered the rope burning her bound limbs as she was tossed about. And then the vehicle stopped.

Koba lay still, scarcely able to breathe. She heard the driver's door open. She felt the cab rise as André climbed out and she closed her eyes. A loud bang on the side of the truck. Her eyes flew open. André's sweaty, red face loomed over her.

'You lie still, you hear me? No trouble or you'll pay for it.'

She blinked, confused, and felt more so when he began to fix a dark green tarpaulin over the truck bed. Soon the breeze was cut off and the blazing blue sky hidden from Koba's view. Was he going to suffocate her? she wondered.

'Tjoepstil, hey? I'm not gonna be long.' He secured the last clip. She heard his footsteps pound away over hard-packed earth.

So this was just an interval, a way to prolong her mental agony. His methods would be approved of by the South African Security Service, she thought. No, she wouldn't let him reduce her to a shaking wreck who messed herself in fear, like the poor woman she'd seen in prison. She would lull herself into a stupor again; it shouldn't be difficult given the stultifying heat under the tarpaulin.

But she could hear voices. They were not close enough to hear her mumbling for help through a gag, she decided; could she make the truck rock to attract attention? But her legs were restrained. She felt sweat pool at her wrists and ankles where her limbs seemed welded together by the heat; perspiration prickled along her hairline and beads began to slide down her temples. She heard a metallic groan. The bakkie struggles with the heat too, she thought.

Then came a light footfall – not André, Koba thought; someone with the caution of a bushbuck. She felt a rush of cooler air as the corner of the tarpaulin above her head was deftly unclipped and momentarily she was exposed to the blowtorch brightness of the day. Then green gloom again and above her appeared a face not unlike her own. She had no time to study the little man; rat-quick, he made a grab for her.

Hn-hnn-hnn! Does he mean to ruin me? She began to struggle. Immediately the man withdrew his hands and whispered urgently to her. His words sounded like a rapid fire of soft clicks.

Jul'hoan? Hnn, he means to loosen me. He is old, face-dents like a granadilla. When my feet are free I'll kick him if he tries to have food with me – kick him so hard he'll fly from this bakkie like buffalo toss-meat.

It dawned on her that she'd seen him before. But where? He spoke again, this time in Afrikaans: 'Yau, little one, you don't remember me and you didn't understand me.'

Now she did, but the gag prevented coherent reply. She nodded, imploring him with her eyes to free her. He didn't seem to notice.

'I am Twi,' the little man said, 'André Marais' boss-boy.' He apologized for frightening her. 'But basie in store near by, I must be quick-quick. I will remind you. We knew each other when you were fresh from your n!ore.' Now there was a Jul'hoan word she *did* know. It meant home – a place where the fruit of the trees and the water in the salt pan belonged to her people. 'Eh-weh, you were so small . . .' Twi pressed his thumb against his other four fingers, making a bud shape. 'Many-many seasons ago.'

Suddenly an image of this man crouching down in front of her sprang to mind. It was years ago and she'd just been abducted and taken to Weltevrede, André's family farm. She'd been locked in a storeroom stacked with sacks of animal feed and fertilizers and she was mute with fear. She remembered that he'd been kind.

Now Twi pushed himself up on one scrawny elbow and scanned the contents of the truck: water containers; lamp; a bedroll; a folding chair; cooking utensils; axe and spade; ammunition.

'Eh-weh, the basie is going camping. Two nights, maybe three.' His expression closed when he spotted a long wooden box lying near by, but he chattered on. 'I have a big-big job, you know, little sister. I am boss-boy at Weltevrede. I have a lorry the basie's father gave to me, a Nissan sw76. It is behind, "resting". Like the basie, also resting.' He winked at Koba.

Koba began to suspect he'd come to boast, not to help her. Was he drunk? she wondered, noting his bloodshot eyes. You wouldn't have lasted long at Impalala, she thought, remembering how reformed alcoholic Deon, her foster father, had kept his staff strictly on the wagon.

'Ja,' Twi was saying, 'I watched basie covering up the bakkie and thought: He is doing a secret-thing; better that boss-boy knows. Eh-weh, the shock when I saw a girl tied like a buck. And it was you, you, the one they took away. Eh-eh-eh!' He shook his head in amazement. 'I never thought to see you again. You must have a guardian spirit with strong n|om looking after you. Come, let me free your mouth.'

At last, she thought, and when it was done, she sat up as best she could in the cramped space and drank from the water bottle Twi handed her.

'You must get away,' Twi was saying with urgency now. 'Basie will be dangerous tonight.' His eyes strayed again to the wooden box, Koba noticed.

'What is in there?'

Twi held her gaze for a moment and she saw a look of pity. 'Branding fingers,' he said. 'And knives for skinning. Basie is not skilled.'

Koba's plan to accept death evaporated instantly. Before she could follow her urge to scramble out of the truck and run, they heard a vehicle speeding down the rutted road. It raced into the lay-by, scattering stones against wheels. Twi flattened himself on the truck bed, pulling Koba down beside him. 'A Ford,' he mouthed.

No matter if it's an aeroplane, I must run away before the Lion returns. But I could be seen; uncle said Lion is near by. Maybe he won't see me, but if *he* doesn't this Ford driver will.

Paap-paap – a jaunty hooter – then a car door alongside opened and slammed shut. A Boer voice boomed: 'Marais, jou bliksem, you started without me.'

Twi relaxed and lifted the tarpaulin to look out. 'sw41 – Baas Schmidt – a bad farmer, but a good drinker. Now we have more time.'

Koba lay very still, forcing the storm inside her to subside. She couldn't bear any more of Twi's time-consuming boastfulness. She needed help. 'Uncle, can you kill a buck with one cut to its throat?'

Twi looked over his shoulder at her, puzzled, and nodded.

Koba reached up and put a hand on his arm. 'I want you to kill me.' She brought her face close to his. He pulled back, aghast. Koba gripped his arm. 'I beg-beg you, uncle. I don't want the pain; I don't want the |Ton to see my fear when he uses me.'

Twi shook her hand off. 'What is the matter with you, girl? What life have you lived that you choose death?'

If you knew, uncle.

But out loud she said, 'To be dead before your baas can kill me will be a sweet thing.' But Twi was flapping his arm at her, spraying angry words. She listened, but didn't hear. This lucky little man didn't understand. He'd never been in a |Ton prison. What did he know of pain? As one of the guards had said, 'Everybody breaks. It just a matter of when.'

She began to sense another presence in the murky space she was sharing with the agitated Twi – a hunched female form dressed in skins. The old woman had a closely shaven head and a raucous laugh. Koba goosebumped. It was Zuma, her long-dead grandmother.

Beware, she can nag for Africa.

Koba closed her eyes as the ghostly old scold talked over Twi: 'You're like a tame animal, one of those pathetic, long-eared ones that can't screw.' Koba knew her grandmother meant a mule, but Zuma seldom bothered with names, preferring instead coarse description. 'Like that miserable animal, you are loaded with heavy things. You are beaten and broken. You have forgotten what it is to be free, to choose what you will bear on your back. Must I remind you, even though I am tired to death?' Koba refused to smile; her grandmother's puns were shameless. 'Don't let me hear you are tired when you still have run in your legs, an appetite for meat, seed for children and a heart for love. Must-be you feel tired *now*, but sleeping under the stars in your own n!ore will revive you. Use what you've got. Get up. Run!'

Koba opened her eyes. Zuma was gone. Only Twi crouched above her. He was telling her to run. She tried to rouse herself, but the effort was too great. 'I can't. I don't know the way. I don't know my people.' In a smaller voice: 'If I did find them, they might not want me, I am spoiled. I cannot go walking-walking-walking in the heat and dust through a land I can no longer read. One Kalahari tree will look like another to my stranger's eyes.'

'I will give you water until you find the Real People. And then *they* will feed you.'

'No, they will refuse me because I am spoiled. I have lost my Jul'hoan skin.'

Twi gave her a calculating look. 'Spoiled? What – by |Ton ways?' He cackled then leaned comfortably back on his elbows. 'Then I,

Twi, boss-boy, truck-driver, I am as ruined as a calabash crushed by a lorry,' and he laughed, showing more gaps than teeth. 'I am spoiled,' he said, patting his rounded stomach, 'by this belly full of meat, by this pouch full of tobacco, by sleeping on a soft mattress full of |Ton money.' He laid his index finger across his lips, merry at having shared his secret.

Hnpf, this uncle is lucky he works for a monkey. He doesn't know the life of most servants. He knows nothing of being a mule.

She glowered at the canvas; it pressed down on her like the weight of her elders' disapproval. Why couldn't they both have left her to suffocate in the back of the bakkie? she thought.

'Because you have a long way to walk yet before you can lie down,' she heard her grandmother say.

4

Impalala, near Hoedspruit
South Africa

30 September 1964

My dearest Koba,

I don't know if this will reach you. I shall send it care of my sister-in-law, Mrs Aletta Marais, at Weltevrede farm, in South West Africa. She was at the station when you left Johannesburg. She was the small woman in the very big hat, who was in front for every picture.

Lettie, if you are reading this, you shouldn't be, it's private. But if you're here, let me assure you I am *very grateful* to you for helping the children. Truly. You succeeded where we failed, so don't take my tease to heart. And please, please, Lettie, help me with one more favour – find a messenger to take this letter to Bushmanland; ask them to give it to any Khoisan person (Bushman) they see. Koba is from the Juǀ'hoan band, which lives in the vicinity of Nyae Nyae. Just tell them to look for the girl who lived with the whites. She might still be wearing a yellow dress. God and you willing, this letter could end up in Koba's hands. Thank you, my dear. I know we haven't always seen eye to eye, but we are, after all, sisters-in-law. That's still true, isn't it, even though Etienne is long gone?

Kobatjie, my heart broke to see you in the pretty yellow dress in the back of a police van. You looked so small sitting next to that policeman they handcuffed to you. I have sent a letter to the authorities to complain. I have argued that you are still a child and they have no right to treat you inhumanely. Well, they have no right to treat anyone inhumanely, but they do, we hear. But you, so small and alone, and after what you've been through! Oh my dear, I shudder to think what detention must have been like for you. I heard such terrible stories during the months I stood outside with the other mothers. Ja-well, I must be careful what I write, Deon says. Still, someone should be brought to account and I will do what I can. Anyway, that's for the future.

For now, I want you to know that never a day goes by when I don't berate myself for taking you from South West Africa. If you'd never come to Impalala none of this might have happened. Oh, Koba, I lie in bed at night crying for the harm my family has done to you and yours. For pity's sake, believe me when I say I only did what I thought was best for you. I thought I could keep you safe. Ja, I know, I should have made a plan to get you back to the Kalahari years ago, but even after only a year it was already too late – we'd all grown to love you.

Well, as you would say, 'my heart is very heavy'. I am trying to believe that it all happened for the best, but I don't know. I wish they'd let me talk to you. If you ever get this, perhaps you will write back, if you ever get pen and paper, or go near a post office.

I had to stop – sorry. Listen, I hope the train journey went well. At least this time you knew what to expect. Do you remember your first train trip with me, from Onderwater back to South Africa? It took even longer those days, and you slept most of the way. I think that is what children do to deal with terror.

Big as he is, Mannie sleeps all the time now. Sometimes I think I can hear him crying in the night, softly, but he won't talk, won't say what happened to him in detention. I'm afraid it may be the same with you. Oh-oh-oh, there is pain and rage in my heart. I would like to walk into the Union Buildings and shoot the rest of the government ministers.

(Yes, Lettie, even your senator, sanctimonious so-and-so that he is – he didn't help us out of the goodness of his heart; he did it to curry favour with that odious Verwoerd-lot. You may scold me for speaking ill of the dead, but that architect of human misery will rot in hell for apartheid. I despise these hypocrites who call themselves Christian and then treat people worse than animals. As I write, I am shaking with anger, but as Deon says, I must calm down. Violence won't give back freedom to the children of this country.)

Koba, I accept that your place is with your people, but I miss you so, my girl. There is a hole in our family now that you are gone. To be honest, two holes, as Mannie is not the boy he was. He's so pale and thin. It's as if Deon and I are living with both your ghosts. I keep thinking I hear you and Mannie laughing under the avocado tree, or I see your young self running through the sprinkler with him. How you revelled in rain that could be turned on at the tap. And how wonderful you looked with diamond drops in your hair.

You know, towards the end, I did wonder if you'd begun to think of us as your replacement family. Presumptuous of me, Deon says. He thought the same about my taking you from South West to come and live here. But please believe me, Koba, I did it to save you. I felt sure you were in danger. I'll say no more; you'll know what I mean.

I feel ashamed now when I think about putting you in that cave all on your own on Pasopkop. I know now Deon thought it was cruel. He says he didn't dare say so; he felt so guilty and I was very angry with him then because . . . well, that's water under the bridge now.

But we did finally talk about it when you two were in detention, so I suppose that's one good thing that came from all this. If you ever felt I treated you as something other than a real person, I mean as a symbol of – well, it's hard to explain and I'll think some more on this and, one day, you and I can talk. I would so like that. There is so much I would like to explain. In the meantime, please don't be angry with me. Please forgive me and please believe that I did what I did because I thought mixing with us would be more dangerous for you than living alone in the bush. Ja-well, I was right.

But now you are going home and I'll try to be happy for you. May you find your people well and may your welcome be all that you expect. You will do good things for them, I am sure of it. They are very lucky to have you among them, as we were.

My thoughts are with you always.

Yours sincerely,
　　　　　Marta Marais

5

'You will escape Baas Marais and then you will find your people,' Twi assured Koba. As she listened to his plan she began to feel optimistic.

'Basie's lorry will puncture.' He drew a long nail from his pocket, grinning. 'Basie will have to change the wheel; then you must slip out and run away.' He raised a bony finger. 'Basie will not be fast for running, but shooting, huw-ah! Even drunk he is sharp with a gun, so you must be quiet as a snake and swift as a hare, little sister.

'Now, when you run, you must go so.' He pointed north-east as best he could in the confined space. 'If you follow in the direction of the morning star for four days you will be near the permanent water. Because it is dry season, Real People will be sitting there waiting for the rains. You must find them before they move north for the mangetti harvest. Eh-weh,' he said, smacking his lips, 'mangetti – better than beer.

'Now, ears up! You *must-not* go near the road when you walk. And you *must-not* go to Tsumkwe. No-good place for a young girl. Our people went there to progress, but they have gone back-back-back. Too much drinking, too much fighting . . .'

'But can't you take me to Nyae Nyae in your truck, uncle?' Koba begged him, worrying that his plan might fail.

He shook his greying head sadly. 'On the road the basie will find us. Then we will both be dead for sure.'

Ten minutes later Twi had whirled away like a dust devil, leaving Koba a replenished water bottle, some oranges, a torch and a tin of tobacco. 'For the people's tobacco-hunger,' he'd said, pressing the tin into her hand. She rearranged herself in the position André had left her in and waited anxiously until he returned to the truck. He ripped the tarpaulin back to leer at her, but he didn't check her bonds. The cab sagged as he climbed in, the starter motor rasped and they took off.

For many miles Koba lay tense, waiting for the tyre blowout. The truck jounced along. Gradually she became aware that the vehicle was dragging towards the right. At last Twi's nail had done its job on the rear tyre. The truck slowed then stopped at the side of the road. André's door opened and she heard him stomp around the vehicle. Then '*Fok!*' as he spotted the flat. Bam-bam-bam as he kicked it furiously and the truck bed shuddered. Rripp – the canvas was torn off. André's bloodshot eyes rolled in his head as he hissed, 'Every time I come anywhere near you, there's trouble. Now you've put a curse on my bakkie, haven't you, you witch?'

Koba saw him raise a huge paw; she hunched up and took the blow across her back. It didn't hurt; he hadn't been able to reach her properly. Beneath hooded eyes she watched him struggle with his rage, contain it, only for it to erupt again as he struggled to free the spare wheel from its casing.

It took a long time and a catalogue of curses before he realized the truck bed was too tightly packed for him to gain access to the spare. Telling her she'd 'pay for this', he slammed down the tailgate and began hauling things out, letting them fall in the dust. Then he leaped onto the truck bed and began tossing out the rest. A black frying pan sailed over Koba's head, followed by a shiny spade and then a bedroll. She heard them land in the veld some way from the vehicle.

Once André had wrestled the spare wheel from its frame he searched for the jack. 'Where's the jack, where's the blerry jack?' he screamed, kicking out at Koba.

That did hurt – her thigh, her ribs, her shoulder. She rolled away to reveal the jack.

'Fokken bitch!'

She thought he might use it to strike her but he jumped out of the truck. She heard thudding, a loud clunk then felt him begin to crank up the vehicle.

Koba knew the procedure; she and Mannie had changed countless tyres on their drives through the bushveld. She knew her best chance of escape would come when André was undoing the wheel nuts. Judging by the amount of cursing about 'nuts tighter than a nun's . . .' – she couldn't understand the word – that was now. She sat up slowly and pulled on her wrist bonds; they fell away.

Like the kaross of a willing woman.

Hnn, Insect, you are beginning to sound like my grandmother.

She lifted her bundle of possessions, using it to test whether the truck bed moved. Apparently not; André was struggling on, attacking the nuts with what sounded like a battering ram. Good, the noise would mask her scurryings, she thought. Silently she slid over the wall of the truck bed and inched herself to the ground on the far side of the cab. Should André glance up, her feet would be hidden from view. He continued huffing and puffing, head down.

Koba backed away from the truck. She wished she dared stop to take off her shoes; bare feet would be quieter across tarmac. She tried to step noiselessly, but that took time. She wanted to hurry in case a car came down the road. This was unlikely; they'd only passed three cars during the course of the journey and they were now in an even less populated area, far from the sweet-smelling orange orchards of the Onderwater area, even further from the sprawling farmhouses with their watered lawns, uniformed servants and two-car families. The people dotted sparsely across this dusty land couldn't afford donkey carts, let alone cars. Nevertheless, Koba could not still the trembling in her legs. Tortoising across the road, bundle on her back, she felt conspicuous. When would she reach sandy ground?

Crunch. Her foot grazed a stone on the verge. It skittered a few yards. She froze, feeling all the saliva in her mouth disappear. The wind seemed to screech down the empty road towards her, loud as a police siren. André's head stayed out of sight on the other side of the bakkie. The banging and swearing continued unabated.

Koba turned. Lying within reach was a bedroll. She considered taking it; it would make sleeping outside on a cold Kalahari night more bearable, but it might smell of Lion. She stepped over it, careful as a cat, then she began to run.

She felt terrified. Now he would surely hear her, but she daren't look back. Which way should she go? The land stretched endlessly away from her, blank, beige, empty as an unused envelope. It offered no hiding place – not a dune, boulder, nor even an anthill in sight.

She heard a shout like a lion's roar. She raced away towards the featureless horizon, angry red in the late afternoon sun.

The minute André realized the girl had gone he grabbed his hunting rifle. How the hell she'd got free he couldn't imagine; he'd tied her up himself, especially tightly. But she hadn't got far; he could see her, yellow dress like a flag out in the veld. He slid the bolt, heard the bullet click into the chamber. He picked her up in his telescopic sights. He'd go for one of her knees then he could still have some fun tonight, he thought, getting the fleeing figure into focus. He chuckled to himself; with the sun behind him like it was now, the shot was almost unfair, he couldn't miss.

'So why not have a bit of fun, boet?' he asked himself. 'Frighten the little bitch first.'

Koba heard a whoosh as something sped past her. A bullet. She dropped her bundle in fright and dodged left. She ran faster. Not fast enough, her instincts screamed. She knew she was still within shooting range. Perhaps if I make like a hare, she thought.

Ha-ha, a dodging target's better sport, André decided, tracking her through his sights. At that moment a large brown buck trotted into shot. André drew back from the sight and lowered the rifle. He saw an eland cow. He gaped. This wasn't eland country, he thought, not since the game fences had gone up. The buck was behaving strangely, trotting back and forth, tossing its long-horned head. Could there be a lion after it? He felt a prickle of unease as he scanned the land. Nothing moved, not even a blade of grass stirred by a breeze. The eland lowered its graceful head and began grazing.

Well-I'll-be-buggered, André thought, an *eland*; just like the old days. He'd get it once he'd dealt with the kaffirgirl. Then he could take the carcass into town to show the okes, otherwise they'd never believe him. No way. 'Wait there, my beauty,' he called. 'I've just got a bit of business to take care of.'

He turned to train his sights on Koba again, but couldn't see her. He lowered the rifle and scanned the horizon where she'd last been. Nothing, not even a partridge scratching in the veld. He rescanned, hand over his eyes to cut out the afternoon glare. Irritation turned to disbelief, then to fury. He whipped from side to side, rifle swivelling above his head like a drunken periscope.

This is fokken stupid. She can't just disappear. Nothing to hide in or behind out here. Wait-a-bit, maybe behind the eland? Bushmen have a spooky connection with animals.

He swung his attention back to the buck. Lucky he'd loaded a .308, he thought. It should tear through the buck and make a bloody mess of anything hiding behind it. Now he saw a soft brown pelt in his sights and the curve of bovine flank. Normally he'd aim for the brain – he was skilled at angles and accuracy – but today he needed to blast his problem off the face of the earth. He steadied his aim.

A flash of light, the shot went wide.

'*Fok-fok-fok.*'

He hadn't missed a mark in years. Now the eland was off, galloping away, grass parting before it like a biblical sea. And there was no body where the buck had been. He swore violently then rounded on the road, expecting to see a passing car, the low sun bouncing off its windscreen. Nothing. He flung himself the other way. A long line of empty asphalt. So what had caused the flash that distracted him? He spun through three hundred and sixty degrees to search the surrounds and saw . . . 'Ab-so-fokken-lute-ly nothing!'

He rubbed his eyes. Had he imagined the flash? No way! It had been real, like someone deliberately bouncing sunlight into his sights. But there was no one out here with him. Neither the eland, nor the fokken Bushgirl, he thought, shaking his head like a dazed wildebeest. Perhaps that last shot Schmidt had poured him had been doctored?

He shouldered his rifle, telling himself he'd had enough of this kak. He stomped across the road and bulldozed into the veld.

I'm a good tracker; I'll follow her blerry spoor – all night if I have to.

After twenty sweat-drenched minutes he had to admit there weren't any tracks – neither human nor antelope. Nor were there fresh droppings nor any sign of freshly chewed grass. It was uncanny. And a wind had appeared and was gathering up funnels of dust and swirling them about him, like a belligerent, invisible maid with a giant broom. He had sand in his eyes, his nose and his mouth. He was livid.

'This is un-fokken-natural,' he spluttered, stumbling back to the truck.

Clunk. André tripped over something lying in the grass – his spade, its head shining in the dying sun. He kneeled down. Could that have blinded him? But it would have to have been held up, angled to catch the rays that reflected into his sights. He felt the hair on the back of his neck rise. He glanced quickly over his shoulder. Too dusty to see. And it would be dark soon.

With the solid, still-warm body of the truck at his back, André felt better. He finished changing the tyre quickly then clambered into the cab and took two aspirin for his thumping headache, swilling them down with brandy from the hip flask he kept in the cubbyhole.

Okay, so maybe the eland was the result of too much Klipdrift at lunchtime; it wouldn't be the first time the booze had made him see things. Once, after a big piss-up at the rugby club, it had been ants the size of Rottweilers. Not too pleasant, gibbering like a baboon in front of his tjoms, trying to climb into their laps screaming 'get them off'. Ja-no, it had taken months and a few kicks delivered to the kidneys of his own scrum-mates to convince the okes he was no poefter.

He had another sip of brandy. Its burn helped him focus. Ja-no, the eland might have been a hallucination, he thought, but the girl was real. Of course she was, that half-Yid, Du Pree, had seen her too. And he himself had touched her; a couple of times. He scrubbed his wide palm on the steering wheel.

'No-dammit! She's my prize. I've waited a long time to claim her. I'm gonna have her. And afterwards, finished and klaar with this Bushman business. I owe that to the old man,' he said.

He'd promised his father revenge when Etienne reeled about, disoriented from the Bushman poison. The boy had sworn then that he, André, was the Marais who could be relied upon – not his pisscat uncle, Deon, nor his mommy-boy cousin, Mannie. What the hell had Pa ever seen in the little wanker?

André still felt a pang of jealousy when he recalled how his father had allowed his young cousin to ride on the stallion with him when he, older and an excellent horseman, was fit only to unsaddle it. And then that son-of-a-commie-bitch had gone and fallen in love, if his mother was to be believed, with the very kaffirgirl whose trespassing parents had caused all the trouble in the first place.

And she was still causing trouble.

Not for much longer. He wrenched the engine into gear and, with the headlights on full, began nosing the truck into the area where he'd last seen her. Round and round he drove in ever-decreasing circles. Nothing. Niks. Fok! He leaped up into the truck bed and swept the area with his powerful torch beam. Twice he picked up movement – once it was a hare, the next time a jackal.

'I'll find you, you hear me. I'll fokken get you if it's the last thing I do,' he screamed across the empty sandveld.

The Kalahari moon stared at him with a baleful blue eye.

Back at the tar road he halted, riding the clutch and accelerator, making the bakkie surge like a racehorse stuck behind starting gates. André looked left, northwards – that was where her home lay. Should he take the road as far as Tsumkwe then cut into the sandveld? He had food and water. Sooner or later he'd find a village or a band of wandering Bushmen. One of them would be bound to have seen or heard tell of a girl new to the area. Aside from anything else, that yellow dress would make her memorable.

He hoisted the handbrake and toyed more with the accelerator, making the vehicle buck. How had she untied herself in the truck, the black witch? But he didn't believe in that kaffir crap. He released the handbrake and took off, northwards.

As he drove, he remembered the unnerving uphill habit of this road. It seemed to rise steadily yet a man never got to the crest. Okes spoke of it, how they all felt the unchanging, uphill slope through their tyres, in their engines, mile after mile on the dead straight road. But there was no hill. He'd proved it, flying over the area, noting how the road snaked along a valley floor between low Kalahari dunes, and even these weren't high, typically no more than sixty foot high along their length, though that was considerable. From the air an oke could see that the dune merged, unremarkably, into the flat, buff sand around it. There was no rise, despite what he could now feel. It was an illusion.

'Fok this,' André shouted, wrenching the truck into a U-turn that bounced it off the tar, into the bush and back onto the tar again. He headed home.

6

Koba crouched low in the burrow she'd found. André had stopped shooting, but she knew he would keep looking for her. She pulled her kaross over her head to better conceal herself.

In chamois-gloom she assessed her hideaway. It had been made by an aardvark. There would be tunnels she could crawl into to hide and offshoot passages exiting elsewhere, but deep underground she might encounter a hyena – there were droppings here. It looked to her as though the aardvark had moved out and the hyena in. Nevertheless, she relaxed a little. The new occupant would be out now, off on its nocturnal scavenging round.

Then the earth began to shake and she heard the thrum of a billion sand particles vibrating against one another. Seismic ripples seemed to be coming towards her. She stuck her head above ground. Two giant eyes were bearing down on her – André's headlights. And here came a searchlight combing the surrounding scrub.

Hyena forgotten, Koba clawed at the walls around her feet, desperate to widen them so she could crawl further in. The roar of the engine grew louder. She felt the ripples reverberating against the tunnel walls. Sand began to loosen and fall on her, weighing her down. She was hidden, but her feet were wedged tight. And something was attacking them. She felt pinprick bites, dozens of them. 'Fleas! I must get out,' was her first reaction, then she chided herself: it was better to be a feast for fleas than for the Lion, she reasoned. Anyway, if the resident fleas were looking for a new host it meant the hyena was out. This might be an uncomfortable hideaway, but it was safe for the time being.

After a while she heard the truck leaving. Koba heaved herself out of the hole in time to see tail lights waggling away in the direction of the road. She jumped up, brushing fleas off herself as best she could. She resolved to sleep above ground that night, well away from the fleapit.

She wrinkled her nose. There was a pungent odour. Hyena had scent-marked bushes in the vicinity. She would have to make a fire to keep the Bone Crusher at bay. But Lion might park his truck on the road and creep back to find me, she reminded herself. She sighed – it was far safer to spend the night in the burrow, though her ankles would get no peace.

As anticipated, Koba spent hours in itch-agony, giving up hope that long before daybreak the fleas would be sated. As she crawled out of the burrow she saw the sky was blue-black and still starred, though on the eastern horizon she glimpsed the green tinge that heralded dawn. It wasn't light enough to set out yet, but neither could she linger in the burrow; the hyena pack might be heading home. If she could find her bundle, there was a torch in it. Step by feel-first step she began to put distance between herself and the burrow.

Must watch where my feet go, must look for dangerous animals. Hnnnn, it is cold, but my ankles burn like embers. I curse those fleas and all their ancestors. I would like to take each one and feed it to a baboon. I would like to roast them in a fire until they pop!

She hugged herself against the dewy chill as she puzzled about what had made André stop shooting at her the previous afternoon. Perhaps her zigzagging had confused his aim? And how had she found the aardvark burrow – it felt as if someone had pushed her into it. She pondered the possibility of help from a spirit guide, but hers was an eland, not an aardvark, as far as she knew.

Whoever helped, I wish they'd found me a hole without fleas, she thought, examining her ankles in the improving light. They looked swollen from scratching. In due course she would find aloe leaf to rub on her bites. Now she needed to find her abandoned bundle; aside from a torch, there was food and water in it.

By the time she located it, the sky had lightened, the blue now pale as a babbler's egg. The avian dawn patrol seemed sparse. Only two long-tailed hornbills flew down to forage, calling each other to 'wurk, wurk, wurk'. Then a scrawny red-billed francolin bustled out of the undergrowth, its caw turning to a frenzied cackle as it spied the intruders. But there was no human sound, no mechanical noise. Koba felt utterly alone. She should set out immediately, get as far away from the road as possible, but she delayed, munching on some dried peaches, drinking a ration from Twi's water bottle, staring at the bag of salted peanuts Mannie had given her at the station. She was able to discern the road across the dawn plain. A ribbon of heat rose from it, silver and spectral above the gold grass. She had a strong urge to creep back to it and follow it south, find a train returning to South Africa, then another, and another . . .

Until I am reversed, back in my cave, back with my Frog-boy and his mother and his father.

Turn from the road; walk, Bushgirl. There is no future there for you. Follow the morning star. Go find where your face will fit.

Koba sighed, gathered up the ends of the kaross bundle and tied them across her shoulder. Then she settled its bulk on her slender hip and set out. But her path wasn't clear; instead of yellow earth meeting blue sky she saw a horizon hemmed in with hostile-looking scrub. Nothing punctuated the khaki-coloured border – neither building, tree nor hill. In every direction the same monotonous nothingness.

She reminded herself that she was San. Like a pigeon she would home in on her ancestral land, Nyae Nyae – eventually. After all, she had what Mannie called an in-built compass. She recalled his fascination with her whenever they got lost on one of their game-trapping expeditions. He'd trot behind, muttering disbelief as she took first one and then, without hesitation, a series of other game paths that mazed through thick bushveld. Her instinct was infallible; she always got them back to her cave. 'It's like you've got a magnet inside you that draws you home,' Mannie had said. 'Like home's true north for you.'

'True n!ore,' she'd said, teaching him Juǀ'hoan for home.

She remembered the place of plenty they'd conjured up as their paradise, their n!ore. There'd be avocado trees and salt pans for her, watermelons and beehives for him. It was a place where they'd speak Juǀ'hoansikaans, or Afringlish, a place where they wouldn't have to hide their love in a cave.

Hnn-hn-nn, thinking about that is like scratching at bites – leaves a sore, swollen place.

7

From a window of the old farmhouse, Marta Marais watched her son drift off towards the hill where Koba had lived on Impalala. She supposed Mannie had been awake all night as usual and, after his pilgrimage, he'd sleep all day. It was weeks now since she and Deon had brought him home from the detention centre in Johannesburg and still he didn't seem back in the real world. He looked like the ghost of the boy he'd been – so thin and pale; even the hairs on his long legs and arms seemed to have turned from gold to grey. It pained her to look at those listless limbs, but at least he bore no sign of torture on them, unlike that poor boy, Moses Malatji. He had a hole in each calf, as if his flesh had been cauterized by a pair of steel rods.

It was because of these wounds that she'd insisted Moses and his mother, Violet, stop over with them. Marta had come to know Violet, and a dozen other anxious black mothers like her, during the days she'd kept vigil outside Jeppe Street police station while waiting for news of Mannie. Violet had been reluctant to detour to Impalala, despite the free ride north; between them lay an unspoken fact – a black head was not allowed on a white pillow. Marta explained that at Impalala they had a spare room in the staff compound.

In fact, she'd housed them in a guest rondavel, much to the outrage of one of the white holidaymakers. Marta was beyond caring. She needed an antiseptic environment and she needed to start the Malatji boy on a course of antibiotics before his mother took him off to a witch doctor back home.

Moses had been held in detention for the full ninety days without trial that the law allowed, a month longer than her own son. She didn't suppose the boys had been in the same cell, because races were segregated in keeping with the government's Separate Development Policy. But somehow they'd bonded in that terrible place; she could tell from the way they sat close together on the back seat during the six-hour drive back to Impalala, how Mannie was careful to let Moses sit forward so his suppurating sores would not be pressed against the upholstery.

Moses stayed a few days while she and his mother débrided his wounds as best they could. Close-up, Marta could see the flesh was dead, blackened, as if it had been sizzled. The women reassured him that the skin would soon close, but Marta knew it would take time and the youth would always have a depression in each calf to remind him of his stay at the South African state president's pleasure. Later, when his legs were cleaned and dressed, Mannie helped him to hobble about. Marta saw them murmuring together under the shade of the ebony tree; Mannie a wraith, Moses like Lazarus, trailing white bandages. Hatred burned in her heart like acid then; she wanted to dynamite the nearest government building – preferably with the full cabinet inside it.

Instead she and Violet sat on the stoep and drank tea from the chipped enamel 'servants' mugs, which the black housemaid, Selina, had set on the tray as a snub. Marta had a lump in her throat at the sight of Violet's crocheted gloves, donned especially for the occasion, clasped around the dirty-looking vessel. If only I'd changed my dress and tidied my hair, Marta thought.

The women sipped the rooibos tea in uncomfortable silence while they watched their distant sons. 'Who'd have thought it, hey? Two boys who don't live that far from each other and it took apartheid to bring them together,' Marta ventured. Violet nodded. 'Have you got any other sons, Mrs Malatji?'

'Huwww!' she said, as if it was a foolish question. 'This one, Moses, she is the fifth-born.'

'You are fortunate,' Marta murmured.

'Huw-so.' Violet laughed. 'Too much lobola to pay for brides. And now Moses, looking for trouble with the pol-is. Aie-aie-ai!' She sucked her teeth, then inhaled the pungent tea through them. A red-faced crested barbet trilled its rapid vibrato from the bird table dangling in an archway. It was the sound of the shimmering heat. 'Mêdem, eh, Missus Marais,' Violet said, 'your boy, *why* she is taken by the pol-is?'

'Okay, so it's ridiculous,' Marta confessed to Deon in the privacy of their bedroom that night, 'but I felt like our son had failed because he'd only been arrested for sexual intercourse, not sabotage.'

Deon sat down on the bed to pull off his built-up boot. A traffic accident had left him with one shortened leg. 'It's not a competition, Marta.' He sounded tired. 'There's no prize for the person who strikes the greatest blow against apartheid, or suffers the most in detention. The government are as crazy to legislate about sex across the colour bar as about separate park benches for whites and non-whites.'

Marta reached across the coverlet and patted his calloused hand. She knew he'd been shocked to discover that his son was having sex with Koba. Deon came from a conservative Afrikaans family. His brother, Etienne, had been a prominent member of the ultra-conservative National Party. Deon had been the 'black sheep' of the family, but not because of his enlightened political views. He'd been an alcoholic. On Etienne's death he'd inherited the farm, Impalala, and unofficial custody of the San girl he'd inadvertently helped to orphan. These factors, plus the stillbirth of his daughter, had placed Deon firmly on the wagon and he hadn't slipped off it since. Nevertheless, it had been an enormous relief for her to hear from his own lips, just two months ago, that he disapproved of Mannie's behaviour because he regarded Koba as part of the family; almost as a sister to his son.

Deon pulled his hand away. 'I don't know why you do this to us, Marta.' Her green eyes widened. 'Why do you *always* have to take in these strays? Do you think you don't have to obey the laws of the land just because you don't believe in them? Jissus, woman, a person would think that by now you'd know the consequences.' He threw his heavy boot into the corner of the room. 'As if we haven't had enough trouble over Koba, now you bring in a suspected saboteur and put him in 'whites only' accommodation, nogal.'

'He's a boy; a poor, injured boy,' Marta protested.

He rounded on her. 'Ja, he's just a kid and ja, he's injured. Probably got strapped into a chair with metal legs and wired to a car battery, poor blighter. But Moses is probably a member of the armed wing of a banned organization. He is probably a trainee terrorist . . . I'm not saying I blame him for choosing that path, but you've got him here going for walks with *our son*! At the very least I could lose my trading licence. God knows how we'll live then' – he ran his hands through his thinning hair – 'already you are driving off paying guests. And I bet you haven't stopped to consider that Mannie could be hauled in for interrogation again, accused of aiding suspected terrorists. Do you want him to go through that again, hey? Do you? Do you want to keep looking into his eyes knowing he's seen things you wouldn't wish on your worst enemy, let alone your flesh and blood?'

At Jeppe Street police station Mannie had seen men in worse states than Moses. They were on the other side of the thick metal fence, their bruises and burns healing, but something about them remained splintered and smashed long after the awkward knitting of their bones. These ones didn't join in the resistance songs that were a feature of black detainees' daily toyi-toyi to the exercise yard.

It wasn't always black men on the non-white side of the fence. Sometimes it was Indians: the 'dynamite coolies', he heard the warders call them. They'd been responsible for the spate of bombings on railway lines and post offices around Johannesburg. Occasionally, his exercise time would coincide with that of the few coloured detainees held there. These, like him, were not Politicals. He heard they were petty thieves or burglars and among their number was the odd fokker like him, men whose sexual escapades took them into forbidden territory. To his dismay, even the inmates regarded the fact that these not-quite-white black men had been caught with white women, as more serious than his own 'crime'.

50

When he'd first arrived at the nondescript blue and grey building, headquarters of the South African Security Police, he'd been questioned by a relay of officers. The only discomfort he'd endured was not being allowed to leave the room to use the toilet. Once convinced that he and his 'kaffirboetie' mother were not involved in politics, they merely mocked him for having sex with 'an animal'.

'What's the matter with the maids on your farm, hey?' they asked. When the youngster stared in disbelief an older officer put his arm around Mannie and explained that a 'Hotnot was one fuck too far'. Mannie exploded then, using every swear word he knew to tell them what he thought of their morality, their policies and their mothers.

'Right, you wanna cheek your elders, behave like a child, I'll treat you like one, boetie. Lines – you'll write lines. *S-i-t down there!*' Captain Steyn kicked a metal-legged chair towards Mannie. 'Write: "I must not fuck kaffirgirls." Write it until this page is full of lines, both sides.' He threw an A4 sheet onto the desk in front of Mannie then turned to instruct his junior officer. 'When this rubbish's finished, make him stand on the paper, only on the paper, not moving, hey, until, say . . .' Steyn looked at his watch. 'Wednesday, five p.m.'

'Two days, Captain?'

'Oh-ja. This one's stubborn. And if he steps off, make him crouch there. On his tocs. For another day.'

Mannie never spoke about this to other detainees. It had been a swaying, swelling, aching hell, but he would learn it was primary school torture by comparison with what they'd suffered. He was relegated to the rank of common prisoner and moved to a communal cell where a man, who was probably younger than his fissured face and trembling hands suggested, spoke to him in a Scottish accent.

Mannie gathered that Dougal was a frequent inhabitant of the cell. He lived rough and was often picked up during police public park clean-up operations. Dougal seemed grateful for the thin mattress on the black iron bedstead and the breakfast of boiled egg and dried bread. 'Put a wee bar in here an' I'd think meself in the Dorchester,' he said, winking. Dougal asked how old he was. 'Nearly eighteen?

There's yer problem, laddie. Under eighteen, yer for Borstal, eighteen-up, prison. Isnae worth doing the paperwork twice, ye ken? Ye huvnae bin charged.'

Weeks later Captain Steyn's underling turned up and said charges would be brought against Mannie under the Prohibition of Mixed Marriages Law, Immorality Amendment Act 23, and he could then see a lawyer and get the visiting rights of prisoners awaiting trial. 'Must be yer birthday soon, laddie,' Dougal observed. It was his second sojourn at Jeppe Street and Mannie thought he looked far worse than the first time. His legs were covered in sores and his whole body shook. 'If yer 'fore Mag'strate Malan ye'll be home fir Christmas,' Dougal reassured him. Mannie wanted to ask what court would be like; would the public be allowed in while intimate details of his relationship with Koba were discussed? Despite or perhaps because of the vulgarity he heard around him every day, the thought made him burn with shame. And fury.

It's only in this fokked up country that it's a crime, he thought. Other places, people over sixteen can have sex. Jissus, they can marry whoever they bloody well like.

An anxious month passed, his birthday came closer and Mannie's resolve to take revenge grew. His low-risk status meant he was allowed into the exercise yard when black Politicals were at large on the other side of the fence. No one imagined that white criminals would want anything to do with the 'kaffir agitators', so the watch was relaxed and Mannie was able to slip his doorstopper ration of bread through the fence. Dougal had told him that coloured inmates were allowed bread, Indians got chapattis, but blacks only samp, a stiff cornmeal porridge. Apparently, government researchers had decreed these the natural diets for the respective racial groups. 'Darkies arenae allowed sweets, neither,' Dougal said. This gave Mannie an idea and he began to stockpile sweets given him by an elderly female warder, who said he reminded her of her grandson. Soon he had a stash of Chappies bubblegum; packets of sherbet and rolls of boiled sweets.

He struck up his friendship with Moses over a tube of buttermilk drops. Moses Malatji had helped himself to one proffered by the white boy, who always watched him through the diamond-shaped mesh.

'Your world far from mine, Dutchman,' he snarled when Mannie shyly mentioned they were from the same area. Mannie switched into Tsonga and fluently insulted a passing white guard. Moses burst out laughing. Mannie saw then that the boy hadn't chewed the sweet, but was cradling it on his hollowed tongue to make it last longer. Mannie thrust the whole tube through the mesh. 'Take it, man.'

After that, Moses called out desultory responses to Mannie's enthusiastic greetings whenever they glimpsed each other through the divide. But he always accepted the sweets, his jaw losing its hard-man set when he popped three at a time into his mouth. One day Moses hailed Mannie as 'bra', township tsotsi-speak for 'brother'. Moses jive-walked towards the fence, a stooped youngster about his own age in tow. He introduced him as Jabu: 'One of those assegai-throwers from KwaZulu.' Though hunched over to keep one arm tightly around his painful middle, Jabu was aloof. Without looking Mannie in the eye he stated that he needed painkillers; he suspected he had a fractured rib. 'The mapuza played soccer with him last night,' Moses whispered about his police treatment. 'He was the ball.'

Mannie was able to get the pills for Jabu and, in due course, things like pen and paper for the messages Jabu always seemed able to spirit out of the prison via a fellow tribesman who worked there. Mannie had the idea of using this messenger to contact his mother.

Though he was not allowed visitors, Mannie's relatives could leave the odd item of clothing or food for him. Thus, shortly after his incarceration, his mother sent him a shirt so peculiar – hippy-style with the widest collar he'd ever seen – that he knew it must be significant. His feverish fingers discovered a message sewn inside it. He read that Koba was alive and was being held at Pretoria Central Prison. They had hopes of making contact with her, too. He immediately sat down to condense his longing for her onto the back of a jam-jar label. He attached it to the note for his parents. He begged Jabu to get these out.

They were slipped into the knee pads of Jabu's man as he polished the red cement floor of the corridor between the cells. The messages found their way into the hands of the woman who stood tall and white amid the crowd of pavement mamas outside the triple-locked doors.

Mannie asked his parents to contact his friend Moses's mother in Phalaborwa to tell her of her son's whereabouts. In the end it was Deon who drove to Phalaborwa, found Violet (not that difficult; the Malatjis were Ba-Phalaborwa royalty and lived near their seat, a sacred hill called Sealeng). Deon drove a trembling Violet to Johannesburg and there she joined Marta.

The day after his release from prison, Mannie climbed slowly up the slope to Pasopkop, passing the contorted trunk of the wild fig tree that grew between massive granite slabs. The castellated hill was unusual among the rounded tors found elsewhere in the bushveld. Pasopkop boasted a crown of quartz, a thick white band that seemed to float on the dense, tan-coloured rock like crystalline milk froth on coffee.

  Years before what Mannie thought of as the Mother Hills murders, before Koba came into their lives, he'd walk up here aged about eight or nine with his father – on the rare occasions Deon was sober enough. Mannie supposed they'd been trying to find a way to reach each other, failed father and isolated child. He recalled a feeling of fear as they stood side by side, not touching, on one of the granite platforms that jutted out across the sunburned savannah hundreds of yards below.

  'Now if it was thorns we were trying to grow we'd be rich, hey?' his father had said, gesturing at the umbrella-shaped acacias that dotted the veld. 'Our money'd be growing on trees, hey?' Mannie hadn't laughed. Their future depended on the corn the farm owner, his powerful Uncle Etienne, expected them to nurture. The crop stood withering in a stony field behind the hill. 'It's not just the dryness,' his father had said, 'it's this stuff.' Deon slapped the rock face. 'Granite weathers down into clay, quartz into sand, and between them not enough nutrients to support khakibos, never mind mielies.' His father had then casually mentioned that some quartz reefs carried gold.

  For many afternoons young Mannie chipped away at the seam, holding every loosened lump up to the sun to see if it sparkled gold. While he worked he dreamed of striking it rich, making the family fortune to save Ma and Pa from the back-breaking grind of trying to farm Impalala. At school Mannie was learning about the Pilgrim's Rest gold rush – that wasn't too far away. And what about Joburg? Weren't the streets there practically lined with gold? One day he'd go.

It was while tracing the quartz seam that he'd discovered the overgrown entrance to the cave and, inside, the rock painting. Ma had been very excited when he showed it to her.

'Oh my goodness! Who'd have thought there'd be one here? This must have been a special place for Khoisan people,' she said. 'Look at the trouble they took to decorate it. How beautifully the buck are drawn; so fine. Can you see that one's an eland?' Ma had copied the painting on her watercolour block, with her own delicate brushstrokes, every single strange figure from the teeming mural. They hadn't told anyone about the painting, not even Uncle Etienne. Ma said they didn't want people tramping all over, scratching their initials onto the wall or drawing hearts with arrows through them. 'It's a sacred place and we must be its guardians.' Her eyes had shone while Pa rolled his.

'I was hoping we might be able to use it as a tourist attraction. Heaven knows we need to generate some extra income. It looks like the crop's going to fail again.' There'd been a ding-dong battle.

But there was always shouting between the old toppies in those days. Funny how Koba being here, in this place, had eventually brought them all together, he thought as he settled, cross-legged, in front of the rock painting. He didn't see the stalking, animal-eared ochre figures that peopled the mural. He was remembering Koba's face when she'd first spotted them.

No, not spotted, he thought; 'beheld' was the word. It had been like watching someone in a church listening to a god only they could hear. He'd struck match after match for her to see by. With every flare she seemed to grow bigger and brighter with hope. But when she understood she was the only living person of her kind in the cave, the light went out. Mannie had felt ashamed to be there as witness.

But he hadn't pitied her. Even when dusty and ragged she had dignity; and she was dangerous – she'd attacked him like a civet cat, scratching and biting when she burst out of the hole her parents had hidden her in on the fateful day of the shootings.

It had taken the death of his baby sister, Ingrid, to bring the children together. He'd braved Koba's hissing hostility and bribed her with an avocado into visiting his bed-bound mother. Her company had cheered Marta – almost too well. He remembered feeling jealous of the growing closeness between Ma and the girl.

Almost a year passed before he and Deon discussed their belief that Marta saw Koba as her replacement daughter. 'That's why there's never enough money in the "train-home" jar, Pa. I mean, we don't have to go to the drive-in, do we? Isn't sending Koba home more important?' Deon had nodded. 'So Ma's doing it on purpose, isn't she?'

'Well . . .' Deon looked uncomfortable. His son was smart and it seemed he'd inherited his mother's intolerance of hypocrisy, but not her blind spots.

'Why don't you buy that girl a ticket home, Pa? Why not, hey?' the furious child had demanded.

Deon considered pleading poverty. It was no lie. Neither was love. 'I'd like to stay married, my boy.'

'It's not funny, Pa,' his son protested. 'Koba's not a caveman . . . even if that *is* her ancestors' place, or something.' His father shrugged, sympathetically Mannie decided. He changed tack. 'I've heard you two arguing about it.' He was pleased to see his father looking uncomfortable again, but why didn't he have the balls to stand up to Ma? 'Why don't we just move that girl into the house, hey? Why don't we, Pa,' he challenged, 'and stop pretending like she *isn't* part of the family?'

Deon was laying the foundations of one of the first rondavels of his new project – Impalala Guest Lodge. There would be six rustic cottages with high conical roofs made of thatch. They'd resemble native huts so that city dwellers would feel they were roughing it while on safari. But the accommodation would be luxurious, with ceiling fans and mosquito netting, a large ablution block with hot and cold showers and a communal braai area with swings for the children. Deon straightened up and wiped his hands on his shorts before laying them on his son's tense shoulders.

'Between you and me, son, I think your mother knows it's useless trying to keep Koba untouched by our wicked ways. I think she'd love to move her into the house and dress her in shoes and socks. But your ma's met her match in that girl.' He felt the boy's bunched muscles ease. 'Ja-no, that pint-size princess says the cave's her castle and she's not moving for anybody!' Deon checked to see his son was smiling then said, 'So, the moral of the story is: be careful what you wish for, hey. But ja-wat, it'll take a braver man than me to point that out to your ma.'

Mannie stood up and wandered around the cave, touching Koba's things. Her collection of scarlet-tipped seedpods that she used to make necklaces; her home-made bow and arrow already strung with cobwebs; her sleeping mat with its shop-bought pillow and blanket – evidence, Mannie thought, that his father had long been under-mining the plan to keep Koba living as simply as she would have in the Kalahari.

Koba had never confirmed that it was Deon who'd given her the zinc bucket, the pocket knife with retractable blade that she kept under her pillow. Mannie picked up her pillow now and held it to his face. She was there, in the sappy, musky smell of golden grass and wild fruit. He'd breathed her in when he dropped into the cave and had felt dizzy with longing. She was mixed in the smoky memory of the fires they'd sat around together, in the halo of lamplight they'd read by. But Mannie didn't want this cave to become a shrine to her, like Ingrid's grave was, with something from the veld placed on it every day by Ma – a wild flower, or a pretty seedpod or pebble. He thought he might break down the day he came up here and found a branch of sickle bush, with its yellow and pink catkins, propped against Koba's pillow. It would mean she wasn't coming back.

The sickle bush was the first plant Koba and his mother had shared muti information about. But it wasn't Koba's knowledge of plant properties that impressed him; it was the fact that she'd learned Afrikaans so quickly. It had been the same with all the subjects Ma taught her.

What was she going to do with her learning? he wondered. Were there schools in the Kalahari where she might teach Khoisan kids? And what would he do? He'd applied to study geology at university, but he'd been arrested before he could write his matriculation exams. Ma said he could sit the exams next year, but he couldn't see himself doing that. Not now. It seemed pointless.

He focused on the figures in the mural. Koba said they were possessed by nǀom, a supernatural energy that came to Julʼhoan healers from their ancestors, or animals, or perhaps it was both – he wasn't sure now. He'd once seen nǀom get hold of Koba when he'd helped her to trance – it had been frightening to watch. In retrospect, that was when he'd realized he loved her; he'd been terrified she might die. It had struck him then that to lose her would be unbearable.

He stirred, stood up as straight as the low ceiling would allow and climbed out of the cave. Slowly he tramped down the dusty path. The morning sun was slanting through tasselled grass heads making them look like lit candles. He wondered if Koba remembered that today was the day they'd settled on to be her birthday. By their calculation, she'd be eighteen.

8

From the road Koba trudged north-eastwards for hours through thick sand. When it gave way to shingle she saw Mannie's angular face in the faceted stone, shining as he talked about minerals. He loved rocks, that Frog-boy, she thought, raising her head to see where the mica clod might have birthed. If there'd been volcanoes here, they'd eroded down to glittering dust. The stunted shrubs were coated in it, too. A hard-hard-hard winter has passed through this land; even the trees with bitter bark have been grazed, she thought. Yellowed seed heads disintegrated as she brushed against them and a dehydrated water pan was scabbed with grey mud flakes.

She heard a high-pitched bark, the alarm call of a meerkat. Ahead, the small mammal stood on its bandy hind legs, tiny hands defiantly folded across its belly. Koba stopped.

I'll watch the Small People while I rest. Hnn, only the sentry, staring at me with her dark-circled eyes; she carries a wound near her tail base – attacked, must-be. Did she try to join the group from the burrow there? Poor-poor little woman.

Koba threw a peanut at the meerkat but she raced off, tail up.

Hnn, the Big Mother comes, Koba thought, spotting a meerkat with hanging teats emerging cautiously from the burrow. The matriarch scanned the sky and a dead tree stump near by for predators.

She hasn't seen me, she's signalled safe to the nest – here comes her man.

A battle-scarred male appeared and hurried over to bury his long muzzle in the matriarch's silver-tinted fur. Hnn, where were you flea-snufflers when I was being bitten? she thought.

The rest of the group surfaced, adolescent meerkats yawning like teenagers forced out of bed. They stood about chit-chatting or stretched themselves like house cats. At some unseen signal they were off, nosing and shoving one another, tumbling away in the dust. Koba stayed perfectly still. Minutes passed.

Here come the babies.

A nanny shoved four young pups out onto the burrow bank. The youngsters stood wobbling, apparently dazed by the outside brightness.

Koba heard the spit call of a threatened meerkat. She turned to see the lone female heading at speed for the young group. Nanny bristled and spat at the intruder, trying to curl her body over all four squirming pups at once. The lone female reached a stray pup and sank her teeth into its scrawny neck, then dashed into the burrow with it. Nanny let out a fusillade of alarm calls. The meerkat family bounded back from every direction. Mother flew into the burrow. Koba heard subterranean scuffles, hissing and yelps. The lone female backed out of the burrow, turned bloodied tail and fled, pursued by the mother. Several adolescent males joined in the chase, four-toed feet balled into fists. They all disappeared from view.

Sighing, Koba stood up. Lone female had only been trying to hide the pups. She'd apprehended danger.

The little drama set her thinking about her own situation at Impalala. For a long time she'd felt like the outsider, watching the burrow, the farmstead, with anxious eyes from her hilltop. Until recently she'd resented Marta for keeping her in a cave, 'like some prehistoric pet', she'd once overhead Deon say. Shame-faced, Mannie had explained the word to her. Not long afterwards Marta invited her to move into the farmhouse with them; Koba had taken the chance to insult Marta in the only way she knew how – by exposing her bare buttocks to her. The memory of it made her blush, even now.

Yau, you felt she was trying to own you, Bushgirl, with her talk of /Ton clothes and hairstyles. You wanted to keep your own skin.

Yes, but my pride kept me from a soft bed for the remainder of my Impalala years.

Your apartheid years.

Koba laughed. She wished she'd had the chance to tell Marta that she finally understood the advantages of growing up in a cave.

At Pretoria Central Prison the inmates had all been black, but for one white woman kept upstairs in a separate cell. This woman wore her own clothes instead of the prison-issue brown wraparound dress and red headscarf. She was exempt from the floor-scrubbing and polishing the black female prisoners were dragooned into.

Shoved in to clean the white woman's cell one day with a mop, bucket and container that said Sunbeam, Koba could only stare at the tin. She didn't even know how to open it. She realized that, like the ǀTon woman who was smiling at her, she had never wielded domestic cleaning implements, let alone in servitude for anyone. 'Get a move on in there,' she heard the warder call from the corridor. She fumbled with the tin, trying to fathom the opening secrets behind the smug smile of the sun logo. The ǀTon woman tiptoed across in stockinged feet and used her painted fingernails to prise the lid off. Inside the tin was a foul-smelling red paste. Koba remembered Selina using something like this at Impalala, but how? She tried to get the mop head into the tin. 'What in heaven's name are you playing at?' The warder stood hands on her hips in the cell doorway. Koba froze. No answer was expected; she hadn't said one word since her arrest; everyone assumed she was mute. The ǀTon woman moved to help, the wardress's hands flapped like birds with clipped wings. 'Mrs Mason, please get back on your bed; you know the rule. And *you*' – she snapped her fingers at Koba – 'get down and do the job properly.'

'It's illegal to make awaiting-trial prisoners work, wardress. That's the rule of *law*.'

'Ag, missus, don't be difficult now, I'm only trying to do my job. Matron will be here for inspection soon. C'mon now, you don't want to get us all in trouble, do you?' The ǀTon woman climbed onto her bed and Koba kneeled to her task over the tin, thinking she'd had enough trouble to last her a lifetime. But it was even more difficult trying to force the long-handled mop into the paste from that angle.

'Stop trying to be funny,' the wardress screamed, coming towards her fast.

Susan Mason leaped up. 'Please. I don't think she's ever polished a floor before. Let me do it, please.'

Koba was never allowed back in the white woman's cell and was never given cleaning duties again. More reason for the other prisoners to resent her.

They'd shunned her from the first; spoke about her among themselves. It didn't matter; she didn't understand their Nguni languages. She'd never learned any because none of the Impalala workforce would have anything to do with her. But it had never occurred to her that Marta herself had risked imprisonment for harbouring her, even in a cave, or for speaking out about the need for blacks to have equal rights. That was what Mrs Mason was in solitary confinement for, she gathered from overhearing prison staff gossip in Afrikaans. Now she understood why the Marais family were socially ostracized.

Shame-shame I never got the chance to tell Marta these things I learned, Koba thought as she plodded on through the savannah, and a shame I'll never get to lie in a soft bed now. Her legs ached.

Too much time in a cell; I have lost my trekking rhythm.

On-on, Bushgirl! In prison you dreamed of walking at will, across spaces without walls and wire, bolts and bars.

Her insect was right. She should relish her liberty, rejoice that she'd left prison and André behind.

But I also leave Marta, Deon and Mannie behind, the one who can bulge out his eyes like a frog to make me laugh when my heart is heavy. Hnnnn, we were like the meerkat couple, nuzzling, cuddling, nesting at night, our bodies pressed close together, brown on white, white in brown, like one.

Stop. This is scratching your bites again, Bushgirl.

By late afternoon fatigue had emptied her head of all thoughts except negotiating her surroundings. Spiny plants to be avoided, thorn trees that offered meagre shade from the crucifying sun. Worse was the constant worry about lions, real ones, whose deadly approach she had no chance of hearing. They could stalk her silently, following the smell of her fear, the flap-flap of her unsuitable shoes. In panic, she ripped off the patent leather pumps and shoved them into her bundle. Walking barefoot was going to be difficult. She no longer had the hardened soles of a typical Kalahari dweller. She hot-footed on and on, dreaming of the majestic mahoganies that lined the riverbank at Impalala. Their fallen leaves provided a soft mat to walk on and their towering branches a cool canopy during the heat of the day. Occasionally there had been leopard lying up in the branches over the river, but they fed on monkeys or bushbuck. Out here, Koba knew she was easy meat for a pride of starving lions.

Finally she found a large shrub whose branches hung all the way to the ground.

None like it at Impalala, but somehow it was familiar to her. Its name popped into her head – lion's shade, her father had called it. Terrified but desperate for shade she circled, checking for spoor. Paw prints a-plenty, but no fresh ones. Carefully she parted the curtain of stiff, thorny-leaved branches and stepped into the shade. Bliss. She flopped down, her back against the stocky white trunk, and breathed in deeply. Hot and dry here, but at least she was safe and out of the sun. She untied her bundle. She was feeling queasy; she should eat. She allowed herself a handful of the Mannie peanuts. Delicious. And salty.

As she munched, she remembered that the roots of this tree could be roasted and ground to make a drink. It was bitter, like the coffee that the |Ton liked. She'd never acquired a taste for coffee, especially not sweetened with condensed milk. Just the thought of it made her feel sick. She drank some water.

'Water, yes. Father said this tree stores it if the trunk is hollow.' She rapped the trunk. 'No, this tree is still a child.'

She began to worry that her water supply would be insufficient for her journey. Then I'll just dig up a water root, she told herself. What if they'd all been dug up already by thirsty people, would she be able to spot the almost-invisible tendril that whispered their underground presence? She worried that her Kalahari eyes wouldn't return to her quickly enough. She pulled her knees up to her chest and dropped her head onto her arms.

She cried for a lot longer than she realized. When she lifted her head, lavender shadows had pooled into every sandy depression.

Too late to walk on now; I must sleep where I sit. A fire will bright me, but the other Lion, André, might be out there.

It had occurred to her that André could swap his truck for a horse and come after her without engine noise or lights. It was better to sleep dark, under the tree; its sharp curtain should deter predators, she decided.

She sat in her thorny tent listening to the sounds of daylight fade. A dove cooed her last lament; the grasshopper choir began to thin out. Finally only a soloist remained, chirruping stubbornly like a drunken bow-player who refuses to pack up. Koba heard the swoosh of a feathered marauder and the insect played no more.

Night fell with bitumen blackness. One minute she could see her toes, blisterfully free of the chafing shoes; the next, she couldn't even see her feet. She shivered, longing for light, but decided against switching on her torch; better to save the batteries for emergencies. Her ears began to ache from the strain of listening for movement. She jumped when a nightjar began its sustained call. It sounded like a small motor.

Call yourself a Bushgirl? Does your intelligence not tell you it's a bird, not a truck? Soon the jackal will yip and the hyena will cackle. Song of the Kalahari night. Now go to sleep.

Koba sighed. She almost wished she was back in her prison cell.

Later, she had a disturbing dream. She was in the prison cell, kneeling on the floor. A lion was riding her, his claws digging into her shoulders, his thorny penis piercing her, burning her, ruining her, when a frog hopped in front of her. With his tongue he caught splashing tears; he licked across her forehead, over her cheeks, cooling the heat there, down her nose, her long, long nose. Now she saw she had a trunk, a muscular weapon she used to pluck the stupid lion from her flanks. She tossed him away, through the walls, and strode out into the night air. There was a storm coming, black clouds flapped towards her like giant bats, and behind them came an enormous animal, its back sleek with rain, its mighty horns made of lightning. She sprang onto its back, thinking an eland would never bear the weight of an elephant. But now the horns were tusks of lightning and the elephant's trumpet was like thunder. She found herself at the top of a mountain, in the centre of the storm. Rain lashed down, the wind tore at her clothes. A dress, yellow in the lightning; at her feet, an eland cow lying stretched out on her side, large eyes beseeching her. And then the eland was bleeding from the neck, and the blood ran down the mountain and washed over the land, like rain. And she was a girl, not an elephant, and she couldn't find the frog.

9

Black nights and blistering days followed. Koba walked and walked, traipsing after the morning star according to Twi's instruction. It was a pitiful guide, that pale star. 'It crosses the sky all day ahead of the sun; it has no branches to carry for shade; it cannot turn aside to rest under a tree. It is chased by the sun and the sun is a death-thing,' her grandmother had said. Koba picked branches and held them over her head like parasols as she walked, but always her arm grew weary.

Dawn was her best walking time. No need for a sun shade then. She'd swish through knee-high grass, not dew-damp but nevertheless releasing a refreshing memory of moisture. Every morning she was sure would be the one when she heard the *thwok-ghrrr ghrrr* of pestles and mortars welcoming her home. Women who looked like her mother would be grinding the roasted mangetti nuts, pouring hot water on the powder to make coffee. Sometimes she could almost smell the bitter aroma.

The mornings passed and she never heard camp sounds. She thought the land unnaturally still. Where was the frenetic bird activity of breeding season? she wondered. Where the parade of colourful males strutting, preening, calling, performing aerial acrobatics to attract female attention? Where was the spring scent? What green there was looked dull in its coat of Kalahari dust.

Drought has this land by the throat, she thought, and immediately began worrying about the danger of fire. One spark and savannah would burn for hundreds of miles around. She would be corralled by white-hot sand and scrub.

She walked faster, scanning the sky for following vultures. They'd know she was lion's prey before she did. And she kept tasting the scalding air, to see if her tongue could detect the veld-fire smoke her dust-caked nostrils couldn't. She rested less often, walking for hours every day, a fierce dehydration headache pounding as she forced herself to ration her sips of water from Twi's bottle. She was beginning to doubt his instruction. Surely she should have found someone, anyone, by now. Has my true n!ore deserted me? Do I walk in a circle?

Late the next afternoon she saw her first baobab tree. It rose from the flat landscape like a colossal tuber. She ran towards it and threw her arms around one of the massive, low-slung branches. 'How my heart has missed you, Giant,' she said, her cheek pressed against the smooth bark. She looked up its soaring trunk. The tree was just coming into bloom. The flowers would stink at twilight. Nevertheless, she would camp there.

'Upside-down trees' people called baobabs because their leafless crowns looked like tree roots. Up their corpulent trunks she had first learned to climb; she had raided her first beehive at the top of an upside-down and learned that for her the taste of honey was not worth the pain of bee stings. She remembered sitting under a sprawling giant with her grandmother, Zuma, hearing the tall tree's tale.

'The great god, Gǁaoan, hungering for baobab fruit, climbed the tree,' Zuma had said. 'But the tree teased him, lifting its branches higher and higher, dangling its fruit just-just beyond reach. In a fury Gǁaoan swelled into a storm and ripped the tree from the earth, flinging it skywards. When it landed, it was upside down, its roots exposed for all to see. And so Gǁaoan left it.'

Koba petted the tree, running her hands over the fat folds in its pink-grey trunk. I can sleep safely here, she thought, out of the reach of lion. I will tie myself to that branch tonight.

People had used the baobab, but they were long gone, the climbing pegs driven into its trunk all but enveloped. And there were no stones stacked at the base of the tree to indicate a hive someone was husbanding. That didn't mean there were no people in a n!ore near by, she reminded herself. Only the bees had moved.

She shinned easily up a narrower trunk. From her perch she could see far into the distance. Flat, dun-coloured dune sand; tall, brittle grass; the usual rim of rugged shrubs on the horizon, further off now, it seemed. Closer, a depression in the sand, darker in colour than the surrounding earth. A pan? Dried out, but she might be able to dig for water. She must remember its direction.

She scanned again. Nothing moved across the Kalahari sandveld, not even a breeze. She sighed. I am not being chased, she thought, but she wished she'd seen some sign of life, slim figures walking single file through the grass, or a curl of cooking smoke on the horizon. Even some Herero cattle herders. She cupped her hand around her ear. All she heard, in the distance, was a cuckoo's plaintive *dee-deederik* call.

She climbed down and examined the sand – big crinkled prints of elephant and some owl bolus. She prodded one with the toe of her shoe; it crumbled to reveal tiny bones inside. Old.

She slept badly and woke feeling stiff and sore. Her whole body ached – from the kicking she'd received from André; the long walks; sleeping curled up in the tree. A combination, she decided. She reached for her water bottle and shook it. One mouthful left. She had better head for the pan.

She set off in air irritable with static. The sky seemed low today, yellow-mauve clouds giving it an old-bruise look. It felt abnormally hot for dawn. The land pants like a dog, she thought, feeling breathless herself.

The pan hadn't appeared too far off seen from the top of the baobab, but it seemed to take for ever to reach. Finally she stepped into the shallow depression. She was excited to see small excavations of sand littering the surface. These hadn't been visible from her lookout. They were evidence of sip-well digging. People had been here. 'People who know about underwater,' Koba sang. She pounced on their drinking straws to check them for recent use. As she touched the long grass stalks they crumbled, leaving lines of gold dust. She thrust her hand into the wells as far as it would go, all the way up to her armpit, feeling the earthen walls. Bone dry, the bottoms crusted over with salt. She sat back on her heels, too disappointed even to sample it.

Koba felt like giving up, like lying down spread-eagled in the middle of the pan and offering herself up as the sun's sacrifice. Let the lion, human or animal, come and kill me, she thought.

Lift your what's-up-front, Bushgirl. Look at that sky. It promises rain.

She raised her face and scowled at the sun. It sulked behind steely cloud. Yes, it might rain. Even a few drops might reactivate a well. She'd wait around here in case. But she'd need shade. She trudged slowly towards a copse of thorn bushes on the far side of the pan. At the back there'd be shade.

As she rounded the thick clump, she saw them – big, grey, rounded. Elephant? It couldn't be. The land was too dry. She narrowed her gaze. *Huts!*

'N!ore; a n!ore!' she shouted.

A lark that had been crouching on the ground flew up. *Prrr, prrr, preee, preee*, it protested. Koba, hand across heart, stared at the circle of low-domed huts. The grassed roofs of the shelters were bleached elephant grey. Her pulse quickened. Six dwellings in all, close together, open doorways facing onto a communal central area cleared of grass and scrub.

Hnn! This is truly a Jul'hoan place. Must be that Real People live here. Cleared earth, freshly swept. Women will do that every-every day, checking for snake trails. Snakes like to share a person's sleeping mat on cold nights. Do you know, Insect, Grandmother told me that one time she scolded her husband for pushing at her back all night with his meat stick. Then she saw she had been lying with a cobra. He-he-he.

There will be Zumas there, among those huts. Maybe Kobas, Bushgirl. All Real People.

The thought made her stomach cramp and her bowel churn. She retched, spewing up the orange she'd had for breakfast.

Yau, now you have made yourself pale and stinking, like a dead thing. Do not be surprised if the people over there run from you.

Just thinking about stepping into the camp made her sweat. Everyone would stare, and even if they didn't notice her sour breath and sticky, pale skin, they might find her clothes strange.

Why am I wearing this yellow church-dress? I am like one of those strange flowers Marta drew – a daffodil – but in the desert. And must-be I look like one, with this.

She plucked petulantly at the frilly collar.

How to explain myself and speak to the people? I don't know enough Jul'hoan words. They will ask me questions, they will press round, they will talk-talk behind their hands. How do I say I was a child, walking with my parents near the Mother Hills, when ǀTon came and killed them? Then I must tell about the ǀTon taking me away to another country, where I lived and lived with them until I had food with a Frog-boy. Then I must say how the police took me, did ruin-things to me, put me in prison . . .

I must explain the government put me on a train and told me to come back to my n!ore. How a lion with three eyes chased me across the veld at night, how I hid in an itching-hole and how I am here now to live as a Real Person. But sorry-sorry, I have lost my Jul'hoan tongue and my proper Jul'hoan-woman ways . . . I think they will not understand.

Her head drooped, too heavy for the slender stem of her neck. Inside she felt empty, insubstantial. She sank down as the sand began to swim before her eyes, individual grains separating, then coalescing again into a spinning mass. Her breathing became rapid; invisible walls pressed in on her.

Koba fought her panic, lifting her head to gulp at the oppressive air. She ignored the flies that paddled gleefully in the sweat beads on her upper lip and forehead. She'd had these attacks before; the first time was when, newly abducted, she'd been locked in a storeroom on Etienne Marais' farm. Marta had helped her to control her terror. Now, she forced herself to take slower, deeper breaths, as Marta had shown her, and eventually she felt calmer. She took the last sip of water from her bottle and stood up unsteadily. She brushed sand off the full yellow skirt of her dress and straightened the collar. Then she stepped forward.

The place was dead quiet. No camp-speech, thought Koba, dismayed at not hearing the *thwok-thwok* of women grinding nuts. She hurried through the gap in the makeshift fence, eager to put thorn scrub between herself and any lion.

She padded up to a hut then inched around the lifeless branches that formed its walls. She froze when she saw a form lying in a doorway. She stared then shivered. It was like looking down on her dead self – a young woman, same height, same age, same thin limbs with what Mannie would have called Wednesday ankles and wrists: 'Whens-dey-gonna break?' he'd tease. This girl had the same narrow brown feet, but the stranger's had thick, hardened soles instead of the blisters blooming on Koba's paler ones. Her gaze ranged warily up the lifeless body, over the beautifully beaded pubic apron made from soft hide and then settled on the facial area. It was covered by a kaross made from springbok hide.

A sense of loss made her whisper one of the few Jul'hoan words she remembered. It was a greeting: 'G‖aan.'

The corpse shot up, fighting to free itself from the voluminous folds. Koba leaped back and stood gawping at the face that emerged. Not mine – better, she thought, admiring the tiny black moles peppering the flat nose and high cheekbones of the resurrected stranger.

She reminds me of those buns I liked to eat at Impalala – poppy seed.

Koba felt herself grinning widely.

The young woman seemed equally astonished by the sight of her, but she didn't smile. Composing her face into an expression of cautious courtesy, she simply said, 'Eh.'

'Eh?' Koba repeated. 'Um, I,' she stammered. How to introduce herself in Jul'hoan? '. . . Er, I, daughter, N‡aisa-late and Tami-late, granddaughter, Zuma-late . . .'

The woman frowned.

Hhn-hn-hn. Spit on my tongue, useless thing. Can I not even speak my family names? She stares at me. Is it taboo to name dead people?

72

I think I have offended this Poppy Seed person. Wish-wish I could explain my grandmother was the Zuma who was an owner of medicine and a storyteller of such renown people came from far to listen round her fire.

No, that is big-boastful. It's good I haven't the words. Wait: nǀomkxao, that is the word for an owner of medicine.

Bushgirl, how you can forget? Are you not one too?

Hush, Cricket. Don't tell of my trancing; it wasn't a Real People's thing. And don't go chirring about that eland spirit guide.

'Zuma nǀomkxao, my late big-mother,' Koba tried. The other woman's obvious incomprehension defeated her effort. They half smiled at each other before the villager shrugged, rose and beckoned Koba to follow.

On her short tramp Koba saw other group members sitting or lying listlessly about. They ignored her, as custom demanded. It was a courtesy, designed to give her time to recuperate in peace after an arduous journey, but to Koba the lack of attention felt hostile.

Foolish me, grown too accustomed to open arms when I step into the ǀTon house at Impalala.

Poppy Seed, whose name was ǀAsa, stopped at an ash-grey fire. She gestured for Koba to sit, then she reached for a tiny tortoise shell that hung around her neck and pulled the grass plug from it. ǀAsa shook some powder into her palm and approached the visitor. She murmured something and sprinkled a line of fine powder onto Koba's dusty head.

My nose remembers this – a visitor-welcome smell. Kind Poppy Seed, but where are her people? Shouldn't some come from the huts near by?

Her hostess began to rake the ashes, searching for something. Finally she unearthed some grey balls from the sand beneath the ashy embers and set them to one side to cool.

Mangetti nuts? I disremember them like this. In my childhood they were fat fruit, steamed to soften the skin. I see me sucking the flesh. They are good-good – better than jam and peanut butter and meat.

These nuts . . . in my child's memory they are pale brown and dented like an old face. We scratched noses and eyes onto them to make them look like the elders. I had a friend, a playmate who could draw likenesses. What was his name?

ǀAsa was saying something in a very soft voice. Her manner suggested apology, but Koba was lost in her own thoughts, hearing her mother's instruction from all those years ago:

'To crack open a nut a person must be sharp with them.' Mother showed me where to hit them with a stone, how to grind them. Will Poppy Seed make the morning drink, the Juǀ'hoan coffee, now?

Coffee? Fool Bushgirl, do you see water here? Must-be Poppy Seed was saying sorry for not having drink to give you!

Koba felt chastened. She had no water left to give. She untied the knot in her bundle and scrabbled around in it until she found an orange. ǀAsa's eyes widened as she held it up to her, and Koba saw the young woman's throat rise to swallow an upwelling of saliva. She accepted the fruit. Koba was taken aback.

Then ǀAsa seemed to sink. Koba wanted to support her, but she felt she didn't have the right to touch this gentle stranger. She stepped back.

ǀAsa steadied herself and, cradling the fruit to her chest, she bobbed her thanks. Their eyes met and the girls smiled openly at each other. Koba glimpsed a dimple in one of Poppy Seed's cheeks. Then ǀAsa turned and hurried off across the camp ground.

Why does she not suck on the orange? Where is she going? Perhaps to share the food with others; they will all be thirsty.

I found no water roots on the way here; people have harvested them all. A shame I don't have more oranges . . . or water. This place suffers.

She looked around the camp. Close-up, the thatching on most of the huts was shaggy; bald in places.

Hnn, old camp, and the people have been too hungry for hut-fixing.

Thirst is worse; gets hold of you and wrings your insides, twists you dry from your throat to your toes. The only way is to move slow-slow. That is how Poppy Seed walks. But she does not look ill. Is she a wife, a mother? With that ǀTon dress on under her skin

74

apron, I cannot see her breasts. Hnn, I did not expect to see a Jul'hoan woman wearing ITon clothes. My dress is not so strange after all.

But IAsa's was worn and faded where hers was travel-stained but bright – too bright under the lowering sky, she thought, feeling unknown eyes staring at her.

IAsa beckoned from a far doorway. Koba eased her feet into her shoes and set off, trying not to limp. A skeletal dog cringed, giving a token growl as she passed. To her left she heard someone plucking mournful notes on a thumb piano; the playing continued unabated as she crossed in front of the musician. Koba heard neither chat nor whispers from the huts she passed, but she sensed people peering from behind the grass walls.

But they will hear my heart beating above the creak of my shoes, she thought. She halted outside the hut her new friend had disappeared into, feeling the air holding its breath.

IAsa was kneeling down beside an old woman, who lay inside the hut. She held a segment of the peeled orange to the woman's cracked lips. This was her grandmother, Zuma, hollow-eyed and -cheeked. The crone sucked and sucked on the fruit with toothless gums, her pleated lids closed in ecstasy. IAsa smiled at Koba over her shoulder and bobbed thanks again.

A flash of lightning illuminated the dark hut. It startled Koba and she spun round to the doorway. In it she saw a policeman, backlit. She screamed. He rushed towards her, the brass buttons on his jacket leering at her in the repeated flashes of lightning.

Metal buttons, biting into her flesh; she is forced face down. She feels the rasp of serge against her thighs.

'Boesman bitch who likes white worm; now you feel some black snake.'

The hut walls closed in around her and she fell into a deep, dark chasm.

Koba's scream brought villagers running; even the dehydrated dog. It thrust its nose through the forest of legs gathered around her prostrate form.

'What happened? Who is this woman? Is she dead?'

'ǀAsa, why did she scream?'

ǀAsa looked up at the concerned faces. 'I was feeding Grandmother the orange the stranger gave me when –'

'She gave you an orange?' ǀAsa's grandfather, the man in the tattered police jacket, exclaimed. 'My mouth is so puckered from lack of liquid, it is like an unused arsehole. I know this because it is weeks since I put something into my mouth that could pass through my stomach and out the back. Where is that orange? Give a dry old man a taste.'

'Dabe.' The old crone, Zuma, waggled a finger at him from the floor. 'Stop talking faeces in front of visitors.'

'This visitor hears nothing. We needed this visitor and her orange weeks ago. She is *late*.' The crowd tittered at his joke as they gazed at Koba's unconscious body.

Dabe relished the fact that old age gave him licence to say things most wouldn't. He could break social taboos with impunity. Wearing the tattered policeman's uniform was one. Though seldom exposed to them, the Juǀ'hoansi knew to fear the men in blue uniforms. Old Dabe had bartered hard for the jacket and the cap from a mine-worker he'd met at a waterhole. Not only was it amusing to see people's consternation when he wore it with his loincloth, but the jacket was practical. On cold days it was warmer than a skin kaross.

'If this girl is dead it will be one joke too many, you old ostrich,' his wife warned.

'No-no. She's not dead,' ǀAsa said, lowering her ear to Koba's chest.

'U-uh-uhnn. Thank –' Old Zuma only just avoided saying the name of the great god out loud. 'You better not touch her, child; something has overcome her. It may be a bad spirit. Go and fetch your mother's new husband.'

'I think she was asking for a healer,' ǀAsa mused, 'but the stranger doesn't have our tongue so it was difficult to follow her.'

'Yet she *looks* like a Real Person.'

'It is so.'

'But she is from the ǀTon. Look at her clothes,' someone said.

'Aie, what's going on?' A woman with skin like brown velvet, worn slightly in places, shook her head at the sight of prostrate Koba. Her

76

mottled cheek was dimpled like her daughter's, but she didn't have ∣Asa's smattering of moles. 'First we have a promise of rain,' N!ai continued, 'then we have a stranger dressed in sunshine lying like a dead thing in my mother's hut.'

'Where is your husband? Go fetch ∣Qui Beard,' Old Zuma commanded her daughter. 'He must check this strange child for bad spirits.'

'He comes, he comes, but slow-slow, you know ∣Qui Beard,' N!ai said. She crouched down next to Koba. 'Aiee, this garment is fine,' she whispered to ∣Asa as she fingered the frill of Koba's dress. 'She looks like a flower in it.'

'Stop that.' Old Zuma flicked her fly switch at her daughter and granddaughter. 'Have you lost your manners?'

Bo, ∣Asa's husband, joined them, his mild face troubled at the sight of Koba. 'Where did you find her?' he asked his wife.

∣Asa shrugged. 'She appeared. I opened my eyes and she was there, above me.'

'People are saying that the stranger may be a rain-bringer.'

'No, no rain. We will only see Rain's hair. It will just hang there, as always,' said someone.

'I don't think so,' ∣Asa replied. 'That sky is pregnant. We haven't seen it so for moons and moons and moons. Must be Big Rain.'

'Yau-no! We can't have Big Rain season – we haven't had the Little Rains yet,' Old Zuma reminded her from her place on the sleeping mat next to Koba.

Koba had come round. She kept her eyes firmly shut. She felt nauseous and the sound of curious voices plus the smell of unwashed bodies was making her feel worse. She didn't want to vomit again. She lay very still.

The group continued debating the vital topic. Little Rains meant they should stay put; Big Rains allowed them to move to new foraging grounds. Meanwhile, ∣Asa pleaded with her husband to fetch the only man in the village who spoke a white language.

Bo was a quiet man, teased for his lack of skill with a bow and arrow, but lauded for his ability with a musical bow. He adored his young wife and hated to disappoint her, but the band's foremost hunter was formidable. 'Don't make buck eyes at me, |Asa-wife. You know Tsamkxao hates |Ton ways. I am not calling him to see a person who looks Real, but isn't.'

'She is Real. And her heart is good. Mine already knows it,' |Asa insisted.

'Rather ask me to stick porcupine quills in my eyes.'

Another young man laughed at Bo's plea. 'Husband-of-my-cousin, you are a worm-penis! How can you not do the bidding of your bride?'

'Yes,' Old Zuma said to her grandson-in-law, 'you stand there growing breasts! Someone be a real man and fetch Tsamkxao.' No one moved. She sucked her teeth in irritation. 'Must I get up from my sick mat? Husband, you go. Tsamkxao will not put his fierce face front with you.'

'Me? But I am nearly dead,' Old Dabe protested. 'Anyone with eyes in their heads can see. Yau, my bag of bones is twenty days without water; my arse' – his wife flicked her fly switch at him – 'er, my *mouth* is so dry my tongue rattles when I speak. Listen: *rrrrrr-r-r-rr*?' People laughed. 'You see, you see? How can I coax Tsamkxao's sting from him without my golden tongue?'

The talk switched to how disobliging their kinsman, Tsamkxao, was.

'Except when it comes to sharing meat,' someone said. Discreet titters. People appreciated the euphemism. Everyone but her husband knew Tsamkxao was N!ai's lover.

N!ai ignored them and pushed her way out through the crowd to stand in the doorway of the hut. 'Looks like my clever daughter was right; the Rain animal is coming,' she said to no one in particular. 'Women had better stay in their huts or they will get his *attention*.'

Old Dabe joined her at the door. His daughter was a bold woman; she'd been like that since girlhood. He wouldn't want her any other way. He put his arm around her shoulders. 'Yes, Rain *will* walk this way. I smell moisture in the air.'

A very old man with protruding ribs and folds of skin hanging across his shrunken belly shambled past. 'The only moisture you smell, old ostrich-egg eater, is your own urine,' he cackled.

'You would know, old penis-pincher.' Dabe grinned back. 'I see you there in the bushes, trying to squeeze something from your little bird's beak.'

'Eishhh! Enough about your shrivelled genitals, you two,' Old Zuma called from inside the hut.

Outside grey clouds roiled across a sky the colour of metal.

'Ladies, get ready to hide, the Rain animal is coming, and he's *bigggg*!' N!ai sang.

'Quick, bring the visitor's bundle in,' |Asa said.

A round-breasted young woman snatched it up and began feeling it. 'Perhaps she has tobacco in there?'

'For shame, Chu!ko, get your paws out of her bag. She will share with us when she is ready.'

10

K oba sat up and examined the hut. It was constructed around a circle of vertical sapling poles, cross struts tied to it with strips of bark. Through the grass walls she could see slivers of light.

It's still day so I haven't been lying here long, she thought. She remembered arriving at the village, not being able to make herself understood, following the girl with the seed-sprinkled cheeks and then nothing. But now she could hear excited voices.

Suddenly, the shaggy walls of the hut lit up with blue-white light, which was gone in a flash.

Lightning. And that damp-dust smell in the air. A rainstorm is coming. Must-be the people are outside, watching the rain's legs.

She registered the first tentative tap of rain on the roof. She crept towards the door and pushed the skin curtain aside. From the shadows she watched fat drops stamp the sand. Dust puffs danced around the ankles of several men and the two old women milling outside. In the doorways of nearby huts she saw the younger women scanning the darkened sky until a crack of lightning sent them shying away like nervous fillies. Thunder boomed overhead as the elders began to bob and skip with excitement. Old Dabe darted about, head feather tossing like a kori bustard's, marshalling children to catch raindrops in their cupped hands.

Koba heard rain tinkling on dry leaves, then it began to fall in earnest. Soon it was pummelling the ground, pounding long silver spikes into the earth. A current of joy surged through the crowd – people were laughing, ululating, shouting with glee above the din of thunder and lightning. Young mothers braved the attention of the Rain animal and held out their hands to catch the water sluicing off the grass roofs, while toddlers squirmed out of their grasp and splashed into puddles. Older children splattered one another. And a dog. He leaped into the air, snapping at the spray, tail wagging back and forth like a windscreen wiper.

Koba watched as every hut was garlanded with old tins, gourds, empty tortoise shells and hollowed-out melons. Anything to catch the precious water. One hut boasted a glass bottle, a diamond set amid rough beads. Another had an upturned hat as its centrepiece.

She held her own water bottle under the stream falling in the doorway, then took a long, luxurious swig.

The water tasted better than any she remembered. Soft-soft-soft throat, she thought, feeling relief flow into her. For now, she was safe.

Even if these are not my people, they will look upon me as a rain-bringer, she thought, eagerly thrusting her hands into the downpour. She felt drops dance on her palms and folded her fingers inwards, making a fist to protect the precious moisture. She held it to her heart, her hand round and shiny like a freshly rinsed baobab fruit.

Watching an old man, whose wizened face was upturned to the clouds in liquid worship, reminded her that her own dust-caked face needed attention.

By now the ground was alive with water. Snakes of it writhed across the communal area, coiling around huts, collecting in hollows that were soon ankle-deep in brown water. And still the rain hissed down, ricocheting into the puddles, leaping up like watery exclamation marks.

Minutes passed, the rain eased, as if someone was slowly closing a tap. No longer were Koba's ears filled with the white noise of rushing water. Now she could distinctly hear dripping. Drop-drip-tinkle, drop-drip-tinkle. It made her want to pee. She stood up, slipped her shoes on and stepped outside, nodding shyly to the younger females, who had also stepped out from their refuges. They tried not to show their curiosity.

How different the camp looked, Koba thought. It sparkled. Wet leaves and grasses glistened in the sun; bushes looked as though they were festooned with tinsel.

Koba passed a mother stripping the muddy vest off her toddler and paused to watch the squab-like woman rinse him in a puddle. The tot was upended, the mother grabbed a handful of wet grass off a roof and wiped between his chubby buttocks, cooing all the while. The boy squealed in protest. Koba smiled, then stepped behind the hut. As she rounded it, she saw her guide.

|Asa was naked, her skin glowing amber from the rainwater. She was using a handful of leaves to wipe across her belly. She waved gaily, beckoned and, plucking a handful of fresh wipes, thrust them at Koba for her own ablutions.

Koba smiled but kept her dress on, letting the rain soak her until the dust streamed off in red-brown runnels.

Ten minutes later the sky reverted to an unperturbed blue and the sun went about its drying business. Steam rose off the wet clothing of the villagers.

To Koba, they no longer stank, but she could smell prison; it emanated from the old man's police jacket. Again she felt nauseous.

How could I have mistaken him for a pol-isman? Loincloth, wrinkled knees, a guinea fowl feather in his cap. Hnnn, my intelligence left me with the lightning.

Still, Koba couldn't meet his curious gaze.

Thirst slaked, the group gathered around Koba, all talking at once. Hemmed in by speculation, she repeated the names of her grandmother, mother and father, but no matter how many times she did this, the villagers did not seem to understand that these were her relatives. Is this a guess-what-the-stranger-is-trying-to-say game, she sighed to herself, watching their energetic exchanges – Policeman said something; Squab bobbed in emphatic agreement; Poppy Seed shook her head, making the beaded hair decoration jiggle across her forehead.

Koba felt crushed. Not since her childhood had she been so helpless. She hated it. Why wouldn't her stubborn tongue wrap properly around the branches of her family tree so people could understand her? Why were her ears so stuffed with |Ton talk that they couldn't discern any meaning in what was said to her?

She felt a wrench to her shoes. The pigeon-breasted woman's toddler was trying to detach the buckles from her shoes. She lifted her foot, hiding the buckle behind the calf of her other leg. They were a present from Marta and suited her better than the yellow dress, she thought. She particularly liked the gold buckles, and was pleased to have preserved their shine by carrying them all the way.

Grass-arse persisted with his plucking, then began to wail as she dropped her bundle onto her feet to conceal her shoes. Koba considered giving him the shoes – sooner or later she would have to share her possessions with whoever admired them – it was the custom, hxaro. She hadn't forgotten. But the shoes would be worn by his splay-footed mother, the squab of a woman who was ignoring Koba's discomfort while greedily eyeing her bundle.

Gracefully, Poppy Seed swung the toddler up to her hip and distracted him by rattling the strands of ostrich eggshell beads around her neck. Koba nodded to her and the girl grinned over his shoulder.

Koba became aware of an altercation. A tall man was arguing with others as they tried to push him forward. He swatted at them. He was, she realized, a new face in the crowd; he was also the only person who did not look at her, not even surreptitiously, yet she felt burned by his scrutiny. She tried to catch his eye to nod a respectful greeting; he turned his shoulder to her. In his hand he held a finely made hunting bow. It had the polished sheen of well-used wood.

This one is the best hunter, Koba thought, but what is his game? He sees me, but will not look. He does not like what he thinks I am.

Still she had a feeling that he, of all the villagers, could assist her. Koba stepped towards him, forcing herself to smile. He was tall, surprisingly tall for a Jul'hoan, almost as tall as her Frog-boy, Mannie, she thought. But this was no boy, but a man of broad chest and fully muscled thigh.

'Do you perhaps speak Afrikaans, sir?' she asked in Afrikaans. He said nothing. 'Do you speak English?' she asked doubtfully. He stared down at her with a look like an eagle's.

Yau-yau, I see you, Koba thought, high above us. You think we are worms or mice for your meal.

'What are you doing here?' he demanded in Afrikaans.

Koba was caught between relief at having an interpreter and alarm that it should be this rude man. Where was the traditional exchange – an enquiry about her journey; the state of the plants and animals along the way? Where was the polite circling, customary among isolated people?

Had she come from far? How was the land – dry or well-watered? And the animals? She would smile and produce some coarse leaves from the tin Twi had put into her bag. They would be received with apparent indifference, but the alacrity with which the locals would produce pipes made from hollowed bone or flattened pieces of tin rolled into cigar shapes would indicate their tobacco-hunger. They would all squat in the shade of a tree and the pipe would be passed around, everyone taking care not to suck up more than their fair share of the delicious smoke. They might be startled that she refused the pipe, but if her eyes met theirs when they stared, they would look away, embarrassed, or laugh guiltily. A woman might dig into the deep recesses of her kaross and produce some mangetti nuts and they would note the relish with which Koba took one, though they would pretend not to.

Someone might remark that he had heard the |Ton had peculiar ways; could the visitor confirm that their driving machines had to be watered? Anecdotes would be swapped, laughter shared; pipes would be placed, stem-up in the sand to cool; and finally they might enquire if they could offer her a place at their fire tonight – that is, if she would be staying a while before she journeyed on to – where exactly?

And so might come her cue for giving an account of herself.

'What do you want with us?' the tall man hissed.

Hn-hn-nnn. Jul'hoan manners have changed, along with their dress, since I lived among them, Koba thought. Should I point out to this rotten penis that I am no trespasser and he no jealous ǀTon landowner; why must he speak to me so badly?

Bushgirl, he is older than you and already hostile; to make an enemy of this man would be foolish.

Meekly she began her story, stopping to give her interpreter time to translate. He kept his gaze focused on the distant scrub and said nothing. The crowd looked expectantly at him; he stared over their heads.

'Er, I am the only child of Nǂaisa and Tami,' Koba said, trying to keep her tone confident. Better he translates me word for word; if he does it only at the end he might leave something important out. He might tell lies about me. His heart is against me. Koba shifted uneasily.

'Go on,' he said.

'Is better you translate as I speak, please,' Koba heard herself say.

'You think a man of the bush can't keep up with your ǀTon story?' he sneered.

Koba felt a tremor in her neck, but she kept her chin lifted and her eyes on his cold ones.

He said no more and the crowd became restive. A few began to question him and the squab woman plucked at his arm to get his attention. He detached himself with a twitch of his golden shoulders. 'Tsamkxao, yau-ah!' Squab scolded, looking up at him from under her stubby lashes.

Tsamkxao – so that is the rotten penis's name, Koba thought, as she saw his jaw clench. He caught the stares of several elders in the group, but would not look away. She felt heartened to see how patiently they met his glare and she almost cheered when his proud head dipped. She heard him begin to speak in Juǀ'hoan, translating what she had said through lips thinned with resentment. Koba began to get interested glances from the villagers. She recognized two words from his speech: 'Zuma' and 'nǀomkxao'. It was the former that had the most effect on the crowd. As one they turned to an elderly woman in their midst, saying, 'Zuma, Zuma'. Koba recognized her as the one Poppy Seed had been tending. The woman barrelled forward on bowed legs, grinning, showing teeth worn down to almost nothing. She thumped her chest proudly and sprayed the newcomer with Zuma-peppered saliva as she pronounced her name.

'You are now her little-daughter, er, "granddaughter",' Tsamkxao explained, as though the word had an aloe-bitterness for him. 'Because you are name-related she will take you to her fire.'

As she was pulled through the throng by her new grandmother Koba wondered if these people really were her flesh and blood. There was a chance, given the limited number of names in each band and the custom of naming children after previous generations. If I find Tamis, N‡aisas and other Kobas in this clan, this might be my true n!ore, she thought.

People crowded round now, close enough to touch her. She was glad custom would prevent that until it was established who she could have an informal, 'joking' relationship with. She hoped it would be her new friend; she'd spotted her smiling from the back of the crowd. Koba relaxed a little. Perhaps she was no longer an exhibit, but a participant – in something she didn't yet understand. No tappings. Must-be I am safe.

Zuma led her to a fire smoking drowsily in the afternoon sun. Painfully, the old woman squatted down and raked some blue-grey balls from the ashes. She dropped them into a nearby puddle to cool, cackling at the skitter of drops they sent sizzling into her fire. All the while she jabbered at Koba, who began to glean that the subject might be genealogy. The woman kept repeating sounds Koba thought must be names, but she was unfamiliar with them. She also kept pointing northwards. Koba nodded, but she had no idea what she was agreeing with.

Finally her hostess held out her hand to Koba. On her palm sat two roasted mangetti nuts. These looked better than the ones |Asa had offered. Koba lifted the nuts to her nose. They had a sweet, smoky smell, one that brought memories flooding back at her:

Mother, her kaross laden with mangettis, walking in front as I follow her back from a grove; the family around our campfire, Father laughing, his teeth dotted with the purple skins he's sucked off the fruit; and Grandmother, sneak-eating more nuts than she is peeling.

But that was at another place – with dangerous, snake-green water. Koba closed her eyes against the prickle of tears. When she opened them, Tsamkxao had reappeared and was being importuned to translate by her hostess. 'Old Zuma says she is glad you kept your skin,' he said, stony-faced.

She smiled at Zuma.

'I said, "your skin" – your Juǀʼhoan ways,' Tsamkxao averred.

'I understood perfectly well, *uncle*. Perhaps you'd be kind enough to tell Zuma n!a'an?' she replied, using the highest respect form. I'll show you, Rotten Penis, Koba thought, watching him from under her lids.

'*Uncle!*' he spat. 'I feel sure we are not related and will never have an informal relationship.' He spun on his heels and left.

Koba felt the old woman watching her stare at Tsamkxao's back. It was cross-hatched with scars.

I I

14 November 1964

Dear Koba,

I should start off by saying I hope this finds you well and all those polititudes a person's supposed to write in letters, but it doesn't seem important.

Not your health, of course that's *vital* and I hope like hell, like mad, that you are okay after prison (I try not to think about what might have happened to you in there), and after what must of been a hang of a long trek back to your people.

I can't even begin to tell you how sorry I am for what me and my family have done to you and I *must* see you again to say so to your face. Before, I was too young to realize the implications of that day near the Mother Hills, but now that I'm older I can see it all started there.

But some things that happened I am *not* sorry about. No way! You are the best thing that ever happened to me; that ever happened to my family. You are, and I must see you again because there is something I need to tell you about but I can't write it in a letter.

If you are holding it in your hands (I wish I was this piece of paper and could feel your touch) then my plan has worked and the minister of the Dutch Reformed Church at Tsumkwe has given it to you. (Do you know, there is not one postbox in the whole of the Kalahari? I checked with the postmaster general's office. But of course there is a church.) Ja-no, if we were together now we might laugh at how we Boere might be verneuking the natives, but we like to do it within sight of God. Ha-ha. (You know, I haven't laughed in such a long time, but I think I would be able to again in your company.)

You might be wondering about the old folks. They're okay. Ma's hair's a lot greyer, from the worry about us, I think. And she misses you. Pa too, but he tries not to show it. The other day I found him up in your cave. 'Just tidying up,' he said. Ma says we should leave you to get on with your own life – to get your old life back, she means I think, to re-integrate with your people. I will, Koba, I promise (if that's what you want), but let me see you once more.

But how? Okay. I am going to come to Tsumkwe. I can't say more about that now. I'll explain when I see you. But please, can you meet me at the church on Christmas Eve, 24th of December, sometime between ten and midnight? I'll also be there on Christmas Day night and Boxing Day night, the 26th of December, just in case you are delayed.

I really, really hope you will be there.

Your loving friend,
> Mannie (Frog-boy)
>> XXXXX XXXXXX XXXXXXX XXXXX XXXXXX XXXXXX

P.S. Because there's no surname for you, in Zhu-twn? Zu-han? Ju? (Jissus, how do you spell the name of your tribe? One day, you and me really must write an English/Afrikaans/Bushman dictionary. You better be in charge of spelling!)

Anyway, with no surname, I had to think about the thing that'd make you different. I guess it's that yellow dress I saw you in at the train station. So, I'm writing to you as:

Koba Yellow Dress
c/o Dominee Venter
Dutch Reformed Church
Tsumkwe
South West Africa

Clever, hey?

12

Mannie told his mother he was going to the coast. 'Which coast?'

'Zululand, then down to Durbs.'

'Durban?' Marta's freckles furrowed into a solid line between her green eyes. Her son had shown little desire to leave the farm since his release from prison. Now he was talking about a seaside town hundreds of miles away.

'Liebchen, is that a good idea?' She tried not to stare at his thin legs sticking out of khaki shorts. Mannie had been captain of the school under-seventeen rugby team less than twelve months ago. The legs of his shorts had been tight as tourniquets around the bulge of his quadriceps. Now they're all knee; like when he was eleven, she thought. 'Ag-please, have a piece of melktert, my boy. I made it without too much cinnamon.'

'Er, thanks.' The white tart wobbled on a plate as she pushed it towards him. He didn't feel like eating it; didn't feel like eating anything much, but especially not something he knew would taste of burned milk. Ma was a terrible cook; he and Pa teased her about it, especially the once when she'd volunteered to teach Koba how to bake. 'Don't. She'll grow up thinking cake is supposed to have a donga down its centre,' Pa had pleaded.

The guest lodge was closed. With temperatures touching one hundred degrees most days and malarial mosquitoes rife, tourists avoided the bushveld in December. This gave Marta time to fuss over her son. 'Like a baboon with a flea-full baby,' Koba would have said, Mannie thought, his longing for her tightening his heart and his balls.

She'd dubbed his mother Leopard-woman because of her freckles, but the name suited Marta in other ways too. She was fiercely protective of her cubs, him and Koba, but since their detention, Ma seemed less sure of herself, he thought. She'd apologized dozens of times for not being there when the police came to arrest them, until Mannie heard himself shouting at her: 'Stop it, Ma, just stop it! What could you have done? Held them off with your broom? With big words? Could you have changed the law of the land?'

Ma wanted to talk about it, but he didn't. It wouldn't help. They were all lousy with guilt – Ma for bringing Koba to Impalala in the first place; Pa because he'd done nothing to stop her, or worse, to stop Koba's parents being shot; him because he'd been caught in bed, his parents' bed, with Koba. No oke wants to discuss details of his sex life with his folks, Mannie thought.

He'd explained to the only person he'd discussed it with – a school friend called David Rubinstein, who had written to him after his detention – that in Koba's culture, sex before marriage was 'no big thing': 'Jissus, Rube, the Bushmen were naked and practising free love long before the hippies even thought of it,' Mannie had written. His parents weren't churchgoers and didn't believe sleeping with someone of another skin colour was immoral, but he was sure they disapproved of him having sex so young. If he and Koba had been married that might have been different. No one thinks Romeo and Juliet were wrong to fuck after the friar married them, he thought, but I couldn't have married Koba anyway, even if she'd wanted to.

Initially, it had been enough just to be able to touch Koba. To have sex with her – that had been beyond his wildest dreams. When it unexpectedly happened he felt they'd discovered a new continent. Here were contours and clefts it thrilled them to explore. Personally, he felt like he was tripping on the LSD he never would have taken.

But now he didn't think about the sex – well, only a bit, probably quite a bit, he'd admitted to David, who seemed to think about it even more than him. Mannie wished he'd dared to kiss Koba long before he did. Then he'd have more than just five honeymoon days to fantasize about. 'I must have the worst luck in the world,' he wrote to David. 'What other oke ends up in tjoekie the first time he has the real thing, hey? I know you say we live in a police state, Rube, but did they have to police my dong?'

His mother's clucks returned him to the tea table. 'You haven't touched your tart,' she said, tucking a strand of her faded copper hair behind her ear. Mannie hated seeing the apprehension on her face. He felt guilty at having to deceive her. He reminded himself that he wasn't a little boy any more; he was a man who had to make his own plans. For safety's sake she should know nothing about them, he reasoned.

'I need to get away, Ma,' Mannie said gently. 'I think the sea air will do me good.' Jissus, you sound like some old auntie talking, he told himself, trying not to squirm. He avoided looking directly at his mother.

'Ja-ja, I'm sure it will do you good; bring some colour back to your face,' she said, sighing. Unable to catch his eye, her gaze drifted across her tangled flowerbeds. Wild flowers were her favourites and she encouraged them to grow here by leaving clumps of bushveld grass and other weeds to grow at will between the more conventional shrubs and creepers – bougainvillea, bauhinia, plumbago. What with scatterings of pink, blue and orange flowers and an avocado tree that always littered the lawn with more fruit than they could eat, she supposed it looked a mess. Over at the guest lodge, Deon planted the beds with carefully coordinated rows of pansies, zinnias and cannas and framed every bed with a border of white-painted stones. She preferred their private space to be more natural. But, today, her garden gave her no peace.

'What about your studies, Mannie? You must get your matric, my boy; life has to go on.'

'Ag, Ma, it's only for a few weeks. Maybe a month.' He rubbed his nose.

'A month? But you'll miss Christmas. Here, with us. I mean, we've never not . . .' She trailed off as realization dawned. Everything was changing, had changed. When that prison door banged shut behind the children, a part of their lives ended.

Mannie saw pain etch itself into lines on either side of her mouth. It had the effect of making her look like a leopard again, one about to lose its cub, he thought. He couldn't talk to her about that. 'Ag, Ma, it's not like we're religious or anything.'

'Christmas is family time!' she pleaded.

He looked at her out of her own green eyes. She felt unnerved to see herself there, reduced to an object of pity. Not quite pity, she thought. She saw a very adult compassion in her son's eyes and she knew instinctively that she'd become redundant. Risking the tears that would send her son fleeing from the tea table, she wallowed in memories of past Christmases. They'd go into the bush together to select the thorny sapling that served as a Christmas tree. She'd then lock herself in the dining room to decorate it. Mannie and later Koba would bang on the door begging to be let in, but the tradition of surprise was strictly enforced; the delight on their faces when they saw the dazzling transformation was too good to forfeit.

Now there'd be no point carefully unwrapping the tree ornaments her parents had brought out from Germany thirty years ago. This year the Christmas sunshine would not blaze on the heavy brass caps of the glass kugels to make the balls glitter blue or crimson or gold. She would leave the delicate cut-glass star, the nearest thing to a snowflake any of them had seen, in its velvet-lined box. And the four lugubriously moustachioed toy soldiers in theirs.

Marta had to dash a tear from her cheek as she remembered that the soldiers had been Mannie's favourites. Chipped from years of being marched across the dining-room table, she'd finally got round to repainting them while he was in prison. She'd also reglued the antlers on the reindeer that Koba treasured. She'd wanted this to be their best Christmas ever – perfect in every way. It had never occurred to her that Koba wouldn't return to them. I'm naive – I always have been, Marta thought, feeling ashamed of the time she'd spent shining the silver. She'd even taken a cloth to the tiny wrought-iron basket that had been her mother's favourite tree ornament as a child, buffing up the miniature dimple-skinned oranges, the bag of nuts, the Christmas fruit loaf that protruded from it.

Loaf. Marta sat up, making a mental note to call the German bakery in Johannesburg to cancel her order for the stollen. Now she was able to look at Mannie, dry-eyed. 'I don't think it would be good for you to be on your own. Not just yet.'

He was ready for this. 'David Rubinstein is coming, Ma, so we won't be celebrating Christmas. Jews don't, you know. But we'll have fun. We're going to hitch-hike and be beach bums for a bit.'

His mother knew of David Rubinstein, though she'd never met him. David hadn't played rugby, or any other sport around which parents might congregate to watch. She did know that David's father owned trading stores all over the eastern Transvaal; the family lived close to Tzaneen, as far as she knew, so they'd never met.

David and Mannie had bonded in the last year of school when they realized they were the only two in the class who didn't agree when a teacher described the lyrics of 'Blowin' in the Wind' as 'commie'.

'Bad poetry, yes,' said David, blinking from behind his round glasses, 'but communistic, no.'

Mannie liked the words, but he didn't dare argue. Rubinstein got the top marks in English, not him. He was good at maths and geography, but even then Ruby, as the other kids called David, scored higher. The Jew was just a brain and he had some with-it music, Mannie thought.

Music had been a problem for Mannie ever since his sharp-tongued neighbour, Katrina 'Cocktease' Botha, had caught him dancing with Koba to one of his pa's records: 'Rock Around the Clock' it was. It was Pa's record, not his, because at that stage he hadn't owned any records. Katrina told everyone at school that not only was Mannie Marais square, but he also danced with kaffirgirls in his front room.

That had meant ostracism. He didn't care, his classmates were ignorant, but *he* was ignorant about being with-it, whether it was clothes or music. All very well for his pa, when he heard the pop songs on Springbok radio to say, 'If that's with-it, I'd rather be without it,' but what was an oke his age supposed to be listening to?

When David lent him some jazz and blues LPs, Mannie had been determined to like them. He'd even played them to Pa and Ma, surprised to discover they'd heard of Miles Davis. That gave him pause for thought – maybe jazz was too elderly? But David said no, it was beyond groovy to like the old stuff now. It was hip.

David was in Johannesburg at university, but they still corresponded. Mannie more often than his friend.

'I thought David had gone to Wits to study medicine.'

Mannie shifted in the old leather-thonged seat of the veranda chair. 'His asthma's been playing up so he's not starting yet.' The chances of his mother bumping into Mr or Mrs Rubinstein were almost nil.

Marta drained her coffee dregs, thinking about the wall that had sprung up between her and her son since his imprisonment. Before, she'd been proud of the way his openness disarmed even the people hostile to her because of her politics, but now his handsome features had a guarded look, almost sullen sometimes, she felt. Try as I might, I just can't reach my boy nowadays, she thought.

Mannie had arranged to meet Moses and Jabu in South West Africa the day after Christmas. Together the trio would cross the Okavango River and make their way to an African National Congress military training camp in Angola. Mannie was hazy on the details and hadn't paid much attention when Moses explained that the best recruits were sent to the USSR for political education.

'We'll see snow, bra, and get a Tokarev pistol. They are number one!' Mannie had been far more interested in the fact that the initial rendezvous point was not that far from Bushmanland. Somewhere in Bushmanland was Koba. He would do his bit for the struggle, he thought, but first he'd find Koba, see her before he went underground, explain a few things. Koba's big buck eyes would shine at him with pride. And maybe, just maybe, she'd go with him, he thought.

13

After a few weeks Koba began to settle into the group's routine. People woke at daybreak and sat talking quietly among themselves. Nobody seemed to need food or drink for several hours after waking, and when it finally came the food on offer was an old tuber boiled into bitter porridge, a mash of mangetti nuts or a handful of sand raisins. Koba was used to having pap. At Impalala, Deon Marais had regularly delivered a sack of maize meal to make the porridge to her cave; in prison, pap had been staple fare. She didn't miss it now; she seemed to have lost her appetite for a morning meal.

The effects of the drought persisted. Mothers had all but exhausted their food supplies. Rain fell intermittently now, but Koba could see the local plant-life needed time to regenerate. But at least the pride had moved off. Koba gathered the lions had been a threat to the group for months. She hoped the men were thinking of going hunting now.

They were doing more than thinking. One hot afternoon a group of men gathered around |Qui Beard. He laid out a kaross for his oracle discs. He would throw them to see if a game hunt would be successful. The fraternity expressed their pessimism, reminding him of the unfavourable conditions – with water so freely available the game herds had scattered over a vast area. Current grazing lands were far from here.

Ignoring the naysayers, |Qui stacked the pieces of hide on his left hand, covered them with his right, blew solemn air on the pile, then with a flourish let them fall onto the kaross. Three of the larger discs, representing the great meat animals, lay face down. IQui immediately declared this a good omen.

Some onlookers disagreed, insisting four face-downs were the only dependable forecast. The arguments went back and forth, finally disintegrating into good-natured banter.

'You men should learn to read. You should ask my adopted grand-daughter for lessons. She is a paper person,' Old Dabe said proudly.

'What would a paper person know of the discs? Or of hunting? Paper cannot fill empty stomachs. It is a useless thing,' Tsamkxao said, sneering.

'They tell me it is better than leaves for wiping,' Old Dabe said, 'but a stopped arse like you would have no need of it.' The men roared with laughter as Tsamkxao strode off.

Soon everyone had returned to their respective campsites and hunt-ing preparations began in earnest. Koba watched men take quivers down from hanging places in high branches. She saw them bent over hunting bows, strengthening them with animal sinew, assembling arrows and dipping the heads into fresh poison. The excitement was palpable; it permeated every corner of the clearing as strongly as the dream smell of meat grilling on an open fire. People laughed, called, did little jigs as they walked hither and thither. Children whooped as they ran errands between huts, borrowing this, lending that. IQui Beard scolded them, telling them to be quieter or they would agitate the meat animals. Koba chuckled. She hadn't seen such joyous anticipation since a sighting of active honey bees sent the villagers running pell-mell in search of the hive.

She dug into her bundle of possessions and found a used torch battery. In her other hand she took a bevelled stone and strolled over to join others, who had a piece of metal suitable for fashioning into an arrowhead. First she loosened the metal casing, careful not to get the battery acid on herself or any of the children whose inquisitive fingers kept reaching for the intriguing object. She heated the sheet of metal and, working swiftly, moulded it into shape. She was pleased with the result – the arrowhead was light, thin and, as a bonus, decorative with its touches of red and blue from the battery logo.

The children marvelled at it; their cries brought adults over to look. Koba tried to ignore the interest her skill was causing by keeping her head down as she fashioned a shaft and fitted it to the arrowhead. People will be talk-talking about me, wondering where I learned arrow-making, she fretted. For once she was glad of her poor mastery of her mother tongue.

If they discover I also *hunted* with my arrows they might reject me.

|Asa's husband, Bo Fingers, approached. He was still in bride-service to his in-laws, so was expected to hunt for their pot. But Bo was neither a tracker nor a snarer. The thumb piano and the five-stringed lute were his gift. His long, thin fingers could fashion instruments from gourds or rusty petrol cans; they could coax melodies of mournful beauty from twine and wood and tin. He could strum rhythms that soothed even snakes, people said. Sometimes, when the others had retired into their huts, or lay curled in sleep around their fires, he would softly play his plaintive compositions, all the while looking humbly at |Asa to see if she approved.

Now Bo held up Koba's finished arrow in awe. With a playful insult a young man snatched it from him. This hunter stroked the arrow's elegant shaft then laid it across his open palm, assessing its balance. Finally, he looked up at Koba with open admiration and mimed begging the arrow for his quiver.

Koba felt uncomfortable. He was old enough to be an experienced hunter and young enough to still be good at it. Her chances of a return on her arrow investment were favourable. But she didn't want to encourage him; his interest seemed to be about more than getting buck meat.

He-he-he. It is your meat he is interested in, Bushgirl, she heard her insect taunting her. *He wants to have food with you.*

She chose instead to give her arrow to Bo Fingers. Just by looking at his wistful expression she could tell he was not a good hunter. The chances of her being able to exercise her right as owner of the arrow to the first cut of meat from the animal he shot were zero. This suited her. She didn't wish to draw any more attention to herself or her arrows.

Tsamkxao kept to himself as he worked on his arsenal, pointedly ignoring the fuss around Koba. When Bo Fingers tried to show him her work, he turned away.

One day you will learn that I can shoot as well as I make arrows, you Big Genital, Koba thought. Tidying her home-made tools away, she took silent pleasure in the fact that he would have to walk a long way before he found fresh spoor. For days she'd been searching for game tracks, but all she'd seen was a francolin near what she thought of as her sick bushes.

Old Zuma's cooking wasn't agreeing with Koba, though she was careful to hide the fact. She was sure it was the sand – every time she bit into anything she detected sand particles. No wonder people's teeth are worn down, she thought.

The next morning, before first light, Koba tiptoed out of camp, keeping a wary eye open for predators. Confident that she was safe, she headed for her copse. Having gone to bed without food she felt less queasy than usual, but she was hungry and determined to catch the francolin. Using Twi's torch, she set a snare. She was so engrossed in the business of trying to do this routine work with limited light that she didn't notice a man approaching. When she looked up he was there, watching her from underneath his policeman's cap.

She jumped but didn't scream. Old Dabe stepped closer, then crouched down next to her. Koba felt her breathing quicken.

Be calm, Bushgirl, this one is not strong enough to hold you down, she reminded herself.

Why is he studying my snare? What will this elder make of my unwomanly work?

The old man took the flashlight from her nervous hand and used its beam to scrutinize her tripwire. He saw a yellow thread and chuckled.

Hmpff, what but my dress could I use? I don't know where the fibre plants grow. Arrghh, don't tug on the thread, it will break . . .

With Old Dabe's final tug it did. He tutted, shaking his head, making the feather in his cap waggle. He was even less impressed with her bait. 'Uhn-uh-uhnn,' he grimaced as he flicked the seed away.

That was not easy to find, you interfering Old Feather! Now I will have to wait for daylight to get more.

Koba sat back on her heels in the dark, sulking that the old man had rejected her attempt to contribute to his group's food store. She felt ashamed being dependent upon the kindness of these strangers.

Lift your lip, Bushgirl. You have accepted hospitality from others before.

That was true. Towards the end of her time at Impalala she regularly ate with the Marais family, much to the annoyance of the black house-maid, Selina, who slammed down the plate of food in front of Koba the first time she saw the Masarwa, the Yellow One, sit down with them. Marta had flushed scarlet up her long, white neck. Deon laid his hand over her fist, which was clenched around her fork, and began an animated conversation about something. What, Koba couldn't remember, but she could recall the feeling of being the cause of the cloud of disapproval that drifted from Selina's domain towards the diners. It was like a bad smell, a choking smoke that any minute might result in her eyes watering. Deon had slipped her his handkerchief and Mannie had cleared the plates before Selina emerged to do so. Thereafter, Koba was invited to the table only on the maid's day off.

Koba prided herself on the fact that she had always brought a gift to the table – a branch laden with monkey oranges, a bunch of the veld flowers Marta loved to draw, a tortoise shell full of honey so fresh bees still wriggled in the comb.

'I was only trying to do the same for Old Dabe and Zuma,' she muttered to herself. She sensed the old man was searching his person for something. She watched him fish a length of finely worked twine from the pocket of his police jacket. Then he produced a pinch of assorted seeds that looked appetizing even to Koba's eyes. He handed her the twine. She understood and, giving him the torch to hold, fastened his twine to her trip branch. He sprinkled the seeds inside her trap, then sat back on his heels and gave her a thumbs-up sign.

Hnn, that is good. Sorry for the insult, grandfather. This snare is better even than the ones I made at Impalala. You mean to help, not harm.

'Keep it, keep,' she said when he handed her torch back to her.

Dabe looked puzzled, then thrilled as understanding dawned. He jabbered gratitude, held the beam under his chin, pulling faces.

Like a boy, not an elder, she thought to herself, giggling.

Old Dabe capered off, drawing zigzags across the dark bush with the torch beam.

Still smiling, Koba returned to the sleeping camp and lay down to dream.

14

Koba was used to silence, to hearing only the voices in her head, sometimes for days at a time. It was difficult to adapt to the din of communal conversation in her new world. And she was seldom alone in the Jul'hoan camp.

No one was. People ate together, sat together, slept together. They hunted in pairs with practised companions and the women foraged in pairs. They clustered shoulder to shoulder when making things and sat, crossing their ankles over one another's legs without discomfort.

But, for once, she was alone, the only person up. She stirred a sleepy fire into life to boil water for baobab-nut coffee, a special treat she intended for her adopted grandmother. Old Zuma, like most of the women and even the children, was having a lie-in. She supposed the departure of the hunters at sunrise had woken everyone prematurely, as it did her. This was the time then to catch up on sleep. But Koba wanted to relish having only birdsong to disturb the vast Kalahari silence.

'Cha-cha-cha,' she whistled under her breath as she padded around the periphery of the camp, checking to see which way the various pairs of hunters had gone. Her mimicry evoked a response from a small flock noisily beaking through nearby undergrowth. '*Cha-cha-cha, kawa, kawa, kawa,*' they bested her. She grinned, pleased that the bird population had become more visible and vocal since her arrival with the rain. From dawn to dusk it seemed the air was aflutter. In every green shrub and tree something twitched, twittered, piped or hummed. Koba strolled happily on.

By mid-morning everyone was up and she gathered that an excursion had been mooted. After what felt to Koba like a tedious amount of discussion, the women reached consensus on where they should go foraging. While she waited for her companions to gather up their children, digging sticks, water scoops and carrying sacks, she drummed impatiently in the sand. The ground felt spongy, as if the individual grains of sand were plumped up. She chided herself. Must not be fierce-face when the land grows green, she thought. When the band was ready, she strode out in step with the other women, relishing the spring of the earth beneath her bare soles.

She'd given the shiny shoes to Squab the day before. The young woman, whose name she believed was Chu!ko, accepted them, arms outstretched, palms cupped, unsmiling. Chu!ko's splayed feet would never fit into the shoes, Koba knew, but she could tell from the way the Squab waddled off, shoes held out of reach of her squawking toddler, that they were highly valued. In due course she would receive a gift from Squab; that was the hxaro custom.

As she walked she sensed the pulse of new Kalahari life; dormant seeds were beginning to thrust shoots through the veld floor, none faster than a green creeper gaily studded with bright yellow flowers. It lay across her path now. |Asa hurried over and, shyly taking Koba's arm, steered her clear of the lush carpet. Koba picked up on a few Jul'hoan words in |Asa's caution: 'foot' and 'pain', she understood. She knew the plant. It was like one that grew in the veld at Impalala. It had evil thorns. Nevertheless, the flowers were pretty. She bent and picked one, offering it to her friend. Smiling, |Asa stuck it into her hair.

After a thorough search of the area the women's karosses still hung largely empty at their hips. The flower in |Asa's hair had wilted by the time the group limped into the shade of a shepherd's bush tree. Its foliage, glossy green now the dust coating had been rinsed off, brought instant relief from the sun. Women flopped down, mothers pulling out breasts to feed hungry children, others digging in pouches for pipe tobacco. They lounged against one another, using fly whisks made from the tail-hairs of antelope to flick away insects that settled on their tangled limbs. All seemed resigned to their fruitless mission.

Koba wondered whether the group would quit the area soon. It was obvious that accessible food sources had been denuded. It would be weeks before shrubs produced nuts or berries, months before tubers grew fat in their subterranean greenhouses. But water-everywhere is a good time for travel, for finding a new place, Koba thought. She would have liked to discuss this with someone so she could make her own plans, but without the necessary fluency in her own language it was impossible.

Koba settled next to Poppy Seed. Remarkably, the young woman had found some fruit; a few shrunken tsamma melons.

I remember these from my childhood – bigger then. Inside, pale green meat, not pink like the big |Ton watermelon. Tsammas are refreshing, good-good when you are thirsty. And the pips are mmm-ahhh, roasted. Mother would grind them into a meal; Grandmother used to moisten the pip powder with saliva and smear it all over her body. Always-always she asked me to rub it across her old shoulders; it gave them a reddish colour she liked. It makes men very hungry, she'd say, winking over her wrinkled shoulder. Heh-heh, they wanted to have food with her because she smelled of tsamma! Must-be the spirit men get no peace when my grandmother is red.

She wondered if Zuma's ghost would ever talk to her again. Not only did she have Insect, she also now had a replacement grandmother. Spirit Zuma could be jealous. Koba recalled the spirit urging her to leave Impalala, warning her that she was losing her Jul'hoan skin. When Mannie became her lover, Zuma had stopped speaking to her.

Or did you just stop listening?

Koba cocked her head now, straining her ears to hear the bustling breeze that used to herald the arrival of her bossy relative. But all she heard was the drone of live women's voices. She felt content to concentrate on what was being said.

The women seemed to be complimenting Poppy Seed on her skill as a forager. The young woman demurred, keeping her face lowered.

'|Asa,' Koba said, finally bold enough to repeat what she heard.

Her effort was audible, causing |Asa to lift her face and stare intently as Koba repeated her name. Then she smiled broadly and asked Koba a question.

I think she asks my name.

Koba said it, tapping her chest. A wave of 'Koba'-punctuated chatter rose from the group; all the Kobas anyone knew were mentioned, along with their known genealogies. Could the strange girl be related to one of them? they wondered.

The litany of names, delivered with a confusion of clicks, was beyond Koba, but she supposed from the lewd gesture her surrogate grandmother was making that they must be discussing the men she would be able to marry. Koba smiled; the two Zumas had a lot in common, but only one of them knew her heart was already taken.

At most fires that evening portions were scanty. The hunters, like the women, had returned empty-handed. Elders grumbled, blaming the band for disrespecting the meat-animals with their jovial hunt preparations. At Zuma's fire, two guinea fowl were roasted; one caught in Koba's trap, the other in Old Dabe's.

But the highlight of the meal was the fifteen small frogs Old Dabe had caught using Koba's yellow thread. This trapping caused great interest and Old Dabe delighted in miming again and again, with increasingly exaggerated actions, how he'd fashioned a hook, attached it to her hemming thread and dropped it into every likely looking pool he could find. The frogs had loved it, taking the thread to be the legs of a dragonfly.

Old Dabe croaked with glee, conjuring up wide-mouthed amphibians queuing to swallow the hook. Then he mimed them flailing their legs to get free of it. That gave Koba a frisson of fear – frogs were close to her heart – but the group was in stitches at the old man's antics. His haul meant everyone could have a leg; even a morsel of meat was better than none, though no one would have dreamed of asking.

Only Koba and Tsamkxao declined the rare treat. Nevertheless, Old Dabe dragged a reluctant Tsamkxao over and made him tell Koba he had named his new granddaughter, Koba the Frog-bringer.

Speculation followed about whether Koba had also brought the rain. Tsamkxao was obliged to translate: 'Old Zuma wants to know if you were born in the rainy season,' he said and, through thin lips, 'To be a Rain-child is very lucky.'

Tsamkxao looked pleased when she replied that she did not know when she was born as she had no relatives alive to tell her.

She heard the women in the group cluck sympathetically. She looked down, fingering her frilled collar.

I do not want their pity. I do not want their attention. Spit on Tsamkxao who enjoys my discomfort.

'Old Zuma asks if you dreamed of rain on your journey here?' Tsamkxao enquired with a sarcastic tone. 'If you did, you may be a Summoner. Perhaps that is why Rain agreed to come . . . *she* say.'

So sure you are, Big Genital, that I, the |Ton-stink girl, could not be n|omkxao, Koba thought bitterly.

Tsamkxao continued. 'Zuma say this is the season of Little Rains but we have Big-big Rain. Did *you* call this rain? she ask.'

It was an important question; all had stopped to listen for the answer.

Koba stared blankly at Tsamkxao pretending she hadn't understood. She needed time to think.

The people are right to worry-worry about early rain – rain too soon means the next dry season will be too long. Even the tsamma melon will wither then. These people do not want another hungry season.

She brooded that there was more to the question.

Can someone in this group visit people's dreams? Have they seen me riding the Rain animal to the top of a mountain and killing it? Do they know I am able to trance? Hnpff, why am I bothering my brain? I myself don't know if my strange dream means I am a Rain summoner.

'No proof-no proof,' she heard the wind sigh. Then a breeze bustle passed whispering, 'What about the unseasonal Big Rain? It came when you did.'

Koba whipped round, staring out into the blackness beyond the campfire. She saw the dark domes of huts, beyond that trees, their spectral limbs still, not signalling to some phantom wind. Her eyes darted round the firelit faces, strained to see into the black hollows of eye sockets, to seek out the whisperer. But the faces looked bright with encouragement. Especially IAsa's.

Tsamkxao demanded she answer the question. People tsk-ed at his rudeness. He ignored them and repeated the question. Koba breathed deeply then said: 'Please tell Zuma I didn't bring the rain. I just followed it here . . . to the Land of Frogs,' she said, looking pointedly at Old Dabe. Tsamkxao translated.

Immediately Old Dabe leaped up and started frog-hopping around the circle. Everyone laughed. Children fell in behind him, competing to see who could hop highest. Old Dabe pulled his mouth into a wide-mouthed grimace and croaked raucously. Tsamkxao sloped off. Old Zuma shook her head and passed Koba a guinea fowl leg.

The girl bit into it, striking sand. She chewed, trying to separate the sand particles from the meat with her tongue, but there were too many. Sighing, she swallowed.

I will get used to sand with my meat; but it is not salt, she thought.

Later, lying back on her elbows staring up at the Milky Way with its smoky veil and scattering of stars like fire-sparks, Koba remembered her grandmother's tale of the girl from the Early Race who flung wood ashes up into the sky. The Jul'hoansi here insisted the Milky Way was not wood ashes, but the Backbone of Night.

She preferred her grandmother's label, but was nevertheless pleased she'd grasped the meaning of the local expression. And this wasn't the only Jul'hoan term she understood – she was hearing the words 'Big Rains', 'strange rain' and 'mangettis' more often, especially tonight.

More and more people joined the circle around IQui Beard's fire. The family shuffled up until the whole village was present. No one else lay back and indulged in the usual postprandial star-gazing. No one repeated the story of how the moon had got its scarred face or how the morning star burned when it herded the sun across the sky. People talked earnestly tonight, eyes downcast.

Koba sat up and listened. Hnnn, they talk of a journey, to a n!ore where the healing comes from a drum dance; and the drum is made from mangetti wood . . . Something is ripe. The mangettis . . . or is it a person? A bride? The pigeon-person, Chu!ko, stares. Eyes are sliding my way. Eeuwhh, greasy-greasy, that Gao Monkey Orange. Surreptitiously Koba touched her fingertips to her ears. Hnn, they are hot from all this talk. One says this place is better, another says no, the one with the drum dance is best. Now his wife says wait; she doesn't like the people there. An old man agrees; people there are ungenerous. Ti!'ay Sour throws bitter words into the pot. Will N!ai boil?

She heard |Asa's mollifying tones, Ti!'ay and N!ai looked shame-faced, but Koba knew that soon the war of the wives would resume. Both women smouldered with resentment.

'We must go to the mangetti groves to find Xoo n!a'an,' |Qui Beard was saying. He glanced meaningfully in Koba's direction.

'The nuts won't have ripened,' Ti!'ay Sour snapped.

'But the year is getting warmer; the trees are beginning to ooze sap. We can sit there and wait for them,' he insisted.

'We'll sit there and die of thirst!' Ti!'ay spat. 'All around us is water now, but in the grove we must walk on our knees to beg the owners for water from the tree-hollows.'

'Xoo will not refuse,' N!ai said from the other side of him.

'She will when she sees how many we are.' Now Ti!'ay looked in Koba's direction. 'Fresh meat attracts flies!'

'Wipe the worry from your what's-up-front.' |Qui patted her knee. 'As soon as Xoo declares who is eligible, the kin will leave and we few can sit in the cool of the groves and watch the nuts ripen. Then . . .'

'Yau, a good-good plan, husband.' N!ai stroked his arm. 'My heart hums in the groves.'

'*And* they are only a day-night walk from Tsumkwe, eh?' Ti!'ay sniped. They were able to ignore her as somehow N!ai had her multi-strand eggshell necklace caught in her hair and needed |Qui Beard to help her disentangle it. Koba watched N!ai toss her head this way and that, displaying the graceful curve of her nape to its best advantage. Hnn, that N!ai, she knows men prefer meat to soup.

In the meantime, something had been decided in the group. Everyone, except Ti!'ay Sour, looked content. Gaps began to appear in the circle as people rose and said goodnight.

Koba grew uneasy, nervous as a wildebeest that finds itself in thinning company, separated from the herd. She scanned the remaining faces for clues and started when another large log was thrown into the fire. All the cooking is done, people go to their sleeping mats, why the wood-wasting? she wondered until it occurred to her that a decision had been made to leave the area.

She gazed up at the night sky again, calculating her options: the Big Rain will have washed away my footprints, but Lion won't give up easily. Better to hide in the herd although it's a noisy place and my heart does not agree with some of its customs.

Use your intelligence, Bushgirl. The Ju!'hoansi do not like women to hunt because they are afraid to lose them. From poison or death by meat animals. There are too few marriageable women in this group. That is why you are eaten by eyes.

Hnn, that man named for an orange, Gao, he is the worst. Brought me a shell full of honey, grinning at me like a baboon from behind a face swollen with bee stings. I hate honey, but Hairs-in-his-ears would not listen, pushing the food under my nose. And every-every time I go to gather wood or set a snare, a man wants to help me. Buzzing round like bees, these men. I don't need them. I have always found my own roots and berries. And when I longed for meat, I learned to hunt.

Is so. Remember that warthog you and Frog-boy trapped in a burrow?

Koba certainly did. It had nearly run Mannie through with its razored tusk. She'd killed it with a stab through its neck and together they'd roasted the sweetest meat and devoured it, the fat running down to their elbows.

Heh-heh. After-after, Frog-boy saw you with a man's eyes for the first time and you knew then he wanted to have food with you.

Koba smiled at the memory of their shy, lustful looks. It had taken a long time for them to consummate their passion for each other. She thrilled, remembering their first explosive coupling.

Bushgirl, your heart still longs for him. Stay among the Talk-talks; let the Buzzings distract. You have spent enough time alone.

And enough time talking to an insect, Koba thought. She would go with |Asa and her family, wherever that was.

But later she lay awake, unable to find comfort in the hollow she'd made in the sand. One of Bo's melodies picked its melancholy way towards her in the dark. It was leading |Asa's voice up, rising like thin smoke, reaching for the stars. And then they danced, entwined until Koba heard notes that led |Asa gently down to earth again and stilled the song with the softest twang. Koba felt it as tenderly as a lover's tap on her naked shoulder. She ached for Mannie, for his lips brushing hers, his chest under her cheek as she lay in his arms, the fresh, musky, man-boy smell of him. Would she ever see him again?

No. And no use wishing to touch stars when a person is planted in the sand, she told herself. She thumbed the tears from her cheeks, pulled the old kaross Zuma had given her over her head and closed her eyes.

15

André Marais hated farming. He loathed every mielie stalk planted on the million morgen of land his father had bequeathed him. He hated ploughing the soil, planting the seed, harvesting the corn, despite not doing any of that himself. Etienne had also bequeathed him an army of farm labourers and several managers to organize it all, including Twi, more mascot than manager, a hindrance rather than a help – not that André noticed.

André had made himself responsible for the business side of Weltevrede Enterprises, an agricultural and commercial empire comprising several farms in South West Africa and a row of buildings Etienne had bought cheaply in Onderwater's main street. These were let as retail premises. André prided himself on being proactive when it came to collecting the rents. It was not unpleasant whiling away the hours in these small shops, being plied with beer or brandy, listened to by storekeepers who pretended interest in his opinions.

In André's book, 'business' beat farming any day except spray day. Crop-spraying was the only agricultural chore André enjoyed. On spray days he had no trouble getting out of bed on time. He'd set off before sun-up, jump into the primed gifbakkie, with which he ferried the giant drums of pesticide, and drive to the airfield. He always gunned the accelerator over the corrugations on the dust road. This helped mix up the chemicals, he felt. He had a mechanic on the payroll whose job it was to keep his Piper PA-18 Super Cub in tiptop condition. While Tertius filled the spray tanks from the drums of insecticide, André downed his first cup of coffee from the canteen, relishing the slightly salty organo-phosphate taste of it. Then he'd amble to his plane, get Tertius to shoehorn him into a cockpit he swore was shrinking, and taxi out in the half-light of an African dawn. He'd be up in his Cub as the sun was rising, racing the rays higher and higher into the copper-pink sky, then banking sharply to the west, waggling a wing at the other dusties only now filling their tanks or spinning their propellers on the apron below. He'd head for his lands, mile upon mile of corn; 'banknote green' his father used to say.

Not any more. The bookkeeper said the lands weren't bringing in the money they used to, but on mornings like this golden one, who gave a fok, André thought. Singing one of his beloved Trini Lopez songs above the scream of the engine, he flipped the Cub into a downward spin, wrenching her up at the last minute to whip across the fields so low he could see dewdrops shatter in the turbulence. He released a gush of insecticide from the wing jets then whooshed upwards trailing vapour like a toxic bridal train.

A few hours later, with the sun higher and the tanks on empty, André landed and parked the plane in the shade of the hangar. Tertius handed him a rolled up magazine. 'Compliments of Tango Romeo.' He nodded in the direction of an ageing Cherokee Cub. 'Jan says check out the poes hair on page seventeen.' André grinned. Lekker-cracker, the day had just got even better. Banned in South West Africa and across the border, magazines like *Playboy* were hard to come by.

'I'll be a while,' he said, heading for the small shack that contained the long-drop toilet.

He'd no sooner got himself settled when he heard a knock on the wooden door. 'André, son, are you in there?'

His mother. He dropped the magazine like it was a mamba. It slithered off his lap and lay half-exposed in the gap under the door. André scrambled off the wooden seat to retrieve it, his haste earning him several splinters in his left buttock. What the hell was Ma doing here? Lettie Marais never came to the aerodrome; she disapproved of flying. 'If God had meant for us to fly He'd have given us wings,' she always said. She hadn't spoken to his father for a week when she found out he was paying for their son to take flying lessons. She still refused to come out and wave when André buzzed over the farmhouse. One day, God help him, he was going to set the wheels of the Piper on the flat corrugated-iron roof of her kitchen and bounce the plane across it, full throttle, just to see her run out.

But now he'd better get rid of the magazine, he thought. Ma might want to use the toilet. She sounded agitated, and upset always went straight to her stomach.

He considered stuffing it down the back of his shirt, but she'd spot the covergirl through the thin white cotton. He was going to have to dump the *Playboy*. He cursed silently as he rolled it up and threw it down the long-drop. Jan was going to be so pissed off, but not as much as his ma if she found him looking at pictures of women's privates. He heard the magazine hit the bottom of the latrine pit and bent to retrieve his trousers.

Almost instantly he heard them coming – a battalion of hornets. This would be the advance guard, the crack stinging squadron from the swarm that nested in the long-drop. Judging by their battle drone, the magazine had hit their nest. André knew better than to stick around. Pants round his ankles, he slid the bolt and rushed out of the shack.

'Run, Ma, run. It's hornets,' he said, hopping past her like an overgrown toddler in a naked sack race.

'André! Heavens above . . .' Lettie's shocked face turned from pink to purple to white as she saw the swarm. But she stood her ground. Weighing one hundred and eighty-three pounds, she was never going to beat the hornets, except with her hat. Lettie Marais never set a foot outside without wearing the right hat and this morning had been no exception, despite the emergency that had brought her to this detested place in search of her son. Now she wielded the wide-brimmed straw hat with its fake fruit like a demented, over-sized Carmen Miranda. In her sturdy arms it became a deadly combination of shield and swat. She suffered a few stings, but hornets fell like flies and quickly the bulk of the swarm retreated into the long-drop leaving the advance guard to pursue André.

He ran towards Tertius, who stood with the pesticide nozzle in his hand. André kangarooed towards him. 'Get them, squirt them; for heaven's sake, do something, man.'

The villagers were decamping. Karosses were stuffed with gourds, ostrich eggs, digging sticks, rolled up sleeping mats and personal treasures. Deep into |Asa's pack went the mirror that Koba had given her, which was coveted by all the women. Zuma wore the woollen hat she'd had from her adopted granddaughter and Chu!ko had the patent leather shoes tied conspicuously atop her kaross. Old Dabe stowed his bird-trap twine in his arrowless quiver and tucked his precious flashlight into the front pocket of his jacket.

Koba had heard children refer to her as '!gao dima ma,' which |Asa had explained meant woman with many possessions. As she lifted her bundle Koba felt it was lighter. She was glad.

She understood that some of her new friends would head for favourite haunts where a prized veld food grew; others planned to visit where they found the company congenial. Still others planned to savour the attractions of Tsumkwe. Koba saw how the elders shook their heads at this and how Tsamkxao shunned those in the Tsumkwe group.

|Qui Beard's group, a surprisingly large one, was going to the mangetti groves, a full day's walk from where they were.

'Goodbye, walk well,' people called.

'Remember me to your relatives.'

'See you in the dry season.' Toddlers were lifted onto shoulders to lord it over the caravan and the small bands set off in their separate directions. Scattering like seeds from a ripened pod, Koba thought with a regret.

Chu!ko, weighed down with her small son and an over-full bundle, fell into step with Ti!'ay Sour. She expected to meet up with her husband, Xeri, at the mangetti groves. He worked in the mines in Johannesburg and would return to Bushmanland for Christmas. Already she had a long list of grievances to welcome him back with.

'So many men in this group and not one to help me carry my things,' she huffed.

Ti!'ay Sour sniffed. 'They are too busy with the fresh meat.' She jerked her head to where Koba was tussling with a young man determined to carry her half-empty kaross for her.

'Except *him*.' Chu!ko admired Tsamkxao's long, scarred back, way ahead in the group. 'He hates Koba. A person can feel the fire when he looks at her.'

'And you think that is the heat of hate?' Ti!'ay snorted. 'Must-be you also believe that the Big Genital would not have the face to eat meat from my husband's fire.'

Chu!ko stopped mid-waddle. Ti!'ay was shameless; she was old enough to be outspoken. To admit knowing one's husband, an owner of medicine no less, was being made a fool of was frankness too far.

'Don't puff your cheeks out at me, wife of Xeri,' Ti!'ay said. 'I am the one who helps my husband when he is doing his healing, when he is alone in his blankets because his other wife is *you-know-where*. I am the one who must sing and sing so the power comes.'

'Yes, but then you sleep and he heals you while you sleep.'

'Hmpff, he heals N!ai too.'

'My heart's easier since you agreed to come with us, Tsamkxao,' !Qui Beard confided as he trotted beside the longer-legged huntsman. Tsamkxao inclined his head but didn't smile. 'When Old Xoo announces who the Koba Frog-bringer's relatives are, we'll explain to the girl which of the suitors she can choose' – !Qui Beard puffed – 'and I can have some *peace*.'

Tsamkxao looked more annoyed than usual as he busied himself with his tobacco pouch. It was beautifully beaded; a secret present from N!ai. There was little leaf left in it, but he ferreted enough out for a mouthful. He chewed quickly; when the bolus was reduced he began to speak, about everything except Koba and the matter of her eligibility. He described the leopard tracks he'd seen in the mud at the last water pan; exactly how many flamingos were standing one-legged in the shallows. This last fact he held as evidence that the rain they'd experienced was indeed a herald of the wet season and not some freak flash-in-the-salt-pan. 'And the bees are awake.

Every-every sunset they go *‡xohhhhh!*' – Tsamkxao made a sound like an arrow travelling through air – 'straight-straight into the hive in the bent baobab.'

The tree was a favourite of |Qui Beard's. When he leaned against its massive trunk he could feel it breathing. He told children it was bent because it had touched a porcupine quill in its youth. He liked to think the baobab would have company in his absence. 'I trust you did not smoke the bees out of the tree-hole, nephew?'

'No; the hive was marked. Gao Monkey Orange wanted the honey as a present for *her*.' Tsamkxao glared back in Koba's direction. She was at the end of the procession, conspicuous in her yellow dress, walking arm in arm with |Asa.

'Eh-weh, I heard the girl does not like honey. Heh-heh, Gao took all those stings for nothing. His face – eye lumps like a warthog!' |Qui laughed.

Tsamkxao spat out the tobacco he'd been chewing. 'She claims to be Jul'hoan. There is no Jul'hoan who doesn't like honey. She says she prefers salt. *Salt!*' He spat again, tongue agitating teeth as he tried to clear stray tobacco strands.

'Salt, eh?' |Qui Beard stroked his scraggles thoughtfully. 'Maybe she is from Nyae Nyae pan? They are salty people.'

'Wherever she comes from, she must go back. Better for us,' Tsamkxao pronounced. Then he strode off, slashing a vicious path through the green grass with his hare hook.

André sat fully clothed, drying himself in the sun. He'd got Tertius to hose him down twice with fresh water in case any of the insecticide had drifted onto him. He didn't think it had; his nose and eyes weren't burning. Nevertheless, his ears and the back of his neck had ballooned from the hornet stings. His mother rubbed aloe sap onto the affected area. He counted himself lucky that only his mechanic and his mother had been there to witness his humiliation. His employee wouldn't mention the incident again, nor would his mother, deliberately that was. She could be spectacularly thoughtless. He sighed, realizing he had yet to go through the ordeal of hearing about the crisis that had driven her out here in the first place.

It concerned a letter his mother had received that morning from his aunt, Marta Marais, jailbird Mannie's mother. She'd asked his ma to get the letter to Tsumkwe where she believed someone would know of the girl in the yellow dress. His auntie was right, someone would. A lot of Bushmen passed through that dump, but few wore fancy white woman's clothing.

Tsumkwe's not that far away, by plane, he thought.

'Can you *credit* that Marta wants us to play postman to her Bushman pet? *We* must run after her kaffirgirl. It beggars belief; it really does!'

André tried to calm his mother. The old girl was indignant. Not about the request, that was easy to ignore, but about the hat remark in the letter. What had his old auntie said? 'Small woman in the very big hat . . . in front for every picture.'

Ha-ha, that sounded like Ma. He hadn't thought his do-gooder Auntie Marta could be so catty. He said so to his mother.

The remark worked like balm on a burn. Lettie pointed out that his aunt in fact had green eyes like a cat's. She segued into disparaging her brother-in-law, Deon: 'he drank like a fish, you know'; his wife 'can't cook for toffee' and his son was 'kaffirboetie and a jailbird'.

'Thank heavens they live thousands of miles from us, is all I can say. The shame they have brought on the Marais name.' Lettie's jowls wobbled and her eyes filled up. 'It's criminal, it really is.'

André murmured agreement and, as soon as she paused to search for her hanky, he said, 'Listen, Ma, I've got to get back to work.'

'With those ears? You look like Dumbo.'

André laughed; he'd been let off lightly. He kissed her and walked off, trying not to wince as his pants chafed his more intimate stings.

He hadn't thought about the Bushman girl for weeks, but now he could think of nothing else. He felt angry, all his fury about the long-drop incident transferred to her. Hornets were the sort of black magic that little witch could conjure up. Hadn't bees chased him the first time he'd tried to track her at Impalala? And she'd Houdini-ed herself out the back of his truck. Then there'd been that eland and, years before, a jumbo where there wasn't supposed to be one, at Impalala. Even now, when he thought about the wreck of his beloved

Bel Air, he felt enraged. He longed to damage the girl, crush her like the elephant did his brand-new car.

André looked at his watch. It was too late to spray now; he'd take a flight north-east, see if he could find her. If she was still in that yellow dress, he'd spot her.

The caravan had reached a large expanse of standing water. It stretched across their route wide, blue and as incongruous as the sea. The group stood around marvelling; the elders trying to recall when last they'd seen this pan in flood. Koba peered into the water. She could see the desert floor and the odd clump of drowned grass. Good-good, no crocodile danger here. She longed to soak herself in this clear water, wash away the grey Kalahari mud that seemed to have become ingrown under her nails, in her hair, in the fibres of her dress. She wasn't the only one. Children squirmed in their parents' arms, desperate to paddle. The adults conferred and the men agreed to go on ahead, leaving the women some privacy.

The women downed their bundles, flung off their karosses and whooped into the water. They shrieked as the cold encircled their warm bellies and backs. In the shallows children yelped with excitement, kicking arcs of water in wonder, windmilling their arms to make maximum noise and splash. Koba waded away from the maelstrom, water lilies rocking gently in her wake. When she was waist deep, the skirt of her dress floated up, ballooning around her. IAsa laughed. 'Will we catch fish under you?'

Koba looked puzzled. Then she remembered the black heron that spread its wings over the water to attract small fish into its umbra. She chuckled as she unbuttoned her dress and pulled it off over her head. IAsa helped her agitate the dirt from it, then they each took an edge and twisted in opposite directions, wringing the water from it.

As they did so, Koba began to feel uneasy. Her skin prickled with apprehension and she knew it had nothing to do with the cool water on her bare skin. Something underwater – a snake, if not a crocodile? She stared down into the crystal clear water but saw only her feet and IAsa's magnified to mangrove root proportions. Another time she might have laughed and pointed this out, but she felt anxious.

And foolish. There was nothing to fear, neither in the water nor out of it, she told herself, yet still she felt dangerously exposed.

André calculated that he had fuel enough for a one-hundred-square-mile search. Though visibility was excellent, ground conditions weren't ideal – the Kalahari bush was thicker since the rain, so it wouldn't be as easy as usual to spot movement below, but if he saw a flash of yellow and could get within striking distance . . . He felt for the revolver he kept in a cubbyhole in the cockpit. Then he pulled the joystick back and let the plane climb into the white heat of the midday sky.

Below were the parallel lines of red Kalahari dunes with their tufts of tall grass and old acacias battling to survive in the valleys between them. Herds of springbok fled the shadow of his plane as it fell across them; stately oryx barely raised their elegantly horned heads. The Kalahari basin dipped away as far as his eye could see; the outer reaches of its eastern rim in Bechuanaland – or Botswana since the kaffirs had taken it over, André reminded himself. North-east was Zambia, another kaffir state. André always felt close to his god when flying on cloudless days like this and now he offered up a prayer of thanks for Rhodesia and South West Africa, still ruled by whites.

The little plane was now over the pans. These shone silver and leaked ribbons of water through the bush looking like strands of silver in peppercorn hair. He leaned back, easing his painful buttock in the small seat. His ears felt hot and the sun was beating on his swollen neck, but he was a man, he could take it. Even under the worst circumstances flying was better than listening to Ma bitch about his auntie or the bookkeeper moan about the expense of keeping an aeroplane. Ja-no, up here, it felt like he owned all three hundred and fifty thousand square miles of the Kalahari, all one million of the basin. And I don't have to see to a single blerry mielie on it, he thought.

Koba's suitor and his friend, Gao Monkey Orange, sneaked back to the pan. Hiding behind a camel thorn they watched the women bathing. 'I saw you trying to steal from the Woman with Many Possessions,' Gao whispered.

'Eh, go ejaculate on yourself, Fat Face. We all know she wants nothing from you.'

Gao rubbed ruefully at his stings. 'Yau, that woman. She will split my face into pieces,' he said, watching Koba sit in the shallows to wash between her toes.

His rival agreed. 'And she has good legs,' he wheezed.

'Those are not legs; they are paths to pleasure.' Gao smacked his swollen lips. 'See how they are not too long, not too thick. Just sleek, like she has eaten well.'

'But not on honey,' his rival jibed. 'You should have gone with the Tsumkwe-lot to learn the ways of town girls, Tiny Genital. Town girls need *real* food.' He gestured down at his breechcloth.

'Screw sand, man. I am not going and leaving you to pick this Kalahari lily.'

'Watch who you push,' the suitor hissed, 'or my fist will make another lump on your face.'

Old Dabe parted the branches and glared down at them. 'Is the prospect of unripe mangetti nuts making you lose your manners, bachelors, or is it the scent of fresh meat?'

André spotted a herd of elephant off the tip of his starboard wing. He banked the plane for a better look. Not jumbo, huts, he thought. But they looked abandoned, though only recently, he chuckled, noting a wisp of dark smoke rising from a fire. Stroke of blerry luck, he thought. A pilot could fly over this desert for hours and see fok-all. He began his reconnaissance, widening his flight path with every circuit, anticipation mounting. Before long he picked up movement – black ants scurrying round a sheet of silver. Water. But he was way too high to see yellow. He pushed the nose of the plane down. At fifty foot he could see detail, women and children gawping up at him, eyes wide, mouths agape. Some of the children waved. He ignored them, searching for a yellow dress.

Koba knew she was in danger long before she heard the roar of the plane engine. Her early warning system had kicked in and her tappings now timpani-ed in her chest. She wanted to run stark naked from the water and hide, but three men had appeared on the far shore of the pan. Were they the threat?

Be calm, Bushgirl, one is Old Dabe.

He was gazing skywards with two younger Jul'hoan men. Still Koba felt vulnerable. *My tappings haven't pecked at me like this since the Lion had me tied in his truck,* she thought. She turned and saw the children pointing up, shouting, 'Vulture, vulture!'

'What is that sky thing?' Old Dabe asked.

'An airplane,' Gao said, 'and it's coming back, so low I think it wants to part our hair. Get *down*, grandfather.'

André laughed to see the three little figures on the bank hit the dirt.

He throttled back as much as he dared and took the Cub back low and slow over the water, whisking the placid surface into ripples that rushed to shore as standing waves. 'Kaalgat!' he whistled. 'Naked, every one. All looking the fokken same.' Two old women hurried out of the water. 'Sies-man, tits down to their belly buttons. Disgusting. Take that, you goggas!' He opened the spray jets and released a trail of pesticide.

Koba saw wheels coming towards her and a veil of white. She dived underwater, pulling |Asa with her. She didn't hear the whizz of an arrow overhead, nor the sound of it zinging into rubber tyre. When the girls surfaced, gasping for air, the plane was climbing again.

André felt rather than heard something hit the plane. Probably a stone thrown by one of the kaffir brats. *Water off a duck's back, boetie,* he thought, checking his dials and seeing nothing unusual. But the fuel gauge showed it was time to head for home. *Damn, all this way, and no Bushman bitch. Ja-well, it had been a long shot anyway.* Next time he'd carry extra fuel instead of pesticide.

Forty minutes later, on touchdown at the Onderwater airfield, he felt the Cub drag to the right. *Fok, had he lost a tyre?* He wrenched the wheel left, over-correcting. The plane swerved off the narrow landing strip, the good wheel hitting a rut. Before he knew it, he'd put the left wing into the ground.

16

'What was that mist? Could it be bad? What did you see?' People crowded around Tsamkxao, coughing, clamouring to know what had happened.

'You got him, you shot the bad vulture with the bad nǀom,' a boy shouted, capering around the tall man, who stood glaring at the sky where the plane had been.

'Xohhhh, in his foot, straight in. Xohhhh!' Old Dabe shouted until he started wheezing.

Spitting to rid himself of a strange, salty taste, Gao confirmed that he too had seen the arrowhead lodge in the wheel.

'How did you know, how did you know we were in danger?' Chuǃko asked, hanging onto Tsamkxao's arm.

'Better you should ask what that ǀTon was looking for,' Tsamkxao snarled.

Koba was helping ǀAsa from the water. They'd avoided immediate contact with the spray, but Koba insisted ǀAsa rinse herself in clean water as fast as possible. 'In case bad . . .' She hesitated to use the word 'nǀom' – not wanting to attribute any kind of power to the plane. 'In case bad*ness* lay on the water – the baby . . .' She could hardly bear to look at ǀAsa's pregnant belly. The men, most of whom had escaped the spray, scooped up children still happily playing in the water and herded the puzzled women together. People milled around gabbling about the bizarre incident, spluttering outrage at being doused with something that made them cough and cry. They'd all seen aeroplanes before, admired jets emitting vapour trails they took as evidence of spiritual energy similar to what their most powerful healers had, the ones who could travel, transcend time and space to confer with the ancestors. But no one had ever seen a plane close-up nor choked on its tail.

'That airplane nearly landed on the Frog-bringer's head,' Koba's suitor said.

'Is our visitor a plane-bringer too?' Tsamkxao called out, trying to catch Koba's eye.

She felt exposed by his stare and avoided him by moving from person to person, urging them to wash in clean water, just in case.

'In case of what?' Ti!'ay Sour demanded. But she was beginning to feel tight-chested and one of the children started vomiting. People mentioned a prickling sensation on their skin, in their throats and eyes. Koba pulled at lAsa's hand, but Bo seemed to think there was no cause for panic, so his wife stood with the rest, hand across her bulging belly while Tsamkxao checked the wind direction and pontificated on the possible drift of the strange mist. Koba twisted the corners of her kaross as the group deliberated and finally moved off to find uncontaminated water.

Tsamkxao and other men stood with bows drawn, scanning the sky, while the bathers dunked themselves, their children and their clothing. Most people could now feel their eyes, throats and skin itch and flare and they were beginning to despair about 'bad nlom'.

'Get into the groves,' lQui Beard urged. 'The airplane might return with more sickening mist.'

Koba could hardly bear to contemplate the misfortune she might have attracted to people who'd become dear to her. Unlike the other Jul'hoansi, she knew that this aeroplane had no supernatural powers, but those who'd seen the veil of white swore a ghostly train had billowed out from the magic wings. Others reported feeling real droplets on their skin. Koba knew it was the poison white men used on their crops. She didn't know if it killed humans on contact. She couldn't stop shivering as she allowed herself to be hurried into the cover of the trees.

The grove stood on a raised dune in an island of pale sand. It was several hundred feet wide and ran back further than Koba could see. The mangetti trees were straight-trunked with stubby branches, too tall to allow a low-flying plane overhead access. The bathers collapsed beneath them and were fussed by their families. Only the old and the very young seemed seriously stricken – Old Zuma had chest pain and several more children had thrown up. Chu!ko's tot wouldn't stop rubbing his eyes. Old Dabe was the first to notice the unusual upwelling of saliva that many were experiencing. 'I'm dribbling like a baby,' he said. 'I hope my teeth will grow back again.'

The women always carried medicinal herbs with them. Now pouches were opened and their contents pored over and a long discussion about which ones were best for which symptom followed. It was decided that they should remain there to treat the sick; they would call on Xoo, the Big-owner of the grove who lived deeper within it, when everyone was better.

Despite feeling light-headed, Koba collected wood for the healing fire with guilt-stricken alacrity, keeping herself well out of Tsamkxao's orbit. But when she volunteered to fill up the ostrich eggshells with fresh water, he insisted on accompanying her, practically elbowing her suitors out of the way.

As soon as they were out of earshot he demanded to know whether the sickening mist had anything to do with her.

Koba wanted to bolt back to !Asa's side. But the group deserved an explanation and this man with the flashing eyes was the only one she could tell with any degree of fluency. Speaking slowly, keeping her eyes focused on the horizon over which the plane had disappeared, she told him that she suspected the pilot was the white man who had killed her parents at the Mother Hills. She kept details of her stay on Impalala scant, but she mentioned that she'd escaped certain death at the hands of this man just days before she found the band.

'But he didn't follow me. I checked. I don't know how he found me here, but I know he will kill me as soon as he can.'

To her surprise her interrogator nodded and squatted down. His eyes were now lower than hers and looked soft with sympathy. 'I know what it is to run from the ITon,' he said. 'When I was young, I was chased by two ITon on horses. They had guns.'

Koba listened as he explained that he and his father had run away from a settler farm where they'd been tricked into working during the last sustained drought. 'The work was hard-hard-hard and my father he never got no money from the white people. But he was working for food to feed his family. The white man said he would give us meat.' All they got was fine white powder, which his mother had to mix with water and cook for them, day after day, Tsamkxao said, his eyes hardening. 'There were no nuts or berries in that place; we were not permitted to hunt the buck. The ITon, they had cattle grazing from one horizon to the other, and always they were slaughtering one fat animal and eating the meat. We could smell it on the smoke from their cooking fire. They ate meat, but did not even smear our mouths with fat. We got only the white powder, thin and tasteless as sand.' In a low voice Tsamkxao described how one day the family all became sick. First his infant sister died, dehydrated from diarrhoea and vomiting. Then his mother, trying to retch up the ITon food. His eyes, now hot with anger, held Koba's. 'There was poison in it. I remember its smell. It was like the white mist today, but much-much stronger.' Koba dropped her head. 'We were much-much sicker than Old Zuma and Dabe. We were dying.'

But he and his father survived and ran away the night after they'd buried his mother. As Tsamkxao described how the horsemen chased them, Koba began to feel dizzy. She could hear the drumbeat of hooves coming after her and her parents all those years ago as they fled from the Mother Hills. Tsamkxao talked on, explaining how he and his weakened father were no match for the horsemen. 'They shot my father when he drew his bow . . .'

Koba felt the ground begin to spin around her. She sat down abruptly and grabbed a tuft of grass, winding it around her hand to anchor herself.

Tsamkxao didn't seem to notice. With hate in his voice he told how he'd been dragged back to the farm behind the horse. 'This,' he said, slapping his back cross-hatched with the cruel scars that had intrigued Koba. The slap jolted her back into the present; she breathed deeply, calming herself as she heard Tsamkxao declare: 'This is how I remember what clawed things |Ton are. You and me, we know the evil they have in their hearts.'

'Not all of them,' Koba said softly.

Tsamkxao reared back, his nostrils flared. 'You, of all people, say *that*?' He rose with one furious movement and stood glaring down at her. 'It is as I thought. You are |Ton-stained. You have lost your Ju|'hoan skin.' With that, he stalked off back to the grove.

17

Mannie had been on the road for ten days. Over eight hundred miles by his reckoning and still five to go until his next stop. That would be Mariental, his last lift had told him.

The tarmac shimmered in a heat haze. Quivering emptiness all the way to a liquid horizon. No human sound, just dry wind and black-faced sheep bleating in the lonely veld around him. He needed something to cheer him up. He set off at a brisk walk, determined to reach the town before nightfall. He'd treat himself to a hotel room and a hot bath, if Mariental had such luxuries to offer.

He'd spent most nights sleeping in the open, not bothering to pitch his pup tent. It was too warm. Several of his drivers had offered him a home-cooked meal and a bed for the night, but he daren't become memorable. 'Blend in, man,' Jabu had advised. 'Make like a white man in snow.' None of them had ever seen any, but if they were sent to the USSR for training they'd soon get sick of it, Jabu said.

A white boy hitch-hiking was not uncommon now there was national conscription. With army training bases all along his route, many drivers assumed he was one of the troepies hitching home to see his sweetheart. Questioned about his unit, he'd become evasive. Then drivers would wink at him and mouth 'AWOL'. Next they'd talk about someone they knew who'd had a rough time during basic training, but now loved the army. 'Afkak's necessary to make a man out of you. You must just vasbyt, boet,' they'd always conclude.

Seems like lately my whole life is lies, Mannie thought, kicking a single stone off the tarmac and into the bush. The most curious drivers were told he was at Wits studying geography and that this was an independent field trip to see Spitzkoppe. It felt like less of a lie – he might well see the fantastic red granite formations; the site wasn't too far off his route north. And he was very interested in geology. If things hadn't turned out as they had, he might have gone to Wits to study rocks, he thought; he had no trouble remembering words like dolomitized. Ja-no, the road trip was definitely fuelling his interest in the earth sciences. Hell, they had some of the oldest rock fossils in the world in the Kalahari. He couldn't wait to see some.

The most astonishing thing he'd seen so far was the deep gash in the earth that was the Sishen Iron Ore Mine. Six miles long, one mile wide and quarter of a mile deep, it was one of the largest in the world, he'd been told by an engineer who gave him a lift on the road between Kuruman and Sishen. Almost as awe-inspiring were the trucks used to carry the ore up the inclines from the pits. These were storeys high. Mannie smiled, remembering how excited he'd been about what he called 'lollies' – lorries – when he was little. His father always stopped to let him stare, open-mouthed, when the big fruit trucks from Tzaneen rumbled through town. 'When I've got a little lightie, I'll bring him to see these,' he determined.

He'd promised his parents that he'd phone them every week and he had once already, from a call box in Upington. It was uncomfortable pretending he was five hundred miles east of where he actually was and claiming to be swimming in the Indian Ocean when in reality he was caked in red dust and closer now to the icy Atlantic. Also, they were all conscious of speaking on a party line shared with Marikie Botha, Katrina's nosy mother. She was skilled at silently lifting the telephone in her house as soon as it rang for someone else. Ma had once confronted her about it and they hadn't spoken since.

Mannie sighed. Christmas was going to be tricky. He planned to be in Tsumkwe by then and who knew if they had phone boxes there. He'd heard it wasn't much of a town. But he'd promised his ma he'd call so he'd have to make a plan. Jislaaik, but the old toppies could put pressure on an oke. He wouldn't be able to keep placating them with telephone calls once he was out of the country. He planned to write them a letter explaining he'd be away for a long time. Jabu-and-them said they'd find someone to deliver it.

Mannie picked up his pace; it would soon be night and he didn't want to have to walk this unlit road in the dark. It was likely to be littered with snakes using the tarmac to warm themselves through the desert night. He whistled now. He was more than halfway to Onderwater; he could be seeing Koba within the week.

18

Back at the grove camp, the victims of the sickening mist were made to gargle, drink and inhale different herbal infusions as the less afflicted, like N!ai, vied to administer the most efficacious remedy. Koba helped, keeping a wary eye on Tsamkxao. She'd expected him to denounce her to the group. They would drive her away, if not that night, certainly in the morning. She tried to formulate a plan for her escape, but it was all she could do to keep Tsamkxao in focus. He was deep in conversation with IQui Beard and neither of them were looking towards her. But she couldn't be sure. Her vision was blurring.

'People are sick. We will dance to heal them,' she understood IQui Beard to say to the sound of general agreement. Men began to gather more wood, building the fire and storing the rest for the long night ahead. All the men except Old Dabe wound dance rattles around their ankles. These were made from moth cocoons strung on sinew. Inside every cocoon a chip of ostrich eggshell clattered as the men began to test them, stomping up clouds of white dust. Women and children eagerly took their places in a circle around the fire. They sat shoulder to shoulder, legs entwined, discomfort from the mist temporarily forgotten. Immediately they struck up a rhythmic clapping and chanting.

Koba sat between IAsa and her friend's mother, N!ai. She tried to clap but did not know the rhythm. She didn't know the words. She thought about her one experiment in trance dancing at Impalala, so different from this. Mannie had done his best to help her create the energy she could already feel building around this fire, but it had taken hours. He'd drummed, she'd chanted, on and on she'd shuffled around their fire until near dawn when, suddenly, she exhibited the dramatic medicine-ownership symptoms. Her cramps, shaking and sweating, had terrified them both. Here there was no trepidation. Even young children seemed filled with joyous anticipation. Harmonic chanting and clapping wove a spell around the circle as every participant focused on the common goal, supporting their medicine man in his astral journey to fetch healing for them all.

Round and round the men danced, their feet lost in a cloud of dust that shone copper in the firelight. To Koba's swimming eyes they seemed to be floating, ungrounded, one set of pulsing thigh and calf muscles indistinguishable from the next, golden pistons pummelling the earth, driving the silver voices of the singers. Or were the singers driving them, conducting the dance with beguiling cries and frenzied hand motions until the men seemed to levitate around the circle? Koba wondered. She couldn't tell, but she shivered with excitement.

Hours passed and the frenzy of dance built. People called out: 'Heat up the nǀom – make it boil.' Koba looked around. Who was translating for her? Not Tsamkxao; he wouldn't help her ever again, she was sure. And he was on the other side of the fire now, tallest among the train of dancers, intent on keeping in step. Koba heard ǀAsa's voice, like a commentary, explaining the action:

'Gao Monkey Orange feels something in his backbone. Tingle-tingle the nǀom enters him. Will he be strong enough to bear its burn all the way up? That one wants to be a healer, but he is not ready.'

Koba stared at her friend. She couldn't see ǀAsa's mouth or anyone else's – faces were difficult to distinguish with her vision so blurred. But her ears seemed sharply attuned. Not only was she understanding the Juǀ'hoan language, she was replying in it too. Her tongue felt agile, rising to the roof of her mouth to meet clicks on demand, curling around tricky Juǀ'hoan consonants as though she'd been born to it.

You were.

Yau, there you are. I thought the insecticide might have killed you. Koba chuckled. But she had no time for conversation with herself. IAsa was talking to her.

'Gao must be cooled. Nǀom boils over in him and he cannot use it.' Koba perceived rather than saw N!ai rise and kneel over a prostrate male form. 'Mother will help him. And see how my mother's husband seizes the nǀom. Up the pain goes to the base of his skull . . . Up, up, he rises above it, climbing the wires to the sky. ǀQui Beard slips out of his skin. He is an airplane. Now he reaches the village of the gods. Applaud him, he has !Aia and can do his work.'

'!Aia.' Koba knew that word. It meant a state of transcendence. Now the healer would have power to see inside bodies, to cure ills. Part of her worried that ǀQui Beard would see she was no rain-season child, but rather a dissembler who allowed people to think she brought luck when she trailed drought and danger. Also, would this mighty healer think her arrogant to have attempted the journey towards ownership of medicine herself? And what would he make of the eland she sensed near her, even now? But these thoughts were jumbled and she felt unable to act on any of them. Even if she'd been capable of leaving the circle she wouldn't have. She longed to be seen, to be healed, and not just of her blurred vision. She wanted to be taken into the group, protected, held at its heart, like she belonged. And she wanted her eland explained.

She saw ǀQui Beard moving around the circle, laying his hands on people. Some swayed, others moaned. She heard him arguing for healing. When he got to Old Zuma he seemed to be losing the battle. ǀQui Beard looked over his shoulder, slick with sweat, as if seeking help. The chanting surged and the clapping intensified. Something unseen disturbed the fire. Sparks leaped in every direction, igniting the dark beyond the dancers. Still ǀQui Beard pleaded and cajoled, but his mother-in-law slumped against her husband, head lolling. N!ai began rubbing Old Zuma's arms, frantically trying to work warmth back into her mother's ice-cold body.

Koba felt a sharply pointed pain in her lower back. She remained seated and tried not to writhe as heat rose up her spine and rushed down her arms all the way to her fingertips. These she felt compelled to stretch towards Old Zuma. The crone's eyes flew open and she sat up straight. |Qui Beard turned and winked at Koba, but she was transfixed by the figure materializing behind him, just beyond the circle of firelight. It was the other Zuma, her grandmother, last seen in spirit form in the cave on Impalala. Grandmother Zuma was singing and clapping, her lined face ecstatic. A younger woman sat next to her wearing the broad, beaded headband favoured by Koba's late mother, Nǂaisa. This figure stopped her clapping and cupped her spectral hands together. She blew across them, sending the kiss towards her spellbound daughter. Koba's heart soared over the fire and landed between them. She felt cosseted.

From this angle she could see another man behind |Qui, supporting him as the healer took the poison from Old Zuma's lungs into his own bony chest. The supporter was Tami, her father, whose own blasted chest looked whole and strong again. He smiled and smiled and smiled at her. Koba was overjoyed. She felt she was where she was supposed to be, at home, her true n!ore, among her own people.

Then she was back in her body sitting next to |Asa. The glowing girl looked at her and said quite distinctly: 'Now you sit among us, at our heart.'

Gradually the singing and dancing slowed. An exhausted |Qui Beard was laid reverently down. He fell into an instant deep sleep. Ti!'ay covered him with a kaross where he lay. She squeezed N!ai's arm, thanking her for helping their husband when she herself felt too ill. 'But I am healed now,' she declared. N!ai hugged her. They crowed their pride in |Qui.

Looking around the fire, her vision sharp again, Koba could see that everyone felt better, including Old Zuma. Trance euphoria had been replaced by dazed elation and, though it was now dawn, most adults weren't ready for sleep. They wanted to continue communing, however drowsily. They lounged about, beamed at the sunrise and at one another, passed sleeping children from lap to lap, admiring them, shared pipes of precious tobacco, or hummed quietly. Tsamkxao ambled over to Koba. Goodwill radiated from him like morning sunshine. 'I have a message for you from |Qui

Beard,' he said, and then in Juǀ'hoan that she understood perfectly: 'The nǀomkxao says you are connected to us with strips of skin – eland skin.'

The band remained dozy and beatific throughout the day and the next night; and the following morning, fully restored to health, they made their merry way to Xoo, Big-owner's home ground. Koba skipped along in their midst, holding hands with ǀAsa, who in turn linked fingers with Bo. Koba felt secure. She understood these people now, understood that they accepted her. And, after her trance experience, she had more confidence in her own prescience. If André was near she'd know and be able to flee. Tsamkxao would keep the group safe; she could rely on him.

He was walking a few steps behind her now, carrying Chuǃko's bundle. She turned and smiled at him and he smiled back. Even Chuǃko managed a half-smile.

Old Zuma was in particularly fine form, her sense of direction among the unerringly uniform trees as acute as that of an elephant matriarch, as she led the party this way and that. She called a halt to the caravan at the entrance to Xoo's clearing so she could 'read the news'. Hands on hips, she studied the sand. It was dented with footprints, barefoot and shod; she studied it with the ravenous interest of a starved gossip.

'That man, what's-his-face, who sits with his testicles in the sand all day while his in-laws go hungry, that lazy one is here.' ǀAsa steered Bo Fingers out of earshot. Zuma continued:

'Aie, a lot of Tsumkwe people have been.' She sucked her few remaining teeth and pointed at a rubber-sole print. 'ǀTon shoes, and this one wobble-wobbles.'

'Beer makes your legs weak.' Tiǃ'ay Sour sniffed. 'Those Tsumkwe-drinkers get so they can't put one sand-presser in front of the other. They can see only sand, because they are flat on their faces in it.' Then, under her breath so Old Zuma wouldn't hear, 'Nǃai knows.'

But Zuma heard her, and sighed. It didn't take long for the trance dance effect to wear off, she thought; best to ignore the irascible relative she'd inherited with Nǃai's second marriage. Nevertheless,

Ti!'ay's sour tongue had put unspoken fears into words. Would N!ai be able to resist the lure of Tsumkwe now that it was within a few hours' walk? The family had avoided the mangetti groves for several seasons, but now that they had to represent Koba in marriage negotiations, they had no choice but to come. N!ai had assured them that |Qui Beard had cured her beer-thirst, but her parents felt that her infatuation with Tsamkxao was responsible for her abstinence. They'd all heard Tsamkxao condemning Tsumkwe, beer and anything else to do with the whites.

Xoo Big-owner's camp looked permanent. The roof of her grass hut had a khaki-coloured tarpaulin fastened to it, and in a lean-to Koba saw rusting tins and buckets impossible to carry in a kaross. More were stacked on a rickety table made from an old billboard advertising Lion matches. Koba tamped down a shudder of fear, reminding herself that she felt not even the lightest of tappings. Her eyes continued to range across the campsite, noting the disorder.

No place for plucking – bird feathers everywhere, like blossom. And bones sucked clean of meat and monkey orange shells from moons ago and broken gourds. Mess!

There was also westernized debris: cracked jam jars, crushed ciga-rette packets, two old car tyres that the children in the group strained to get to, hessian sacks half-buried in the sand, a rusty piece of corrugated iron similarly interred.

Serene amid the refuse sat a white-haired old woman. Her gleaming back was curved like the mahogany handle of a walking stick and her legs, stretched out in front of her, were covered by a kaross. She was staring into the rustling treetops and didn't seem to have noticed her large band of visitors. Zuma stepped forward into the clearing.

'Xobo!' the Big-owner exclaimed, hand fluttering over her heart. She peered up at Zuma. 'What are we to each other?'

'It's me, Zuma, your |Gautcha pan cousin.'

'Mi !xa xobo!' Xoo clapped. 'My Zuma?' The old face shone, wrinkles radiating out from glaucous eyes.

'My heart is glad-glad to see you,' Xoo said, raising kindling-stick arms up to her old friend.

Zuma clasped Xoo's hands between her own. 'Xoo, kxae kxao, I hope the new season finds you well now the year grows warm and the trees are oozing sap. How are your legs?'

'Sister, my legs are like logs. Soon wood worms will live there and gnaw at them.' She dismissed commiseration with the wave of a narrow hand. 'How are the people? Did everyone survive the thirst?'

'We are alive once again; before the rain, we were dead.'

'Here too, here too. Now we have a few of the rain's things.' As she gestured towards some fungus growing in a damp patch at the base of nearby tree, Koba marvelled that she could see them. 'But for moons, the sip well was dry. Tell my old ears, how are the animals near IGautcha pan?'

They bemoaned the scarcity of buck, plant-food and tobacco then cosied up to a favourite topic, the lack of generosity among relatives, especially theirs. Zuma's kin looked on indulgently. Old smoke had the right to waft where it willed, even if it caused irritation. Then Old Zuma told her cousin about the aeroplane incident. The old sage was all ears, exclaiming, shaking her heavily beaded head, muttering about bad ITon nIom. Zuma assured her they'd exorcized all bad spirits and had in fact brought along a visitor who her son-in-law, the healer, IQui Beard, believed had healing gifts herself. 'She is named Koba,' Old Zuma said, pointing at her, 'and we come to ask you who she is related to because you are old and know these things.'

The girl sat with eyes downcast while Zuma explained what she knew of Koba's story. They all heard Xoo cluck and grow increasingly animated. From under her lashes Koba saw Xoo's top half bustle as the old woman grabbed a short broom of twigs and swept the patch of sand directly alongside her lifeless legs. With a gnarled finger Xoo began tracing, muttering all the while.

People crept closer, agog to hear to whom Koba was related. It had serious implications for her suitors. Koba was interested only in establishing who her parents' closest kin were; she wasn't looking for a husband, but this was probably not the right time to explain that; she thought it would seem ungrateful. Xoo shooed everyone off and beckoned for Koba to sit closer. 'Against me, child, so I can know your heart.' Koba shuffled forward.

Xoo's emaciated hand with yellowed nails long as pincers worked its way across her lap and up her torso. Bit by bit, it found her face. It was like letting a crab climb her, a crab rotting in its shell, Koba thought, trying not to flinch. She held her breath as Xoo's milky eyes brooded over her like two blind moons. They see straight through me, she thought, and she will know my heart belongs to a white man and that I am a dangerous dry-season child. Koba drew back.

Xoo cackled; Koba felt spittle on her chin. 'I see your grandmother, yau, I do – Zuma, who was a strong nǀomkxao; Zuma, mother of Nǂaisa, Nǂaisa who married Tami. That Zuma had but one grandchild, a girl. It is you!'

ǀQui Beard nodded vigorously. He'd seen that venerable woman too, he told Xoo, around the healing fire, with another spirit woman; they'd been there, large as life, and Koba's father too. That one had helped him, held his back when he took the sickness into himself.

People nodded, patted Koba on her back, stroked her arm. Immediately some of the women began tracing the branches of their family trees out loud to see if they touched Koba's. Suitors' representatives contradicted one another and some begged Koba to try and remember aunts or cousins twice removed. She was relieved to have public confirmation of her parentage, but felt alarmed at being the centre of attention. She tried to sidle off.

ǀAsa pulled her from the throng and hugged her, whispering, 'Now you don't have to marry that greasy Monkey Orange.' Koba laughed. She didn't intend to marry anyone, but she felt suddenly happy. She and ǀAsa held each other around the waist and spun around under a clear, uncomplicated blue sky. 'I am home, *home*!' she sang.

But dare you stay? A lion stalks you. You may escape but you could bring this death-thing to your people. How must Tsamkxao save them?

Koba stopped. ǀAsa looked puzzled. 'What's the matter? Has a scorpion stung you?'

'I, er . . .' She cast about, looking down at the ground. 'Yes . . . No, er . . .' Koba saw Old Xoo beckoning her. 'I must go.'

*

The crone sat alone now, motionless amid the traffic of people dashing across the clearing to greet old friends already there, or to secure vacant spots to set up home. 'Sit,' Xoo commanded. Koba hunkered down, her heart thumping.

It is my heart, not my tappings, she told herself. She had to lean in to hear Xoo's voice above the jovial hulabaloo.

'Our hearts are glad that you have come back to us.' Koba heard the words like the creak of an ancient tree limb in the wind. 'And that you have a child hitting fists inside your womb.'

Koba was shocked by Xoo's words. Had the old woman actually used the Jul'hoan expression for pregnancy? Perhaps she'd misunderstood. She didn't dare ask; she didn't want certainty.

She fled the old woman and the crowd, found a lone tree and leaned against it, dumbfounded. Her mind raced over the last few months, searching for evidence. Yes, she'd been throwing up – wasn't it the sand and bitter food? But she hadn't menstruated lately. Not unusual. Her breasts? They'd felt tender, even after her bruises from André's kicking had faded.

Hn-hn-hn-hn-hnnnn. Xoo Big-owner has seen. What will I do now? And when, *when* was this seed planted?

She wanted to remember the silvered nights she'd lain with Mannie when their love made anything seem possible. But all she could think of were the rough, dark men tearing at her in the prison van.

19

Koba stood with arms clamped around her middle, feeling the sudden certainty of the child heavily in her womb.

How will my heart be towards it if I hated its father? And if it has green Frog-boy eyes and my skin, will Xoo and Tsamkxao, will anyone, accept the child? I cannot bear this thing alone, but I don't know where to turn.

In the space of a heartbeat she realized Marta and Deon would accept her, no matter whose baby it was. Mannie, too. But how could she get back to Impalala? André might catch her; or the police – she'd been expressly forbidden re-entry into South Africa. In any case she had no money for the train fare and it was too far to walk, even had she known the way.

I want to run-run-run; from here, from this thing in me, from my life that is always-always so hard. I wish that the Lion had killed me. I wish that this child could kill me.

She sat on the ground, drew her knees up to her chest and let her head slump between them.

Cheerful activity continued across the clearing as people made camp: some went for firewood, others to search for plant-food. Children unearthed one of Old Xoo's tyres and bounced on it while young men wrestled, pretending to grab one another's testicles. A young buck from the resident group scooped up a pair of withered mangetti nuts from the ground and threw them into the air. Thak-thak: they hit branches. '*There* are yours, cousin, hanging in the trees.' Gao pinned his opponent to the ground. 'Ejaculate on yourself, cousin-of-Koba,' the new suitor spluttered, choking in Gao's stranglehold.

'We hear you are cousins with her, Gao Monkey Orange,' another one teased, '*your* testicles are not wanted.'

Gao grabbed at him. 'I'll feed *yours* to the vultures.'

People passing by stopped to watch the young men horn-locking like kudu bulls. It was good sport. Tsamkxao stepped into the middle of the mêlée, hissing: 'You are rolling around thasi nl'ang! Has your intelligence left you? How do you think a young girl feels to be spoken about like this? See how she buries her head. Show some respect or I will teach you some.'

Wrestlers and onlookers gaped at his livid face. Since when had he become a paragon of good manners? Behind his back the young suitor pulled faces.

'Has Tsamkxao's wind changed direction?' the |Gautcha pan-band asked behind their hands.

'Must-be. Last moon he hated the Frog-bringer,' |Qui's people said, sniggering in reply.

As Tsamkxao strode off, blatant laughter broke out.

A few minutes later Ti!'ay found cause to wander past Chu!ko, who was unpacking her kaross. 'Told you so,' she said, tapping the side of her nose. Chu!ko glowered at her.

Koba remained lost in her thoughts until she felt a touch on her shoulder. She looked up to see N!ai indicating she'd like to sit beside her. Koba nodded vigorously. Worries and questions rattled in her head like eggshell shards in a cocoon. Who better to answer than her surrogate mother? She had best circle the subject, try to get from N!ai the information she needed without revealing her condition, Koba decided. She took a deep breath.

'|Asa's mother, I have a thing I want to ask . . . not a personal thing, just a woman-thing.' N!ai nodded. 'It's about, er, pregnancy, but is not about |Asa,' Koba hastened to add. N!ai nodded again and waited, hands open in her lap. 'I was thinking, wondering . . . can a child grow twisted in the womb if, if the mother is afraid?' She stole a glance at the older woman, but N!ai looked unperturbed. Koba rushed on. 'I have heard the women say this. They say that if you are afraid you will have a bad birth.'

'Eh, you are afraid you may be buried.' N!ai spoke it as a gentle statement of fact.

'Me? I . . . No.' Surprise stemmed Koba's tears, but her lips betrayed her. She felt them quiver.

'Hush-hush.' N!ai patted her. 'It is just the baby inside making you tearful. It can also make a woman angry. These things are known.'

Koba realized she didn't mind this woman knowing she was pregnant. And angry. Fury was far, far better than fear.

'Yes, I am angry! Why did I have to be a child alone on a hill with no one to teach me about woman-things?' Koba was breathing fast. 'Why did my heart take root among people whose kin killed my parents? It makes me cross-cross that these people should feel more like mine than the Real People, you Jul'hoansi. But the worst-worst thing is that my heart is soft towards a ǀTon boy. I call him Frog-boy.' Koba fierce-fingered tears from her cheeks. 'But this *thing* in me, this child . . . I'm afraid it is not his seed, but the seed of bad men who ruined me in the prison van.'

She was panting now, sobs escaping between snatched breaths. A release. A relief. She'd told her secret to someone, her shame-thing, the one that made her want to crawl away and hide. And N!ai hadn't castigated her. But she found she couldn't look into the Jul'hoan woman's face for fear of what might be hidden there.

Koba buried her head between her knees again and now she began to sob solidly. She registered N!ai slipping an arm across her shoulders; it swelled her storm.

N!ai rocked Koba for the long time it took the girl to quieten.

Eventually, through hiccups, Koba said: 'Bad-bad things happen to me. I don't know why.'

'Must-be you have cold n!ow; you are not the lucky rain-season child we took you for,' N!ai murmured.

Koba sat up. 'So bad things will happen all of my life because of n!ow that flowed into me from my mother's birthing waters?'

N!ai shrugged. 'The old people say we must expect the scorpion to sting us. That is his work.'

Suddenly Koba felt glad she couldn't stay with the group. She didn't want to sit in the sand with them, accepting the stings of the scorpion – from André or any other plagues like drought, disease or hunger. She looked closely at her companion. It struck her that defeat marred N!ai's pretty features, her dark eyes seeing only the now, not a future. She'd gathered from campfire gossip that during her stay in Tsumkwe N!ai had been what Marta would have called 'a good-time girl'. Was this woman content with her quiet life now?

Koba looked down at her own toes, half buried in the sand. Already they had what she thought of as the sand-presser look, with splayed toe pads. Underneath, her heel was hardening. But she'd seen another way of walking, of being.

I cannot clean, but I can read books and do sums. I can see me working behind a desk, like Marta sometimes does, at the lodge; I wear a smart skirt and a pressed blouse, not this yellow thing. I could do work, in a building, every day.

Not with a baby on your back.

The thought stunned Koba. She would be fending not just for herself, but for another human being. But I know nothing of mother-things, she told herself. And should she and the child survive the trauma of childbirth, what then? How did women alone manage? Koba wondered. It was no use asking N!ai; she'd raised her daughter among the Ju|'hoansi where children were a shared responsibility, a communal joy. What did mothers alone do, to get their children meat to eat? Koba asked herself.

I don't want a child of mine to live on nuts and berries alone. It must eat meat to grow strong.

Hnn, already you worry for Little Fists. Already you speak like a mother, Bushgirl.

The truth stung. Koba sat absorbing its implications. Quickly she realized she didn't need the smart skirt or the pressed blouse. She needed people who cared for her; who would help her care for this child. But they were beyond her reach. Self-pity doused her ambition. 'Why do people always ruin others?' she asked in a small voice.

'Those are things the old people never told us about.' N!ai shrugged.

Koba stared at N!ai's inscrutable profile. 'So I must not beat fists against things I can't change. Hunger and cruelty and this ruin-thing?' She gestured down at her belly.

N!ai turned to face her. 'I can tell you this one thing. I also feel small here, like a tree without water enough to grow tall. But here I am straight. In Tsumkwe,' she said, sighing, 'I was twisted.' Then her dimple appeared, revitalizing her face as she flashed Koba a wicked smile. 'I long to be twisted sometimes. The taste of beer, aieee, my mouth still remembers it.'

Koba felt disconcerted. Should she explain that there were better |Ton drinks than beer? But she'd never tasted beer. And she'd never been to Tsumkwe. Her experience of life in towns was restricted to what she'd seen from the back of a pick-up on the few occasions she'd driven into the small ones around Impalala. It was then she'd glimpsed the odd young white woman hurrying into a building wearing a smart skirt and crisp blouse. Maybe |Asa's mother was right. Tsumkwe and beer were better than Nyae Nyae; better than bushveld towns. She didn't know; she didn't know anything any more except that she had to leave.

'Wipe away your worry, little-daughter. We will help you bear the child. We know woman's work and will teach you.'

Koba gulped. She didn't want to tell N!ai that her presence posed a danger to the group. Only Tsamkxao knew and so far, for some reason, he'd kept her secret. She owed it to him, to all of them, to leave before André returned. But where should she go?

She lifted her eyes to the treetops and scanned the sky, as if the answer might lie there. If she wished hard enough the spirit of her grandmother would return, would whisper the answer on the wind, she thought. She sat listening, so hard she felt she could hear lizards licking the air as they climbed the tree trunks, but she didn't hear spirit Zuma giving her a solution. Once again, she was on her own.

She supposed she should stand up; go find her bundle and set off – somewhere. But there was comfort to be drawn from sitting a while beside N!ai.

The older woman seemed in no hurry either. N!ai stretched her legs out on the sand, reached into her kaross and extracted a heavy ostrich eggshell necklace from its folds. The beads looked magnified to Koba, but once she'd blinked back the tears, she recognized it as one her surrogate mother had been working on for a while. It was special – multi-stranded with finely worked beads that were carefully gradated from small to large. It was almost long enough to hang down to a woman's navel. A birth present from mother to daughter, Koba thought jealously.

N!ai opened a leather pouch and shook some loose white beads onto her thigh. 'If your heart is not sure of this, I can tell you of many ways to ruin a pregnancy,' she said as she searched for a bead of the right size.

Sergeant Hendrik Du Pree was teeing up his golf ball at the practice range on the Onderwater army base. The kommandant had made it clear that the local policemen were welcome to use the sandy range anytime they wanted to. Du Pree used it whenever he could. Golf was a game played next door in South Africa by rooinekke and Jews, and Afrikaners who wanted to get on. He planned to get on very well; a transfer to South Africa, a promotion, eventually a brigadiership, why not? B. J. Vorster, the new minister of police, was good at this golf game and everyone knew Vorster was destined for big things. Du Pree was young, at the start of his career, and determined to learn all the skills necessary to get to the top. If this moffie sport was one of them, he'd master it.

His drive landed well short of the hand-painted two hundred yards sign.

'Ag nee, man, Du Pree,' Dirk, one of the permanent force army officers, said. 'My sister could hit further than that.'

'Ag kak, Dirk. I gave your sister such a seeing-to last night she can only hit high notes today. Your mother and your granny too.'

'You fokken wish, Yid-balls. Now show us how that SAP sharp-shooter training has paid off. See if you can hit Philemon over there.' The officer pointed to a black man in a brown army overall who was scurrying about the range picking up balls.

Du Pree laughed. 'Pass me my Colt then.'

Dirk chortled. 'Nee, man, that's too easy. Use the bloody driver.'

'I might hit your kaffir. I'm feeling lucky.'

'Okay-okay. Hi, Philemon, sit die deksel op,' the officer shouted to the black man. Du Pree convulsed with laughter when the man reached for a saucepan and put it, upside down, handle foremost, on his head.

And bugger me if I didn't actually hit the pot, the jackpot, Du Pree thought, still laughing to himself twenty minutes later as he drove his Volkswagen home. What were the chances, hey, what were the fokken chances of hitting a kaffir right on the head with a golf ball, from two hundred yards off?

He became aware of the young man with his thumb out at the side of the road. He pulled over.

'You sure you're going my way, boet? The army base is back there.'

'It's north of Onderwater I want to go, sir,' the youth said.

'Oh, with that number one . . .' he said, indicating the young man's army-style crew cut. There was no reply.

'Ja-well, hop in, man.' Du Pree leaned across and opened the passenger door. AWOL, Du Pree thought, I'll tip off the military police. But out loud he said: 'Not much north of Onderwater; Tsumeb and then some kaffirs who cover themselves in red mud. But they are way out west.'

The youth explained that he was a student of anthropology on a field trip to study the Himba tribe, the ones Du Pree was calling redskins.

'Let me guess, the University of the Witwatersrand, hey?' The boy nodded, a bit too eagerly, Du Pree thought. He studied him out of the corner of his eye, while he kept up a teasing banter about all students at liberal universities being communist-sympathizers. But why, he wondered privately, would such a student sport an army haircut? The fashion at places like Wits nowadays was for hippy-hair. Some of those miscreants had hair so long you couldn't tell from the back if it was a Mister or a Miss. What kind of men wanted to dress like that? Du Pree thought.

But this wasn't one of them. This little coward was running away; he could smell the fear on him. He'd telephone Dirk, get him to let the military police know.

Mannie was feeling uncomfortable. The man next to him had the innocuous look of a honey badger: small dark eyes, friendly turned up nose, a compact body. But Mannie suspected the joking mouth could deliver a dangerous bite. And the oke never stopped talking. He seemed to have an endless supply of rude jokes about kaffirs and cunt. Nevertheless, Mannie felt he was being silently watched. Off-duty pig? he wondered. He was thankful when the man said he'd have to drop him off just before Onderwater as he had an errand to run.

Late that night Du Pree learned that the military police had found no sign of the youngster on the road to Tsumeb or anywhere else in the vicinity. They had no reports of anyone AWOL from the base, so the search was off.

And mine has just begun, Du Pree thought. That youngster was talking twak and I'm gonna find out why.

Abort Little Fists? Koba crossed her arms over her chest and manacled her elbows with steely fingers. What if it is Frog-boy's child? she thought.

What if it isn't, Bushgirl?

N!ai sat sewing beads. 'You could cook food at someone else's fire,' she said without looking up, 'you could ride a donkey; you could sleep with a man who is not the child's father.' The idea was so outrageous Koba had to laugh. She relaxed her grip on herself.

'Why you laugh, Frog-bringer? Many men want to have food with you. You are not lazy, you are not thin; you do not wander about at night visiting other people's fires like a bitch. Now that we all know who you share blood or name-relative with, the Eligibles will be asking |Qui Beard for you. He will ask you to choose.'

Koba bristled. 'I don't want to share a sleeping mat with anyone but Frog-boy.'

'You said Frog-boy is not possible. And not permitted?' Koba nodded. 'No point to hunger for what your heart can't have. Take a husband from these. You'll grow fond of him in time.'

'With respect, mother of |Asa, I don't want a husband from here.'

'Not even Tsamkxao?'

Koba's eyes widened. Why was N!ai suggesting her own lover? She looked down, embarrassed.

Your heart has softened towards that tall Ju|'hoan man since you both spoke of being |Ton quarry, Bushgirl. And he is strong enough to protect you. He would never accept a child with green eyes, but if you got rid of the child . . .

She felt N!ai's nudge. 'You are always looking for Tsamkxao out of the back of your head. He looks for you the same way. That one stamps around like a bull elephant trumpeting your no-goodness, but he is just an elephant in musth. He wants to have food with you. Now he knows your family were Real People from |Gautcha pan, he will let himself look at your beauty.'

Was N!ai proposing that four people should share sleeping partners? Koba felt so shocked she couldn't meet N!ai's matter-of-fact eyes.

'I am going to share my blankets only with my husband again,' N!ai explained, grinning. 'If you want Tsamkxao, little-daughter, you should smile at him instead of putting that fierce face front. Try now. He comes.'

Tsamkxao strode towards them, his rippled torso gilded by the evening light. 'Daughter of Tami-late, you left Xoo's as if a swarm of buzzings were after you.'

'They were,' N!ai remarked dryly.

Tsamkxao allowed himself a grin. It split his face into two sunny halves, each more dazzling than the sunset.

Koba blinked.

'Come, I've made a fire for you and the wood is talking,' Tsamkxao said. 'Tonight we will celebrate that Zuma-late's granddaughter has returned to claim family rights to the biggest mangetti tree in the grove.'

20

After a night of rain and hail, Dominee Venter was surveying the damage to the vegetable plots in Tsumkwe. Cornrows lay flattened and the flowers of the squash plants had been shredded. There'd be no crop from either of these: but, worst of all, the topsoil had washed away. In desert sand like this, humus-rich soil was hard to come by.

Venter comforted his protruding chin with his gardener's dirt-ingrained hand. Between them, he and the Bushman affairs commissioner had devoted eight years to teaching the indigenous people agriculture, but it was a fruitless task. Out in the veld Bushmen were peerless when it came to husbanding the wild food resources; he'd been on foraging walks and seen how careful they were to avoid disturbing a plant they said was still a child. But they cared little for farmed food.

And on the rare occasions he did manage to get a Bushman interested in vegetable gardening, the harvest was inevitably lost to cattle or goats belonging to the Herero herdsmen who had settled on the periphery of the town. These half-starved beasts regularly broke into plots where they ate the melons and trampled the corn. A person needed the patience of Job for this work, Venter thought.

Listening to the rain rattle on the roof of the church house the night before, he'd felt agitated. Without doubt, most of his parishioners would have forgotten to protect their young plants. 'You'd think,' he said to his wife, 'that with all they know about plant-food they'd be able to care nicely for a few vegetables, but no.'

'Ag, Fanie,' she said, 'it's not the lack of knowledge – we've explained to them often enough. It's that they don't care. They want food that comes in bags or boxes or tins. They think when they come to town their days of having to get food from the earth are over.'

'Ja-but, they are going to suffer, Elsie. When those women's husbands stop tracking for the army, they are going to be hungry.'

She sucked her teeth, making her dentures clack. 'A person doesn't know what's worse, isn't it – them having money to spend on booze or not having any money at all? You should of seen the state of Gumtsa's children in the classroom today. Filthy with fleas, too tired to concentrate. The good Lord only knows when last their mother fed them. I took them back to their shack and what did I find? She'd used the bread we gave her to feed her children for making beer! Ja, chunks of it floating in a sour-smelling bucket. I wanted to throw it at her, I really did.'

Her husband shook his head as he cut into the lamb chop on his plate.

They chewed in sorrowful contemplation a while, then: 'So, what about that letter what came?'

'What letter?'

'I put it on the sideboard.'

'No, my angel.'

'Ja, Fanus, I did.'

'Sorry, angel. I didn't mean you didn't, er, put it on the sideboard. I mean I didn't see it.'

'Wait-first, I'll get Fidelity to fetch it.' She rang the bell next to her place setting and a small black woman wearing an oversized headscarf and overall opened the dining-room door and came in. She stood waiting, hands clasped in her lap.

'Fidelity, fetch that letter from the sideboard for the dominee.'

The woman took the three steps across the room, picked up an envelope from a yellow-wood dresser, took three steps back and handed it to her mistress. 'Thank you. I'll ring when we want the plates cleared.' The minister's wife settled her glasses on her nose and, staring at the envelope, read out: '"To: Koba Yellow Dress, care of, Dominee Venter." Fanie, do we know anyone of that name?'

Now, as he picked his way around puddles in Tsumkwe's only street, Fanie Venter wondered about the person the letter in his pocket was addressed to. She might be Damara, Herero, Kavango, Himba, Nama, Tswana, Owambo – from any tribe except the Bushman. So why send her letter to him? Everyone knew he worked only with what the university-types called the San. San did not have names related to the white world. Up until a few years ago they'd had little official contact with it, unlike the other Bantu tribespeople. The latter often had names foisted on them by the church or a school. Venter was always surprised by how often these became self-fulfilling, like their own maid, Fidelity. He didn't know her Kavango name, but he did know she had a faithless husband who'd left her to provide for their six children single-handedly. She hadn't failed them.

He stopped to study the freshness of a pile of mule dung. (Ja, still some goodness in it. He'd come back later with a spade.) He shambled on. Names? Yes, in one of his early parishes the church had employed a Sotho man to work in the garden. He was called Born-in-a-queue; a patient man, that one. His mother had been queuing to get her passbook when the child came. Ja, poor thing, she'd probably had to go back and stand in the queue again afterwards, baby on her back, Venter thought. Thank the Lord the Bushmen in his mission didn't have to carry passbooks. Their peripatetic paths across an area as hostile as the Kalahari defeated even the rigour of the Bantu registration authorities.

The Tsumkwe town-lot were easier to keep tabs on. They didn't move further than the nearest shebeen, more was the pity. He saw it as a personal failure that they looked different from their country cousins. Shaggy-haired, dull in skin and eye, they were pathetic scraps of humanity who'd given up the hunter-gatherer life for the squalor of a town that no white man who hadn't sold his soul to God or the devil would live in, Venter thought. He did what he could to keep them alive on church charity and he kept encouraging subsistence farming, but they had neither the aptitude nor the inclination. They wouldn't water or weed.

He mourned the fact that every year more of them drifted in from the bush in the hope of getting a share of the handouts. Their fatalism was the bane of his life. If the crops failed, they just shrugged their delicate shoulders, as if there was nothing they could do about it. But, dear God, how will it end for these little people? he wondered, looking past the two small concrete blocks that housed the clinic and the primary school, away to the wilderness crouching beyond.

He'd come to a camel thorn tree that marked the centre of the hamlet. A few of his flock squatted in its shade. Venter approached them. He found San words difficult to reproduce; many contained click consonants; too often his tongue popped off the top of his palate when it should have been tapping the back of his teeth. This amused the locals. They called him Tongue-young and predicted that intelligence would come to his organ if he kept practising Jul'hoan words. 'Ag-no, I'll be dead before my tongue's even a teenager,' the elderly cleric would reply.

He was at ease, however, with the banter permitted between friends and used it now: 'Surely you have forgotten me?' He took off his hat and bowed to the group. They feigned indifference. 'Perhaps you no longer care because I speak only of vegetables? Perhaps you will refuse to talk to me?'

A man with hair that stood up in dusty spires responded with a slow grin. 'No, clearly you are the one who has forgotten us; didn't we see you talking with vegetables just now, instead of with we Real People?'

Group laughter, more thrust and parry and then the inevitable shrugging when he said there would be poor yield from the vegetable crops damaged in the storm. Everyone agreed it had indeed been a ferocious downpour. See, the sand was still pockmarked from the drops. They all tried to remember when last they'd seen lightning like it, or heard such thunder. On and on and on the conversation went with not a mention of crop care.

Venter lamented the waste, but stopped short of reprimanding them. Though they looked like them, they weren't children, he reminded himself.

Instead he asked about Koba Yellow Dress. A woman with a scarred face, palsied on one side, slurred that she had heard there was a strange young woman who had come from the |Ton. They called her the Frog-bringer as she'd brought the Nyae Nyae Big Rains and small jumping meat, it was rumoured.

'Must-be she who has ruined Dominee's crops,' someone said, laughing.

'Your crops,' Venter tried, but Palsied Face hadn't finished.

Whether or not this person wore a yellow dress she couldn't say, the woman persisted. What this 'yellow' was, she had not been told.

Venter had long been intrigued by these people's seeming inability to understand colour as Europeans do. It wasn't that they didn't know colours or have words for them, as far as he could tell; it was more that they thought of colour only in relation to familiar objects, animals or plants, he'd decided.

Much discussion followed until Venter hit upon an idea. 'You know those flowers, Mma,' he said to the woman, 'the tall ones that grow in the church garden? The ones with dark faces that follow the sun all day?' She nodded. 'The frill around their faces is yellow.'

Palsied Face tutted. 'It's no good for a person to look at the sun all day. She will lose her eyes.'

Venter hoped not. An adult Bushman, presumably, who could read and perhaps write Afrikaans, now that was something you didn't see every day. He left the group still speculating about the Frog-bringer and walked on to the trading store.

Crushed cartons of Chibuku beer littered the outside. He sniffed the rancid air. The devil's brew. How he wished it had never reached this part of the world. But if they didn't buy it here from the hard-nosed Herero woman who ran the store, they'd make their own from the bread they were given.

'The Lord only knows what the solution to the Bushman problem is,' he muttered to himself.

*

Du Pree had his own problem – he suspected that the young hitch-hiker he'd picked up might be a terrorist trainee. The more he thought about it, the more he was sure that the story about doing research among the Himba was bullshit.

The little liar hadn't known the location of the tribe. Anyway, Christmas was coming; what moegoe would spend it in a stinking kraal in one-hundred-degree heat? No-man, the wanker's story doesn't wash, he thought.

He'd seen a memo from the counter-insurgency unit yesterday. They reported that the ANC might use the People's Liberation Army of Namibia to smuggle recruits across the South West African border. From there it was simple to get them away to commie training camps in Tanzania or even the USSR. What if the 'student' was going to meet one of these in Tsumeb?

Despite recent arrests, Owamboland was crawling with South West Africa People's Organization activists. A few months earlier, heliborne police had raided one of the liberation army's training camps, killing two would-be terrorists and arresting nine. In retaliation, the terrs shot up the Oshikango border post, Du Pree remembered. Within weeks his colleagues in the area had rounded up the bastards. All thirty-six of them. But it was feasible that some had escaped across the border and were waiting for weapons. MK, the ANC's armed wing, was well-supplied by their Russian masters, he'd heard. What if PLAN was trafficking MK recruits in exchange for weapons? Could the kid be one of the first deliveries?

Du Pree considered taking his suspicions to his superior officer, but at this stage he had nothing to go on besides gut feeling.

And the boss will think me a fokken mamparra for not searching the youngster while I had him in the bakkie.

Du Pree had telephoned the stations in Owamboland, but with the big game reserve at Etosha pan, there were often whites in the area, even at this time of the year, they pointed out. If he could supply an identikit picture they would keep a lookout.

Du Pree sat down to telegraph the records department at Security Police headquarters in South Africa. If the student's a political activist, they'll have something about him on file, he thought.

21

A red moon rose over the mangetti grove that night. 'A great meat animal has died somewhere,' people exclaimed. 'We could find the body and feast.' Tsamkxao and Gao Monkey Orange determined they would go and search for it. Everyone urged them on; it had been a long-long meat fast.

'Take along the two grooms who sit around my fire,' Old Dabe said, indicating IQui Beard and Bo Fingers. 'These two have sat so long not doing their bride-service, their testicles have grown into the sand.' Old Dabe's son- and grandson-in-law did not demur. They had a duty to the family pot and vowed not to return until they had fulfilled it.

'I won't sharpen my meat-tearing tooth yet,' Old Zuma declared.

'Grandmother doesn't believe they'll find a carcass,' IAsa whispered to Koba, 'not because she does not think them good hunters.' Koba nodded, straight-faced. 'Old Zuma thinks redness in a moon is blood from someone who has died,' IAsa explained. Koba hoped it didn't signify the blood N!ai had warned her of if she took the pregnancy cure.

Koba had been glad to hear Tsamkxao was leaving the camp. His now blatant ardour for her was flattering but confusing. She wanted to make the decision about drinking N!ai's potion without considering him. She didn't yet know whether or not she'd still have Little Fists growing inside her when she left. N!ai's account of the abortion pain – 'pain that will make you writhe like a snake in the teeth of a mongoose' – terrified her. 'Aie, it is the same if you carry the child until the end,' N!ai had said. 'Most women survive; Real women bear it alone. They give birth quietly behind a bush. It is the Jul'hoan way. We use things to stop from crying out.'

This didn't allay Koba's fears and she was anxious to learn more about these things before she had to face her ordeal, whatever it was. She felt a few more days among the women, to soak up their wisdom and lean against their hearts, would serve her well. There was time; her tappings were still, which meant neither she nor the band were in any imminent danger.

Nevertheless, in the morning, she would take herself off somewhere private to consult her oracle discs. They might also help her decide on her direction when she left the camp.

She sat with Bo Fingers and IAsa long after most people had gone to their mats to dream of meat. Bo took out his lute and tried to teach them a tune, but it was so mournful that for different reasons neither girl could bear it.

'You are not going away for ever, husband. Play us a happy song.' He played her favourite and IAsa sang:

> 'We live in the groves
> And what little bird calls dzui?
> And we're surprised.
> My dear Koba and I,
> On a gathering trip
> For mangetti nuts.'

Koba allowed her shoulder to touch IAsa's sitting close beside her. This was the last person she could discuss the abortion with; her friend was in the glorious bloom of pregnancy, her stomach bulging like a golden calabash. But Koba needed to talk around the subject, however circuitously.

'IAsa, if a bad thing happened to you and you could stop what grew from it.' IAsa looked puzzled. 'I mean, would you accept it, or would you throw away the . . . the bad thing's *result* . . . even though it might be dangerous?'

|Asa looked across to Bo, then back at Koba. The Frog-bringer's new fluency in Jul'hoan had revealed what a serious person this young woman was. She and Bo had decided there couldn't have been much joy in Koba's life with the whites, but they didn't like to ask. And now this deep question, deep even for a solemn person, |Asa thought. It struck her that her friend had been in a strange mood all night. And she didn't look quite like herself either. With her usual generosity, Koba had been gift-giving. Tonight she'd given her beautiful dress to her mother, N!ai. Now Koba sat wrapped in the tattered kaross her grandmother had given her when she first arrived. Her friend's face looked too naked unframed by the frill of the yellow dress. |Asa determined to make her a necklace. She would raid her mother's store of beads tomorrow. Now she needed to answer the strange question.

'I had to accept my parents' liking for beer – that was a bad thing; it killed my father. I cannot change that.' |Asa sighed. 'But if I could cure my mother's thirst for beer, I would, even if it was dangerous.'

'It might be,' Bo said and went on to describe the drunken frenzy he'd witnessed in various men. 'Beer is bad. A person who is drunk does not know people.'

'Is-so,' |Asa said softly. 'Even a mother does not know her own child. And husbands and wives, they start off talking nicely, but they can't finish.'

Koba had long wondered about |Asa's childhood. 'You lived in Tsumkwe with your mother and father?'

'Eh . . . But I disremember it,' |Asa said quickly. 'My mother brought me here to live with my grandmother. I waited and waited for my N!ai-mother to come back to us, and then she did. Things come if one waits.' |Asa patted the stomach orbing over her skirt. 'We women must always wait, isn't it? We wait for meat, for our moons, for babies. For men! Especially for men,' she said, laughing.

Koba began to drum her fingers in the sand.

|Asa ignored her. Her impatient friend needed to hear this. 'That time you found us at |Gautcha pan, Koba, nearly dead from thirst, we had waited a long-long time for rain. But it came and it brought its barra things: flowers and fruit, fresh grass. And you.' She leaned lightly against Koba's shoulder. 'You are our lucky rain-season person.'

Koba felt ashamed. 'No, |Asa.'

|Asa's hand closed over hers. 'This |Ton tapping – always you are busy with it and your heart is restless. My friend, I don't know many things, the old people haven't told me everything, but if you could learn to be still, and wait, I think your heart will be easier.'

Koba let out a deep sigh. I don't have the luxury of having a man who longs to be the father of my child, she thought.

Koba managed to steal away from the grove just before daybreak. For the first half-hour she was tailed by a hyena, its hunched brown shape trotting doggedly behind her. It turned tail when she threw sticks at it. That was all she could do, shouting or banging on tree trunks to frighten it away might bring people out to investigate.

She hugged her kaross closer around her and hurried on. Reaching a camel thorn copse she decided to sit with the safety of a thicket at her back until daylight drove the hyena back to its burrow.

It didn't take long. In the newborn light she saw it slink off, taking the smell of death with it.

She shook her discs out of the old pouch. They'd belonged to her grandmother. Koba had used them successfully before, though not in public. They were intended for hunt prediction and were thus the preserve of men. Her grandmother, however, had taught her to read them for other things.

Koba held each one in turn on her palm, naming them: Little Fists; Lion; N!ore; Journey; Heart and Unknowable, the wild card, the mist behind which even the oracle discs could not see; a possibility to be respected, her grandmother had said. Now Koba performed a stacking, blowing, throwing ritual similar to the one she'd seen |Qui Beard use. The discs fell, landing soundlessly in the pale, morning sand. Koba searched for Lion. If that tawny disc lay face up she needed to be on the alert. It did, but further off, and not on top of N!ore, that was the important thing. The people were safe; she could trust her tappings.

But N!ore was lying face down; the only disc that was. She felt desolate to see its back turned to her. She sat for a moment thinking of all the things she hadn't done with the group, all the things she would have liked to share but now wouldn't. She might have described to them the wonder of a radio, a hippopotamus or even the sensation of sucking on a block of ice. But, she reminded herself, the Ju|'hoansi were quick to mock those who set themselves above others.

Perhaps she could have told |Asa and Bo Fingers that her favourite song was made by a lawn sprinkler. She loved its *chu-chuk-chukka-chukka-chukka* sound as it spat water over a lawn, rattling on leaves broad enough to use as sunshades. But, turning a piece of metal, using just a wrist-twist to make a rainbow of rain, would simply confirm her as the rain-bringer in their minds. She didn't want to keep that lie alive.

Koba turned back to her study of the discs. A grouping in the sunset direction: Journey, Little Fists and then Heart. Their relation to one another was as important as their falling order. She'd noted these and would think about the meaning, open her mind to let it become clearer, as her grandmother had taught her. It took time. And she must not forget that Unknowable loomed large on the horizon too.

She gathered the discs and stood up. She'd got what she came for, direction and peace of mind. André was out there beyond the mangetti trees but for now he slept like a lion hidden in the long grass.

An hour later, just one hundred miles away across the Kalahari sandveld, Gerrit Wolfaardt was on his way to work. He was in charge of grading the long stretch of dirt road between Onderwater and Tsumkwe. What had started as a standard maintenance job had swelled into a major repair operation since the heavy rains. Floodwater had gouged chasms into the surface and created mud islands elsewhere, leaving sections of the road impassable. He was picking his way around potholes, cursing the job, when he saw a sight to gladden his heart, company, thumbing a lift, a white man about his own age, to boot. He flung open the door of his pick-up and invited the youth into the cab.

He babbled on about himself non-stop as the truck bumped along the endless road. He complained about how lonely it was in the Kalahari. 'It's so wild, so empty up here, that when you step off this road, man, you step into the Dark Ages.' He couldn't wait to finish the job and get back to civilization, he said. His companion gazed at the lumpy road that stretched like a botched surgical scar across the pristine land and said nothing.

This was the last leg of Mannie's subcontinental trip. He knew this dirt track led to nowhere that whites wanted to go and he'd imagined walking a long way. Now he was sorry not to be doing so. But at least he could be sure of being on time for his rendezvous. In fact, he was a little ahead of schedule, so he'd need a place to lie low until it was time to meet Koba, he thought.

He asked Gerrit if there were any whites in Tsumkwe. The buck-toothed young foreman whistled disgust. 'Man, there's only four in the whole dorp! And I say "dorp", but you mustn't imagine a town with tarred roads and shops and a bar, hey. There is nothing there. Fok-all. Just the four old toppies: the Bushman affairs commissioner and his wife, a real pair of old suid-westers, you know the type.' Mannie didn't, but he nodded anyway. 'But they've gone to Luderitz for Christmas – lucky for them they got out just before the rains washed away the road – so that leaves just the dominee and his missus in Tsumkwe. And a lot of kaffirs.' Gerrit laughed.

'Ja-no, a nice old boy is Venter, and his missus is a kind lady, but all they can talk about is the Bushman and their blerry vegetables. I tell you, it's more of a jôl sitting in camp with my kaffir road crew than going to the dominee's for supper.

'Anyway, what was I saying? Oh ja, no one can get in or out now until I fix up that road. And that won't be soon. Tomorrow, ou maat, me and the kaffirs knock off for Christmas, so I think you better forget about going to the reserve at Kaudom. Better come back to my posie. But, like I say, I'm off, like a *cracker,* tomorrow. Going vry-ing.' He rolled his hips on the seat and winked at Mannie. Then he stared at him as if the boy's sunburned face had given him an idea. 'Hey, you know what, forget this dustbowl, man, come down to Upington with me. I'm sure my tjerrie can find you a lekker girlie to have a jôl with.'

Mannie declined. He'd camp in the bush and walk the rest of the way, he said.

'Ag, don't be stupid, man. But if you want to live like a monk, I've got a pull-out bed in the caravan, a shower fixed up in a tree and my cook-boy makes the best mealie pap this side of Upington,' Gerrit said.

On her way back to the grove Koba spotted the strangest spoor she'd ever seen – hyena pads, human hands, sticks and something being dragged. She shivered, imagining a giant spider with two hands, hyena paws and a massive abdomen dragging across the sand. Most unsettling of all was the stench of rotting meat.

Had the hyena taken a child? Her belly contracted with fear while her nose told her it was a corpse long dead. The Tsonga people at Impalala believed ghosts walked during the day. Selina, the Maraises' housemaid, once told Mannie to beware when playing near the river. The evil tokoloshe went there to fetch corpses from crocodile dens and paraded them 'for the sun to see', she'd cackled.

Has your intelligence left you? There is no tokoloshe. The Tsonga also told their children you *were the evil one. These stories are to frighten children. You are not that frightened Bushgirl any more. Be a Bushwoman made of metal.*

Koba squared her shoulders and began to follow the trail. Soon she discerned whistling. Not a hyena then, but some insects whistled through their abdomens, she thought. She worried that the loud noise came from an abnormally large insect. Her skin goosebumped; had the discs evoked something? The Unknowable? Reluctant to meet it, she slowed down.

Something large and black crept very slowly through the scrubland ahead. She froze, scalp prickling as she saw a hunched body and bent limbs. Five. She considered turning tail, cowering away like the hyena, but if she'd awoken this bad spirit she should drive it off too. She crouched down, trembling, scanning the vicinity for a tree trunk thick enough to bang on. Then she heard the spirit sneeze, an ordinary, man-sized *atchoo* sound. Koba stood up. This was no giant spider spirit; it was a man dragging himself along by his hands, trailing a heavy sack; he was whistling, but through the gritted teeth of someone in pain, Koba thought. She approached quietly, aware of the rotting smell getting stronger as she did.

'Greetings,' she called out in Jul'hoan.

The spider started and tried to scuttle round to face her – a black man, not Jul'hoan, with tribal marks on his cheeks like whorls on dark polished wood. His eyes seemed feverishly bright. He said something to her and mimed a rapidly beating heart. She did not recognize his language.

'Do you speak English?' he called.

'Y-yes,' she stammered.

'Stop then. Not good to come closer. I don't want to offend such a pretty nose.'

A rotten spider flirting with her in the middle of the bush; she had the urge to giggle. 'I help you?' she suggested across the halt between them.

'Only if you got some Old Spice.' His smile spread the whorls so his face seemed to spin with merriment.

Old Spice? Old Spice! She shook her head, amazed. She knew that name. It was the smell Mannie's father kept in a bottle in the bathroom at Impalala. It was quite nice, even if it was pretend. Why did Spiderman want it?

'Is my leg; she is stinking.'

Koba looked at the limb. The bottom half was missing and there seemed to be a raw wound where the knee should have been. She felt afraid again.

'Lions?' she whispered.

'No-no, wehk.' He laughed. 'In the gold mines. I lose the leg inna accident. I got a replacement,' he said, waggling a prosthesis at her, a half-leg, made from heavy pink plastic that ended in a clumpy black boot, 'but I don't like the colour, so I going to change it.'

Koba burst out laughing and immediately felt ashamed.

'I am not pulling your leg, Kalahari flower, I am going for refitting. What colour I should get? Green, to match this?' He airily indicated his pustular stump as if it was a fashion accessory.

Koba sat down where she was and stared at him.

To Mannie, the roadworks camp looked like something from a science fiction film. Metal behemoths, diggers, scrapers and rollers, were corralled behind high wire-mesh fencing, their massive buckets and blades like monstrous appendages. A caravan shaped like a space pod blinked silver in the sun and the split, creosoted timbers of what was no doubt the ablution area looked like a dark rank of troopers with lances aloft. Childish to fantasize like that, he knew, but he longed to scale the machines, to sit in their high cabs and conquer their controls. He tried to engage Gerrit in discussion about them, but his host clearly saw them only as a maintenance-intensive means to an end.

The roadworks camp was the perfect hideaway. The black workers did not question his right to be there – Gerrit's effusiveness made him appear to be their baas' best friend. In the highly unlikely event anyone passed by, the outsider would assume he was part of the crew; having been on the road for as long as he had, Mannie guessed he'd acquired the weather-beaten look of a white man who spent all day outdoors. He'd check in the morning when he had his first shave for weeks, using a mirror.

'You sure you don't want to change your mind, Monk-man?' Gerrit called out of the window of his pick-up on the morning he left.

Mannie grinned, but shook his head.

'Then stay and be a wanker.' And with a loud parp on his horn Gerrit and most of his crew were gone, leaving only Mannie and the nightwatchman. The old Zulu's earlobes, which must have once contained enormous ear plugs, now hung down to the shoulders of his army greatcoat, which he wore even in the one-hundred-degree heat of the camp. Mannie found him better company than Gerrit had been.

He felt he'd heard far too much about his host's girlfriend, Annalies: 'thirty-four, twenty-four, thirty-four'. Apparently these were the inches around the feminine parts of her body; they were also the perfect vital statistics for a woman to have, Gerrit said. 'More than a handful is mos a waste, isn't it, man?'

All the girl-talk had made Mannie long for Koba. Where, in that vast empty scrubland, was she? And why the fok had he been stupid enough to imagine she'd be sitting on some street corner in her yellow dress just waiting for someone to hand his letter to her? There were no street corners in Tsumkwe, said Gerrit; there was only one street and the Bushmen there spent most of the time lying drunk in the middle of it. 'Can't say I blame them,' Gerrit had remarked. Mannie didn't think Koba would hang around a place like that. She was more likely to be out in the bush. But where? The place was the size of a small country. Even if he had a vehicle he wouldn't know where to begin to look.

As the sun baked down on the caravan, turning it into a scorching metal oven, Mannie began to despair. What had felt like an adventure while he was still on the road now began to seem like a big mistake.

What if, miracle of miracles, Koba did get his letter but decided *not* to meet him? He broke into a sweat and knew it wasn't just the temperature in the van.

If I'm honest, he thought to himself, I couldn't tell from our last meeting whether or not she still loved me.

It had been at Johannesburg station. They'd been released from their respective prisons less than an hour before. Koba had to pose with a government senator, who was using her to show the new Homeland Policy at work. The press were all there; it wasn't every day they saw a Bushman in South Africa; the last ones had been wiped out in the Cape during the previous century, the newspapers reported. They called for Koba to pose semi-naked. Readers had seen the dummy of the massively steatopygic Bushman woman on display in the national museum. 'Did this one have inbuilt water storage tanks too?' one hack asked the frowning senator.

Mannie had been unable to get near to Koba until she was aboard the train, next to her guard. Eventually the big black man had allowed her to lean out of the window to say goodbye. Mannie remembered that he'd tried to kiss Koba, but she'd drawn back.

Was that because she no longer loved him or was it because everyone could see them? He'd pondered that for months. He wanted to ask her as soon as he saw her, if he saw her.

He couldn't bear to think that he'd come all this way and wouldn't see her. Ever again. Instead he dwelt on her last enigmatic words to him: 'You gave me salt. I gave you honey. It was not nothing.'

He smiled. His girl and her salt. How old had they been when they started bartering with each other, he and the wild child his mother had brought to live on their farm? Ten, maybe eleven? Already Koba was expert with bees, he remembered. She could raid a hive without getting a single sting. She'd pull out the chewiest honeycomb and always leave some for the little bird that guided her to the hive. Yet she didn't like the taste of honey herself. She liked salt. They'd had plenty of that at home, in boxes with a drawing of a boy chasing a chicken on it, saltshaker in his hand.

Mannie lay back on Gerrit's bed and listened to the metal frame of the caravan groan as it expanded in the heat. He repeated to himself her parting words: 'You gave me salt. I gave you honey. It was not nothing.' *It* was not nothing. What was 'not nothing': their affair?

But she hadn't said that, exactly, and he wasn't sure he would have either. 'Affair' seemed so adult; so dressed up, like something on a screen at the bioscope between a woman wearing gloves and a man in a suit. He couldn't ever imagine Koba in gloves or him in a suit. He didn't even own one. He'd anticipated buying one when he went to university; there were occasions there where an oke had to wear one, Rube had said. But now he wouldn't be going. Mannie sighed. He didn't want to think about that now. He wanted to think about Koba. Jis, but he missed her. All the months without her had made him even surer that he loved her.

He thought now about their first kiss. Ma and Pa had been away. Second honeymoon, he'd teased them. 'First,' Ma said. 'We were too poor before.'

'We're still too poor,' his pa had said, grinning, 'but this woman is worth getting into debt for.' And he'd led Ma shyly off.

Mannie remembered that he'd been alone in the house, studying for his school-leaving exam, when Koba had jumped in over the windowsill – she never used doors. They'd listened to music, danced a bit, shared a smoke and then they were kissing and he'd wanted to touch her all over, like he'd never wanted anything in his life before. And she'd let him.

'She unbuttoned that old school shirt of mine that she always wore,' he said out loud, as if he still couldn't quite believe it, 'and let me touch her tits. Jissus, Koba's body!' He groaned.

Mannie felt hard thinking about it. He didn't know what her vital statistics were; he didn't care. To him, she was perfect and delectable. Her bottom a golden peach, her nipples plump sultanas, and, oh God, her cunt! Eating there was like lipping open a guava.

Conscious of his erection, he looked round. He met Gerrit's girl-friend's ice-blue eyes taking a dim view from the photo frame next to the bed. He turned his back and began to masturbate.

In a lively baritone the Spiderman was explaining to Koba that he was from southern Rhodesia and was trying to get to Johannesburg. Yes, it was a very long way, he agreed, but he hadn't planned to walk the whole way. He was going to get a lift in a helicopter, so if she could just direct him to the nearest army base.

'A helicopter?' Koba knew the word but she'd never seen one and certainly not in this area. Why should there be a machine like that in the Kalahari skies?

This time the laughing Spiderman wasn't joking, she learned. 'For the bush war, to help the Boere find the terrorists. Freedom fighters to you and me, flower.'

Koba registered the words, but didn't understand their meaning.

It was his turn to stare. 'How it is that a Masarwa, er . . . Bush . . .'

'Bushman, Jul'hoan,' she interjected.

He smiled at her obvious pride. 'How is it that such a flower of the Jul'hoan people can speak English, maybe the Boer language too' – she nodded – 'but knows nothing of the white man's wars happening in her land?'

Koba tried to explain her history as succinctly as she could. Though most of the detail was omitted, it felt good talking to this stranger. Something about the Spiderman made her feel she was talking to someone who understood.

She stood up. 'I will help you back to the Jul'hoan camp,' she said. 'We will make muti to heal your leg. Come, lean on me.'

He smiled. 'What do they call you, little flower?'

'Koba,' she said, heaving him up. 'What is your name?'

'Trust.'

22

'Another strange thing she brings us,' Chu!ko muttered when Koba returned to the grove with Trust. Koba did not introduce him as an old acquaintance, but Chu!ko noted how easy she seemed around him. Koba explained that the stranger had walked all the way from a land far north. No one had ever heard of it. She said he was seeking a ride in a flying machine that wasn't an airplane but looked more like a bubble – no one had ever seen such a thing, – to a place far south to fetch a new leg. Even |Asa looked sceptical. What was clear to everyone was that he needed treatment. He had a raging fever.

Infusions were brewed and poultices applied after his wound had been débrided and cleaned. Together the women built him a shelter some distance from the main camp. Out of Koba's earshot the community speculated whether she had deliberately gone into the bush to meet the stranger and planned to set up house with him when he stopped stinking. After all, some women said, she could choose anyone she was not related to and she was obviously not related to that ugly black thing.

Chu!ko leered at him from behind a tree. 'Perhaps the bone missing from his leg lives inside his |Ton trousers and when he stops stinking we will hear him making her a happy woman.'

'That will make Tsamkxao unhappy,' another observed. Chu!ko flounced off.

'Eh-weh, that one. Her husband needs to get his genitals back here quick-quick,' Old Zuma said. 'We are all suffering from her meat-hunger.'

Fed and rested, Trust announced he had to move on.

'Your eyes are still bright with fever,' Koba protested.

'That is not fever, it's admiration,' he flirted. Chastened by her stern look, he explained that he needed antibiotics. Koba conferred with N!ai who said the closest source of white medicine was Tsumkwe.

'I'll take him there.' N!ai dimpled.

'Don't go!' her daughter and her mother immediately shouted.

'Hush, I won't be there long. I'll be back before it is time to meet my grandchild.' She patted her daughter's belly.

'Which direction is Tsumkwe?' Koba asked.

N!ai pointed. Not towards sunset then, Koba thought. But the train station lay that way and, eventually, Impalala. She pressed her hand to her stomach. No, it wasn't possible. And the discs had shown that her heart lay west, not south.

'Don't go, Mother. It's a bad place,' |Asa begged.

'The man is sick; he doesn't know the way. With the men gone, who else can help him?'

N!ai put on the yellow dress and braided a new ornament into her hair. She tried to hide her glee. Going with the cheerful half-man now meant she wouldn't have to explain herself to her husband. Or Tsamkxao.

My back-work with him is over, but I will miss our moonlight meetings, she admitted to herself. Tsamkxao needed to get on with wooing Koba, she felt. He was the best match for the girl. They were both handsome people and together could have a beautiful Jul'hoan baby if Koba would just get rid of the one she was carrying.

N!ai pressed a small horn filled with the cure into Koba's palm as she said goodbye.

Koba put her arm around |Asa, who was trying not to cry. She'd be going soon herself, but she needed to see Tsamkxao first. She had a plan she believed would keep the group safe should André come searching.

But what about Little Fists, Bushmother?

Koba's hand tightened over the horn. She knew what to do now.

Dominee Venter was very surprised to see a Bushman woman in a bright yellow dress standing at his back door. Before he could confirm her identity he was addressed by the man standing next to her, a man on crutches. 'Good aftanoon, suh, I'm-a looking for a lift to Johannesburg any time soon. I have-a no money, but I am a good carver and I can make the driver something, anything, from wood or stone to pay him.'

'A lift to Johannesburg from here. That would be a miracle, my friend.'

The man grinned, his teeth dazzling white in his tribally scarred face. 'That is why I am-a knocking on your door, reverend.'

Fanie Venter laughed. 'Even if I stayed on my knees for a week, praying, I wouldn't find you a lift at this time of the year, son. The road to Onderwater's impassable in some places. We've had rain like Noah's.' When Trust laughed, Venter warmed to him even more. 'Ja-no, they're grading it, but they haven't finished the job yet. Not by a long stretch I'm afraid.

'And I'm sorry to say that even in the dry season we don't get much traffic through here. Sometimes it's weeks before anyone comes . . . or goes. I'm very sorry. But listen, you don't look well. What happened to your leg?'

Trust gaily related details of the mining accident that had ended his employment. Venter nodded, marvelling at the man's good humour and fortitude. 'My guess is it's inflamed, hey?'

Trust nodded.

'Listen, go sit under that tree and Fidelity will bring you some water to drink while I fetch you some antibiotics. My wife always keeps some. But I'd say you need a doctor and the nearest one's in Onderwater.'

Even if they could get through on the road, Venter thought, he wasn't sure Kleinschmidt would treat this man. He'd turned black patients away before. Perhaps if he wrote a letter for the man.

He returned to find Trust and N!ai resting in the feathery shade of his jacaranda tree. The Kalahari was too dry for it, but he lavished it with water. He'd brought the seedling from his hometown of Pretoria and now it was over eight foot high and in October had graced him with a cloud of sweet-smelling purple blossom.

He handed Trust the pills and N!ai a letter. 'Where did you learn to read, Mma?' he asked.

She reared back from the letter as if it might bite her.

'Er, Koba Yellow Dress?' Venter asked.

She looked uncomprehendingly at him. Trust explained that there was someone of that name who could speak English, but she was in the mangetti groves.

'If you give-a the letter to this one, she will take it for Koba. I will explain her.'

Venter felt relief. He thought he'd seen this particular woman before in Tsumkwe. A transient, who didn't attend service. She'd been in the company of a troublesome man, who'd brought in animal hides to sell. They were both big drinkers. He didn't like to think that a Bushman who had learned to read and write English was wasting herself on alcohol.

But this Koba, she sounded like what he called 'bush-Bushmen', judging by what the nice cripple had said. Bush-Bushmen didn't drink, at least not until they got into Tsumkwe, he thought bitterly.

He had long been at odds with Steiner, the Bushman affairs commissioner, about his policy of encouraging the wild Bushmen to move into town. The government promised them rations and employment, but work was scarce, so Tsumkwe had become a rural slum. He'd like to discuss the problem with a Bushman who could perhaps write a letter to the government, stating her people's problem in her own words. Could this Koba be that person?

Lettie Marais was sitting on the veranda of her farmhouse, Weltevrede, her cheeks flushed from cooking. She could hear the clatter of tins and pans coming from the kitchen where her staff were clearing up. It had been a big baking day. Tomorrow, after the Christmas service, a table would be laid in the church with all the baked goods made by the

Ladies' Committee on display. Her mosbolletjie pyramid would be the centrepiece. This year, her raisin yeast had given rise to buns that were particularly puffy, so she was confident that the Etienne Marais memorial trophy for best baked goods would go to her. She'd established the award after Etienne's untimely death, choosing the cut-glass rosebowl herself and having it engraved. She supposed she shouldn't enter the competition, but baking had been such a comfort to her in her widowhood and Etienne would have been proud to know she'd won the award every single Christmas since his cruel passing six years ago.

She had briefly entertained the hope that she might impress another man with her baking skills. At Deon's behest she had re-cultivated acquaintance with one of Etienne's fellow MPs, handsome Denis Bezuidenhout, whose influence her brother-in-law had hoped would get his son released after that distasteful episode with the Bushman girl. But after their successful charm offensive, she'd heard no more from Denis. They'd had such fun dining out, so why had the man not responded to her letters? she wondered. Lettie remembered the glorious day they'd had their photograph taken with the senator. Yes, there'd been a bit of bother about the number of badly parked cars she'd encountered on their way to the publicity thingy, but the Mercedes had barely grazed them. Surely Denis didn't hold that against her.

She dabbed at her eye with the corner of her apron. It wasn't just Denis. She always felt a bit weepy around Christmas-time. Without Etienne it was hard, she thought. It was the small things she missed most, like his advice about how many buns to make.

'D'you think six dozen's enough, ouseun?' she asked her son André, sprawled in a rocker opposite her. 'Those Dreissen children eat like locusts. Their ma, Astrid, you know *that* one, *home-perm*.' Lettie's hand strayed up to her own salon hairdo. It was an elaborate beehive featuring koeksister curls that gleamed with lacquer. It was finished off with curlicues of hair plastered to both of Lettie's wide cheeks. 'The very latest,' the stylist had assured her, but Lettie wasn't sure kiss curls were the sort of thing a respectable widow should be sporting. What would Etienne have thought? And Denis? She fingered the crisp curls as she continued: 'Ja, Astrid doesn't bake and . . .'

'Ma's made enough to feed an army.' André scratched his belly where it showed between his shirt buttons. 'Ma always does.'

'Well, a person's got to do what they can, isn't it? It would be a crying shame if anyone went hungry.' She smoothed her apron over her broad lap.

'Ja-no, especially when it's going to be lunchtime before they can stuff themselves again,' he said, smirking over the magazine he was reading.

'Ag, you're such a tease. Now be nice to your old ma and go see what's taking that lazy girl so long. I've rung for the coffee twice already.'

André put the magazine face down. It was his favourite copy of *National Geographic* as it contained a feature on the Himba tribe complete with full-colour pictures of bare-breasted women. He found them a little too buxom, but a naked tit was not to be sniffed at by the porn-starved, he thought. After the loss of the *Playboy*, the dusties refused to trust him with their contraband. He cursed his luck that he couldn't go and get his own copy, as he levered himself out of the chair with one arm strapped to his chest. He'd dislocated his shoulder when he crash-landed his plane a few days ago.

He lumbered back into the house. A shout, muffled apologies and soon Lettie heard the satisfying tinkle of china as one of their kitchen maids trembled out with the tray.

Lettie relaxed back into her chair, tittering as her son made a face at the retreating back of the elderly black woman.

They heard the telephone ring.

'Is it us?'

'Three shorts and a long, ja. Want me to go while I'm up?'

'Ag-no, seun, it'll be for me; one of the ladies from the Nagmaal committee.' Lettie heaved herself up, wincing as her two-way corset bit into her flesh. Three-way's what I need, she thought, but out loud she said, 'If it's Dagmar, it'll serve that operator, Truda Groenewald, right. Truda listens in on all the telephone conversations, you know. This one'll send her to sleep. Dagmar will witter on for hours about how much bicarb she put into her cheese scones, you listen.' Lettie creaked up the passage like an overstuffed sofa.

'Hullo, Lettie, is that you? It's me, Marta.' Lettie's heart sank into her two-way. Her sister-in-law never called her; this was bound to be something the operator would relish.

'Um, hullo, Marta, season's greetings to you-all. Clever of you to call today and avoid the Christmas rush. I'm sure no one will be able to get a line tomorrow, hey? I got your card. Very nice. Did you get mine?'

'Yes, thank you. Listen, Lettie, I've got a problem –'

'Ja, it's very hot here too. We haven't had rain in six weeks now, though I believe they've had some up north.'

'Lettie . . .?'

'Ja-well, maybe it will move down, the wind's blowing from that direction.'

'*Aletta!* Will you stop and listen to me? Please. It's Mannie. He's missing. I think he's up in Bushmanland trying to find Koba.'

'Who?'

'His girlfriend, you know, the one he went to jail –'

Lettie coughed loud and long, hoping she'd been quick enough to drown out Marta's words. Was the woman mad, talking about things like that in public? She could almost hear Truda Groenewald cocking her ears.

'I'm very worried about him,' Marta was saying. 'He said he was going on holiday with a school friend, but I've just seen the boy in town and he knew nothing about it. Mannie's not the kind to lie, Lettie. I'm so afraid he's involved in something dangerous. I've got to stop him, but it's going to take me a week or more to get to you. The railways at Christmas! Please, ousus, please, can you see if you can find him in the meantime, stop him doing anything, you know . . .'

'Liewe magies, Marta!' The temerity of the request made Lettie abandon discretion. 'Do you think I run a missing persons bureau up here? First the one in the letter –' Too late she remembered Marta's letter hadn't been addressed to her. 'N-not that I –'

Marta cut in. 'My son is going to be where Koba is. Somewhere around Tsumkwe, but if you ask the police . . .'

Lettie slammed down the receiver.

*

Back on the veranda Lettie fell into her chair and began to fan herself with her apron.

'Is Ma all right?'

'No-I-am-*not* all right.' Lettie hissed like a pressure cooker. 'That aunt of yours has got no shame. It's not enough that she wanted me to take a letter to a Boesman, now I must find your cousin hiding in some love-nest with her in the Kalahari. Can you believe it?' Her face worked its outrage around her mouth, ungluing her kiss curls. 'After all the trouble I went to getting that *damn*, excuse-my-swearing, boy out of jail!' The left kiss curl levitated on her air of disgust. 'The cheek of that woman beggars belief, it really does.'

André had dropped his magazine and sat intent in his seat. 'Mannie's with the Bushman girl?'

'So his mother thinks.' Lettie resumed fanning her red face with her apron.

'Where, Ma?'

'Tsumkwe, his mother thinks, but –'

'I'll go,' André said.

Lettie stopped flapping her apron. 'What?'

'I'll go and look for him.' He stood up, sending the chair careening across the floor.

'Where are you going?'

'To Tsumkwe. I'll start looking there.'

'You can't go now,' she wailed. 'Tomorrow's Christmas!' The phone rang again. 'Oh for pity's sake! André, get it. I am *not* talking to Marta again. Truda Groenewald has heard enough to keep her gossiping until next Christmas.'

André lifted the instrument off its cradle on the wall.

'A call for you from the police station in Onderwater,' Truda said, trying to sound uninterested.

It was Du Pree. After a cursory exchange of seasonal wishes he said he had reason to believe that a young offender, Manfred Marais, was in the area, in contravention of his prison release conditions. 'I'm wondering if you've seen or heard from him, him being *family*?' Du Pree asked. André repeated what his mother had just told him.

Du Pree sounded very interested. 'Hmm, well, I'll send someone up there.' Du Pree's tone became sly. 'But there's not much chance of your cousin finding her, is there, Marais?'

'Damn-and-blast-it!' André shouted as he slammed down the phone. His mother's head appeared at the end of the passage, but he ignored her. He had to get moving before that smarmy little Yid started poking his nose in Marais business. Grabbing a rifle off the wall, he pounded down the passage and out to his pick-up. It was a curse that the plane was out of commission. The wing spar had snapped when he planted it trying to land on two wheels. Tertius said it would be weeks before the new part arrived.

André turned on the ignition. Driving wasn't going to be easy; the off-road parts would tax his shoulder, but what could he do? Opportunity had knocked loud and clear.

Mannie had arrived in Tsumkwe earlier than expected, thanks to the roadwork company's nightwatchman. When the old man realized the boy was going to walk to Tsumkwe he'd suggested he travel like a white man instead. 'Take one,' he'd said, using the gnarled head of his fighting club to point at the collection of heavy machinery slumbering in the works compound.

'I couldn't, grandfather,' Mannie said in passable Zulu. 'Stealing.'

The old man shrugged, making his elongated earlobes shake like dewlaps. 'The boss is away, the machines they can play. I see how you touch them, like they are women. You will take care of them. Ride one; go find a real woman, young bull.'

No one would know, not out here, Mannie had thought. And it wasn't like stealing. He'd have the machine back long before anyone could miss it.

'Pick your Christmas box, umfaan,' the nightwatchman had urged him.

Mannie had, wandering between them as if in a giant toy shop. He'd finally settled on the bulldozer. He drove it all the way to Tsumkwe with his foot flat on the accelerator, its huge claw retracted like a knight's visor.

But after two hours of standing in the dark around the back of the Dutch Reformed Church, Mannie's exhilaration had worn off. One more hour and he was giving up on Koba, he told himself.

He tried not to feel depressed. She could yet appear; if not, there were a few more nights to go before he had to set off for his rendezvous with the comrades. He'd promised in his letter that he'd be in the same place at the same time for three consecutive nights, so that was what he would do.

He looked up at the church tower, modest by Dutch Reformed standards. No frilly bits, a single bell. It would ring tomorrow.

He'd never spent Christmas alone before. He'd hoped he and Koba would spend this one together. Somewhere, anywhere, but he was beginning to have doubts. He stared up at the moon. Was Koba looking at it too now, longing for him like he was for her? Maybe she was fast asleep and didn't have a clue he was here.

Oh Jissus, this was a bad idea. It had seemed perfect when he'd thought of it at home. And it had gone so well with his lift luck and the use of Gerrit's caravan and all. But now . . .

He looked at his watch. Another fifty minutes to wait; another fifty minutes to Christmas. And in less than six hours Ma and Pa would be up and waiting for a telephone call from him. There wouldn't be one.

He hunkered down and dropped his head into his hands.

N!ai had had a marvellous evening. Earlier, she'd managed to sell the heavy ostrich eggshell necklace for five rand. It had bought her a big calabash of the shebeen queen's special brew. It kicked like a kudu going down the throat and tomorrow she knew she would feel as if her head had been trampled by the whole herd, but for now she had a song in her feet and a new dress on her back. She would go home tomorrow and prove that she wasn't a slave to the beer. Just one more drink.

Headlights off, André let the truck roll into town. It was deserted, no lights burning, not even Christmas ones at the church. Miserable old git, this dominee, André thought. But the kaffirs knew how to party. He could hear shouts and laughter and kwela music coming from their camp.

That's where she'd be, waiting for her boyfriend. Maybe rolling around in the dirt with him right now, the filthy bitch. He'd have to root around to find the jailbirds, but he'd brought along a couple of bottles of brandy that should earn him some pointers from the locals. André was just deciding where to leave the truck when movement caught his eye. He hunched over the steering wheel, eyes staring down the dark in the street – could it be? Had his luck finally changed? A woman alone, no shoes and – yes! – a yellow dress. Mustn't be hasty, he told himself. Other kaffirgirls could wear yellow dresses. He nosed the truck forward for a better view. The woman stumbled. He turned his headlights on.

'Well-fok-me! All my Christmases have come at once.'

It was the Boesman bitch all right and she was drunk, so drunk she hadn't even noticed the truck. There wasn't a soul around to see. He floored the accelerator and in seconds the pick-up was on top of her.

The woman turned and seemed to step towards the grinning grille, a yellow moth drawn to the lights. Metal met soft body parts, a small cry as the slight figure buckled between the wheels.

André turned his headlights off and looked about. Nothing. He eased the truck into reverse and backed up slowly over the body. *Kerrump, kerrump.* First the rear tyres then the engine-heavy front ones. Just to be sure, he thought to himself. Then he quietly put the truck into first gear, turned the wheel gently so as not to hurt his shoulder and drove out of town, lights still off.

Mannie had thrown himself onto the ground when he heard the low growl of a vehicle engine.

Police.

Though he was around the back of the church, he felt exposed against its moon-white wall. Better off in the shadows between the squatter shacks, he thought, but suddenly a pair of headlights was trained on the open ground between the church and the shacks.

He fell onto his front as he heard the engine accelerate and took his chance, leopard-crawling across the open ground. A faint cry froze him. The headlights were off, so he sat up on his haunches. He was in time to see a pick-up reversing carefully over something lying in the road. A soft thump, then a *pffut*, like a polite burp. But that splitting sound?

Jissus, liewe Jissus, could it be bone cracking? He rose and ran towards the road in time to see the pick-up driving away, headlights off. He looked down. A yellow dress?

'*No! Nawwhhh!*' he screamed.

Nearby a door opened; footsteps running. He ignored them as he felt for the head, the beloved face, cupped it in his shaking hands. It was like holding a sackful of marbles. Beneath the warm skin he felt fragments of skull shift. He began to sob.

'Dear God in heaven, what happened?' A narrow old man in a long white nightshirt shone a torch on the body.

As it illuminated the dented face, Mannie gasped. 'It's not her. Thank heavens, thank heavens. This poor woman. But oh Jissus, Koba's still out there . . . but so's *he*!'

23

Mannie couldn't stop shaking. Murder, and he'd witnessed it. The sound of the bakkie soft-thumping over the body would echo in his ears for a long time to come. Though he'd assured the minister he hadn't seen the vehicle number plate nor the driver, which was true, he had a sickening feeling he knew who it had been. André.

Koba believed André blamed her for the death of his father, Etienne, after a hunting trip in South West Africa six years ago when the hunters had encountered Koba and her family on Marais land. The truth was that he, Mannie, could have prevented his uncle's death. He'd confessed this to no one but Koba.

On that day, nine-year-old Mannie had been alone on the driver's seat of the wagon being used in the hunt. He was petrified by the events unfolding around him: his father was drunk, his cousin had shot a Khoisan man, who now lay bleeding in the sand not far from the wagon, and his uncle had a Khoisan woman in the back of the wagon where he was displaying her genitalia to a giggling André. Facing front, young Mannie had seen the wounded brown man crawl towards the wagon. He'd kept silent when Koba's father took aim and shot Etienne with a poisoned arrow. His uncle's death throes still haunted him.

It seemed to Mannie that Koba's return to the Nyae Nyae had cast her back into the lion's den. He had to warn her, but where was she?

*

Earlier, Mannie and the minister had carried N!ai's body into a storeroom at the side of the church.

'I'll send a message to the police,' Venter had said, 'but if they come, it won't be for days, so we can't leave her lying out there, not in this heat.'

Mrs Venter had arranged the yellow dress so that the skirt covered the woman's mangled leg. She'd bound her splintered skull in a faded orange tea towel fastened under the jaw. Mannie was glad they'd placed one of the kneelers from the church under the woman's swathed head. Somehow it felt as though they'd made her comfortable.

They retreated to the church-house kitchen where the reverend in his long nightshirt wandered around with a candle like a distracted Wee Willie Winkie. He was trying to locate the oil lamp they kept for emergencies.

Mrs Venter, in a dressing gown with all the chenille washed out of it, was spooning sugar into a glass of water for Mannie. 'It's good for shock,' she said, pushing it across the table towards him. Then she sat down, folded her arms across her massive bosom and turned the flickering light reflected in her spectacles on him.

'Now, son, what I don't understand is: why were you in the church-yard at that time of the night?'

Mannie twiddled the glass between thumb and forefinger, watching the liquid swirl round. Even if an oke's not religious, he shouldn't lie in a church, he thought, not even in a kitchen next door to one. But how much could he safely say? He took a gulp of water and plunged in.

'I was hoping to meet someone.'

The couple blinked like a pair of frazzle-haired fledglings. 'Who?' they chirruped.

'A girl.' He blushed.

'What girl lives out here?' Mrs Venter squawked her surprise.

Mannie wanted to bang their grey heads together, but he'd been brought up to respect his elders, even those whose politics defied logic. There are girls in the town, he thought irritably, but they are brown-skinned, so I suppose they don't count.

He reminded himself that the Venters were good people; he'd seen that. Nevertheless, they were keepers of the Afrikaner faith and

188

therefore of apartheid principles. His tone was mutinous when he said, 'An old friend. I wrote her a letter asking her . . .'

'Koba Yellow Dress!' the old woman exclaimed.

Mannie felt his whole body tighten with urgency. 'You got the letter? You gave it to her?'

'Here it is, son.' Slowly Venter laid the crumpled letter on the table between them. It was bloodstained in one corner. 'That poor woman in there' – he gestured with his pipe towards the storeroom – 'was going to deliver it to your Koba.'

The glass of water swam in Mannie's vision. He hung his head, ashamed to realize he felt most sorry for himself. All this way, all this trouble and Koba knew nothing about him being here. She wasn't coming.

He swallowed the lump in his throat and managed to mumble, 'She's in terrible danger.'

Over the next half-hour Mannie stumbled through an explanation of the problem without, he fervently hoped, giving away his identity or other compromising details. This meant he couldn't name André. He was grateful that the Venters seemed to accept they were better off not knowing more facts. Maybe faith was like an elastic band, he thought. It could stretch to hold many things at the same time. He wished he had faith just now, so he could pray to someone to keep Koba safe.

I've got to warn her in case André discovers his mistake; she'd be better off getting well away, he thought. He told the Venters that he must find Koba and soon.

'Now, there I can help you, son,' the reverend said and he repeated the information that Trust had given him about her whereabouts. He felt sure he could find Mannie a horse and a guide to take him to the groves later that day. 'And someone will have to tell the woman's family. They'll want to come for the body. Ja-no, you better go, my boy. But not now, you need some sleep.'

Mannie protested – he was too keyed up – but he was asleep almost as soon as his head touched the pillow on the narrow guest bed.

*

By lunchtime Fanie Venter had found him a horse and a relatively sober Jul'hoan guide to take him to the mangetti groves. Mrs Venter handed him a package wrapped in wax paper. 'Christmas lunch,' she said. He stared at the tinsel she'd used to tie it. He wanted to cry. What would Ma and Pa's meal be like without him and Koba? Jis, they'd be worried if he told them what had happened, but they'd be able to help. He couldn't tell them though, not without endangering his comrades. Quickly he shoved the package into the saddlebag.

The reverend was leaning against the hitching post, sucking on his pipe.

'So, the boy,' the pastor said, using his pipe stem to point to the prunish old man who would ride out with Mannie, 'will find out who the woman's family are. Her name was N . . . er, anyway, he knows. You'll have to explain to them as best you can. And I gave you back your letter for your girl . . . er, friend, didn't I?'

Mannie nodded. In the privacy of his room he'd gingerly opened the bloodstained envelope and reread his letter. It made him cringe. He sounded so young and stupid in it. He was grateful Koba hadn't read it. Ja-no, he'd rather talk to her face to face, like a man.

'You know what doesn't make sense to me?' Venter was saying. 'How did that, er, hit-and-run driver get his bakkie into town anyway?' Mannie tensed. 'I mean, you'd need a tank to get through on the road at the moment.' Mannie let the girth he was buckling swing free.

'Or a bulldozer,' he replied in a small voice. His face had turned scarlet, all the way to the roots of his lengthening brush cut. 'I, er, the thing is, Dominee . . .' He took a deep breath then spoke in a gush. 'I borrowed the bulldozer from the roadworks camp and flattened a path through the bush where the road was too bad. I never thought . . . it didn't occur to me . . . Oh, Jissus, he must have used that to get here.' He slapped his hand down on the saddle; the horse shied. 'Sorry, sorry,' he gentled the animal. 'I swear I was planning to take the bulldozer back, Dominee. I still will. And I had the nightwatchman's permission.'

'The *nightwatchman's* permission?' Fanie Venter's eyebrows rose up high on his domed forehead.

'I dunno what I was thinking,' Mannie mumbled. 'I'll explain to Gerrit, and I'll pay for the d-diesel I used. I, er, like machines. Quite a lot actually, so, er . . . ja-well. I didn't need a lot of encouragement, I suppose. Um . . .' He looked up. The reverend looked very stern.

'Okay.' Venter cleared his throat. 'No harm done, I suppose. We'll keep an eye on your *transport* until you get back. So, go safely, hey? And God bless, son!'

Koba was laughing as she watched the line of girls perform the dance called the Caterpillar. In perfect unison, they moved their shoulders, necks and heads, thrusting out their chins to reproduce the body roll of a caterpillar in motion. They did this twice then made a tiny hop forward, until the 'caterpillar' reached a tree trunk. Then they repeated the dance, hopping backwards. It looked just like a worm reversing; Koba clapped her hands in delight.

'Why don't you join in, little-daughter of Zuma?' Tsamkxao called from the shade, where he was expertly scraping a gemsbok hide. He'd had great success on the hunt and tonight everyone would eat well from the large antelope. Now he was giving careful attention to the skin so it would dry well. Nudging and winking at one another, people near by speculated about who was going to be gifted with the beautiful white-striped kaross. Unaware, Koba waved across at Tsamkxao. She hadn't found a chance to speak to him alone, but she felt sure she would tonight. She and |Asa wandered off together, following the caterpillar dancers.

Boys, giving smaller playmates a ride on an old kaross they were dragging across the sand, first spotted the horsemen.

'|Ton, |Ton!' the children shouted.

Tsamkxao jumped up, knife in hand, and ran towards them. Mothers who'd been lazing in the shade leaped up and scooped little ones from the kaross and retreated deeper into the grove with them. Other men gathered around Tsamkxao, staring across the sand, their hands across their brows to shield their eyes from the low sunrays.

'The small one is a Real Person,' Gao Monkey Orange said. 'It's Old Tashay, who moved to Tsumkwe with his family two seasons ago.'

'Who is the tall |Ton with him?' Tsamkxao growled.

'Put your fierce face away; you have frightened the women and the children already,' Old Dabe said. 'Hasn't Xoo Big-owner said |Ton from across the water come here sometimes to ask her questions? Must-be it is one of them. They give tobacco to those who speak into their machines so don't you frighten the smoke off, you Big Genital.'

Tsamkxao ignored him. The foolish old man had already forgotten the airplane incident. And he hadn't been there when Tsamkxao and his father had been pursued on horseback by white men with guns.

'I don't think this |Ton is one of Xoo's questioners,' a local man was saying. 'Those ones are heavy people; they drive lorries. This one looks too young to be heavy. His shins will still be ostrich-red.'

Tsamkxao scanned the mule's saddlebag for a rifle. Seeing none, he sheathed his knife, but he kept his hand on it. He said not a word when Old Tashay and the nervous young white man got off their mounts and greeted the reception committee.

'We have bad news about the daughter of Old Dabe and Zuma n!a'an,' Tashay said.

Old Dabe kept very still. Tsamkxao moved closer to him.

Tashay kept the details of N!ai's death brief. As he spoke, Old Dabe began to quiver like a frail tree in a wind. Tsamkxao took hold of his elbow.

'This man knows more about it,' Tashay said, indicating Mannie, 'and he needs to speak to a girl who is new among you. He calls her Koba and says she wore a yellow dress.'

'Dead? Dead. My daughter is dead!' Old Dabe wailed. 'Don't tell her mother, don't tell Zuma,' he cried. 'It will kill her.' But already the old woman was hurrying towards the group, anxiety working her face.

'Yau, yau, yau!' she began when she heard the news. 'I told her not to go to Tsumkwe; I told her. Evil lives there. Don't tell N!ai's daughter. The baby must not know it will have no grandmother. Aieeee!' She fell onto the sand, banging her fists on the ground.

*

Koba, |Asa and the other girls hadn't heard the commotion. They'd been singing the Caterpillar song louder and louder over on the periphery of the grove as they looked for the delicious worms.

'Koba Frog-bringer must come, and N!ai's daughter, *now*!' said a young boy who'd run to find them. Holding hands, the girls hurried through the trees after him.

As Koba stepped into the open she saw a tall blond man, a man who looked very white among the brown villagers. There was something familiar about him. Then she realized it was Mannie – a taller, thinner version of her Frog-boy, standing not two hundred metres away. Why or how she couldn't imagine, but she found herself running towards him as if drawn to her magnetic north.

Something about the stance of the people in the crowd around him made her halt abruptly. Why was Old Zuma on the ground, Old Dabe being supported by Tsamkxao? she wondered. Why were people staring at her? Heart hammering, she waited for |Asa to draw parallel, then she slipped her shaking arm around her friend's expanded waist and walked slowly forward, hardly daring to look where her eyes most wanted to.

Mannie could see Koba coming over the heads of the people milling around him. It was Koba, he was sure, though she looked completely different from the last time he'd seen her. Her hair was decorated with beaded rings that hung over her forehead, around her ears and down to her shoulders in places. Instead of his old shorts she wore a small, beaded pubic apron made of animal skin and a much bigger, tattered hide cloak draped over one shoulder and down her back. Her breasts were bare, the nipples very dark and large in the middle of each golden pear. She looked radiant. But her beauty scared him; it was almost wild. Suddenly he didn't know what he was going to say to her.

He watched her enter the crowd, absorb the news, reel from it. He saw how a pigeon-chested young woman with a baby at her side pushed Koba away from the bereaved family. Koba looked shaken and afraid, at once part of the crowd and yet ostracized from it. He wanted to rush in and carry her off, yet she wouldn't look across at him, not once, though he knew she felt his gaze. It was like staring down at something happening just below the surface of a clear pool of water. Everything was visible, but seemed distorted. Sound was muffled, indecipherable; faces blurred; actions seemed slowed. He was there, but he felt separated from everything below.

He wasn't aware of how long it was before people began to pull the weeping old couple and the pregnant young woman back towards the trees where he could see huts and hearth fires. Only then did Koba come towards him and he was acutely conscious that some of the group kept looking back at them. One unusually tall Bushman squatted down in the sand not too far away and watched them intently.

'Greetings, son of my mother, Marta,' Koba said softly to him. He was taken aback. Ma would be pleased to hear Koba thought of her as that after all, but did that make *him* her brother?

'Er, hullo, Koba,' he said and found himself sticking out his arm for a handshake. Fokken fool, he thought to himself, this is not a blerry garden party. On the other hand, kissing or hugging her was clearly out of the question. If they shook hands then at least he'd get to touch her.

She put out her small hand with what he hoped was a twinkle in her eye, but it might have been the residue of tears, he thought. He grabbed it, burying her hand in his, hanging on to it, staring into her eyes. 'How are you, how are *you*? I'm *so* glad to see you. Jissis, am I glad to see you!'

He felt her hand flutter in his, dry and soft as a trapped moth. 'Er, sorry. Hell, man, sorry. Ja . . .' He released her. 'Koba, I'm so sorry about what happened to your, er . . .?'

'Name-relative,' she said. 'What happened?' she asked him in urgent English.

'What? Oh, right.' He glanced across at the man who was still watching them, then proceeded to tell her what he'd witnessed in Tsumkwe and his suspicions about André. By the time she'd told him about her escape from his cousin after he'd taken her captive on the road out of Onderwater and about the incident with the plane and its poison, they both knew André was on her trail.

'Sooner or later he'll realize he's killed the wrong person and he'll come after you, Koba.'

'And you.'

'He won't find me. I'm going away. I came to tell you.'

The sun set with a crash of crimson and gold, and within minutes Mannie's beloved voice came at Koba out of the dark as he told her about his meeting in prison with Jabu and Moses.

He sensed her stiffen, but he couldn't see her face. Then the tall villager was beside them holding a two-pronged flaming torch. He hissed at her in Jul'hoan. Light flickered across his tense face like a serpent's tongue. He and Koba seemed to be arguing; finally the man stalked off.

'You can't stay out here,' she said to Mannie. 'There are hyenas; maybe lions. Bring your animal and I'll give you a place for the night.'

Koba settled him at the shelter made for Trust. She built a fire and boiled some water she'd scooped out of the tree bole with a tortoise shell. He watched her, remembering how efficient she was around a camp. The place was neatly swept and looked well organized, unlike some of the others. The firewood was stacked on one side, divided into logs and kindling. Koba hung a skin bag from the tree, too low for him to avoid hitting his head on, but just the right height for her to reach into. He supposed it contained the things she wanted to keep out of the sand. He remembered how she disliked sand in her food.

She brought out gourds and shells of various shapes and sizes and began mashing and mixing. He didn't recognize the veld food and noted that there was not one man-made item among her utensils. Nor could he see a bottle, a box of matches or a torch anywhere. He wasn't sure why, but the absence of these things made him uncomfortable. He fetched the Christmas lunch package and handed it to her. 'Merry Christmas,' he said.

Koba stared at it, at the silver tinsel twisted around the wax paper. It was something from another world – one that smelled of candle wax and cinnamon and cloves, where a table was laid with more food than four people could eat, even in a week. There, Deon and Marta had given her and a sun-haired boy packages wrapped with silver string like this. The boy had grown; he stood tall and handsome, giving her his frog-eye look. She hadn't expected to see him again, but having him here made her feel happy beyond her imaginings. The decisions she had to make, the terrible news she'd received, seemed secondary.

It is not right to be happy; you have brought death to the band, Bushgirl. Now is the time for guilt and sorrow, not for joy.

She tried to shake sense into her love-struck head, but stopped when she saw Mannie looking at her questioningly. He would think she was mad, tossing her head like a wildebeest trying to get rid of flies on its face. She unhooked a strand of beads that had become tangled around her ear, hoping she looked normal, if not pretty.

Hnn-hn-hn, how can I look beautiful for my beloved when I have no time to prepare, no mirror to see in. May he use only his heart to discern me.

She sat down next to him, as close as she dared. She needed to be sure he understood. As much of her situation as she could tell him, anyway. 'You know I gave that dress to N!ai, the late-woman?'

He nodded. 'I guessed so.'

'It should be me lying broken in the Tsumkwe place, isn't it?' He looked distressed and didn't reply. 'Only *we* know, me and you. *They*, late-N!ai's family, they know nothing of the Lion who has hunted me.'

He gazed at her dear face. Her brow showed copper corrugations in the firelight. He wanted to run his hand over her forehead to wipe away the worry.

'What would they do if they found out?'

'Hnn.' She frowned deeper. 'I think they would blame me for bringing this death-thing to them. The woman's daughter, |Asa, is my friend. I think her heart will harden against me.'

It took him less than a minute to realize that he was going to change his plans. He felt overjoyed at the prospect. 'Koba, you don't need them. *I'll* look after you. Let's you and me go away together.'

Glee engulfed her. She felt it course through her body and ignite the excitement she'd been trying to suppress from the minute she'd seen Mannie. Hope leaped in her chest like a bright flame, dancing up and up. It was going to be all right. They could go together; she, he and Little Fists.

Little Fists! Now that she'd seen him, this beautiful person, she knew she was going to grow the child. It might be his. Even if it wasn't, she knew she could love the child and she had no doubt he would accept it. He said he'd look after her. But she wasn't ready to tell him about the baby yet. That would mean telling her shame-thing. Tonight was not the night for it.

She passed him a bowl of mangetti nut mash. 'What about going to join the Spears?'

He immediately admitted that he'd never really wanted to join Umkhonto we Sizwe. 'It's just that they were leaving from here, you see, where you are.'

She raised an eyebrow.

'Okay, maybe that wasn't the only reason, at the *time*. I was thinking like a child; freedom fighting sounded noble, you know . . . and, er, romantic. I could imagine myself fighting for justice.'

'And driving a tank.'

'Ja, that too.' He blushed, thinking about the bulldozer. 'Anyway, look, I gave Moses-and-them the wrong impression and I'll do my best to explain to the okes. Better still, I'll introduce them to you.' She smiled. He put the tortoiseshell bowl down and placed his hand on her arm. She thrilled to his touch. 'I've just had this bakgat idea. Listen: if we go to Swaziland or Botswana or some country like that, we could still help in the Struggle, couldn't we?'

'What is this Struggle?'

'Against apartheid,' he breezed. 'See, Botswana's not that far from here, a few days' walk maybe.'

'Is it towards the sunset?'

'No, other way – east.' He was jiggling his foot up and down in excitement. 'The country's soon gonna get independence. Jabu and the other Politicals said Rhodesia would be next.'

Koba drew back and pulled her kaross closed across her chest. Botswana was the wrong way. The discs had said her future lay in the west. And now Frog-boy was talking about things she barely understood – ZANU and ZAPU. She felt stupid, again the little Bushgirl who had to be shown which end of a pen makes marks on a page.

I am a nothing-thing pregnant with a shame-thing . . . Real People are looking at us. I feel their eyes in my back like stabbing sticks.

'Koba, don't you see,' Mannie was saying, 'there's no apartheid in Botswana. The president, Seretse Khama, has got a white *wife*. We could marry there, no problem.'

Koba drew her knee up to her chest and began stirring some ashes with a thin twig. How could she explain that she needed to go in the opposite direction? The oracle discs had shown sunset, that was where her heart lay, next to Little Fists. She wanted the child more than anything now, more even than the man-boy whose face shone beside her. But she could tell him about neither the oracle nor the child, just yet.

She stood up. 'There are things you don't understand.'

'But, Koba –'

'Hush, now. I can't be with you; I must be there,' she said, gesturing to distant fires between the trees. 'We will talk in the morning.' Noiseless as a bushbuck, she slipped away.

Mannie sat stunned. What had he said that was so wrong? Why couldn't she see his idea about Botswana was a brainwave? It solved everybody's problem. She could get away; they could be together; they could still do work for the anti-apartheid cause; *and* they could make Ma and Pa happy, he thought.

'Can't be with you,' she'd said. Did she mean tonight, tomorrow, never again? he pondered. He picked up the twig she'd been playing with and twirled it between his fingers. He could hear a Scops owl prrp-ing near by, some flit-scurry sounds in the tree canopy above and sporadic ululating. From the bereaved family, he supposed.

That was it – Koba needed to go and commiserate, of course she did, he thought. He'd been babbling on about their future happiness when her relative had just died.

Mannie stood up, cursing his insensitivity. He'd go and pay his respects too, and whisper to her that he understood and he'd wait. Picking his way carefully in the dark over tree roots and around trunks, he followed the sound of the ululating and arrived at the sorrowing fire. He recognized the old woman who'd fallen on the ground at the news of her daughter's death and a few others, including Koba's pregnant friend. But where was Koba?

He backed away, too shy to approach without her to interpret for him. He stood in the dark, looking about. There was a low hut not too far off. A big gemsbok skin was stretched on a frame outside it. This would be the tall Khoisan's place, Mannie thought. He'd seen the hunter scraping furiously at the hide just before dark. He remembered now that the man, Tsam-something, spoke Afrikaans. The oke was hostile, no doubt about it, but he had no choice but to talk to him if he wanted to find Koba, Mannie decided.

In the light of the hunter's fire Mannie caught the gleam of two gold-buckled shoes placed side by side in the doorway. Those were Koba's shiny shoes, the ones Ma had given her. Good. He'd knock and ask for her, he decided. Knock? Where's a person going to do that on a grass hut, you moegoe? he reminded himself as he approached.

He heard grunts and gasps, a woman moaning. It was the sound of sex – a man and a woman making love. Even with his limited experience he couldn't mistake the sound.

Mannie turned away, stumbling over tree roots as he ran.

24

N !ai's family were huddled together, rocking and moaning their pain. Their faces looked thick from crying and they were all hoarse-voiced from keening. Waves of pain emanated from them, each one a body blow to Koba. She couldn't bring herself to step into their space.

They gave me kindness, I repaid them with grief. I am not a rain-season child, I am worse than drought. People survive drought; they do not survive |Ton. Better I creep away and take my death-thing with me.

But they deserved an explanation; the whole village did, Koba felt. Now, more than ever, she needed to talk to Tsamkxao. She would consult him about the best place and time to confess to the group. He'd been furious with her for letting a white man into the camp, but if she explained her and Mannie's suspicions about N!ai's murder, he'd help her, she felt sure. After all, she reasoned, the last thing he'd want was for her to endanger the band further.

As she drew close to his hut she heard him making loud love to a woman inside. She saw the shoes. Chu!ko. Koba felt the insult for N!ai. She backed away and looked beyond the hut to where Mannie's fire glowed reassuringly bright.

But her first duty was to the band so she had better go and consult Xoo, she decided.

The old woman sat alone amid the detritus of her camp, smoking a wooden pipe. 'Is that you, granddaughter of Old Zuma?'

How does this blind old mother know someone stands here? She thinks I am ǀAsa. I would like to be, to take the tears from her.

'No, Xoo Big-owner, it is Koba, daughter of Nǂaisa-late.'

'Aie, I know; you are the one they call Koba Frog-bringer.' She smiled so that the fallen apples of her cheeks lifted; she looked almost girlish. 'Come closer, child. I am nearly dead, you know. I cannot be expected to shout to far-offs. Come and sit with me, put some wood on my fire. No one ever comes to visit me, no one ever brings me food or firewood, even though I am so old I am pitiful. Ehhhh-weh.'

Koba fetched a log from Xoo's well-stocked pile. She stoked the embers and blew the fire into life. Then she sat back on her heels. 'My heart is heavy, kxae kxao,' Koba murmured.

'Eh, I feel you are crushed like grass an elephant has slept on. We are all flooded with sorrow tonight – aiee-aiee-aie.' Cupping her own elbows, Xoo rocked herself. Eventually she spoke. 'Crack open your story, little-daughter, if it will lighten your load.'

Koba did, faltering at first, but eventually with a flow that spoke of grief too long stoppered. She claimed culpability for the sickening mist and for N!ai's death and did not spare herself the shame of admitting she'd consulted the oracle discs and seen danger there. 'But I looked the other way, down at my own belly. I was thinking only of . . .'

'The baby you have decided to keep?'

'Yes.'

Xoo clapped and rocked herself again, this time ululating softly. 'Life for death, life for death. It should be so.' Then she stopped and gripped Koba's arm. 'If this bad person is close you must-must save yourself and your child.'

'I will.'

'Where will you go?'

'Towards sunset is where the discs said.'

'And the handsome ǀTon you have tucked away at your fire?'

'He goes towards sunrise.'

Xoo sucked her teeth. 'Let me see these discs.' Hesitantly Koba produced them from a pouch around her waist and laid them one by one in Xoo's lap. The old woman's fingers crabbed across them. Swifter than Koba would have thought possible for her, Xoo gathered them together and flung them into the fire. 'They are wrong-things!'

'But . . .' Koba felt shocked. They were her guides; they'd belonged to her grandmother. The Jul'hoan taboos did not apply to her; she was leaving. With rising anger she watched them curl up, then crisp in the fire.

'Follow your heart, not the discs,' Xoo said. 'Go and tell your |Ton you will go with him – towards sunrise, sunset, it doesn't matter. Go wherever you and he and Little Fists can live in peace.'

'Hnn.' Koba felt unsure now about Xoo's judgement. 'M-mustn't I . . . shouldn't I tell everyone? Beg forgiveness –'

Xoo cut her short. 'Is there is a bad thing *you* did, not one that was done *to you*, little-daughter?'

'The discs,' Koba said quietly.

'The discs are gone.'

Koba sat back. Suddenly she realized what a relief that was. She could leave her past behind, walk off into a future with Mannie. Her stay with the group had been an interlude. They would always have a place in her heart, like Marta and Deon did, but this was not her n!ore. She wanted to make a new life in another place for her child. She should return to Mannie and tell him. Unable to help herself, she gushed about her beloved.

'His name is Mannie – "small man" in one |Ton language, but he is not small, he is tall, but not ugly-tall.'

'How is his heart?' Xoo asked, sucking on her pipe.

Koba blushed, hoping Xoo's sharp ears weren't able to detect skin warming. 'Better than mine, Big-owner. *His* heart did not lose hope. It drove him from a place of plenty, with water and meat to eat every day, to come and find me. He walked many-many-many days. His heart has not thrown me away since we were children together.'

'Go to him. Time is short. Go before the day brings its sorrows.'

Koba placed a kiss on one of the bald patches on Xoo's woolly grey head and left.

Like a moth she flitted back through the trees towards the light of Mannie's fire. There she stopped, breathless, surprised not to see

Mannie's horse outside the hut. Had it broken its tether? She peered around, but the animal was nowhere to be seen. She stepped into the hut. Empty. On top of the neatly folded blanket was a piece of paper.

My dear Koba,

I am writing this on the only paper I've got – an old letter to you. I've tried to cross it out but the pen's not working. Sand in the nib. Don't read the old letter; it's rubbish. What I want to say now is this: I am sorry that I came here and disturbed you all. I can see you have a new life and I wish you happiness. You deserve it. I'll go now and get on with what I'm supposed to be doing.

Listen, please warn your boyfriend about André. He needs to take care of you; get you out that lunatic's reach. You should think about Botswana.

I'm going to miss you, Koba.

Your loving and respectful friend,
Manfred Marais

Boyfriend? Koba knew the word. It meant Mannie. But who was this 'he' who should protect her? She read the letter again, slowly, convinced she was not understanding it properly. 'I'm going to miss you' – that part was unmistakable. It meant he had gone and didn't intend to see her again. She sat down on the blanket, the letter shaking in her hands.

'Why, why?' she wailed.

Mannie thinks I have another boyfriend. Tsamkxao?

She sprang up, indignant that he could think she'd give her heart to another so easily. And what evidence did he have for his belief? she wondered. Then it came to her: Chu!ko's shoes. Mannie knew them as hers. The shoes she'd given Chu!ko. But this was a simple misunderstanding, which she could explain. She would go after him. He couldn't have been gone long.

*

The horse's trail was fresh, the imprint of hooves in the dew-covered sand obvious in the dawning light. But Mannie had galloped. She could imagine him whipping up the animal to keep it at full stretch. The horse would have obliged, probably petrified to be out in the predator-scented open, Koba thought. She didn't have time to worry about that herself. Judging by what people had said of the route, even if she ran she would arrive in Tsumkwe many hours after Mannie.

Run she did, her feet finding the dark hoof-hollows like they were stepping stones. Come sunrise she found she was still jogging. 'Like a tireless jackal. Love makes my feet light, my limbs liquid,' she sang. Her kaross streamed out behind her like a wing; she felt she was flying.

As the heat increased, the miles seemed to lengthen. She slowed, feeling the sun bearing down on her. There was no time to rest. She picked up a branch with a spray of grey-green leaves and carried it like a sun shade. Eventually it felt too heavy to hold aloft. She knew she should stop and rest under one of the thorn trees along the way, but there was no time. She stumbled on.

'He loves me, he came to find me, now I must find him,' she burbled to herself. Every panted breath seemed to scald her parched lips. She needed to drink, but there was no time to stop and search for water. She had to find Mannie before he moved on.

We will go to Botswana and find work and help with the struggle-thing and live and live. Live and live. Live, live, live, like in those story books Marta showed me. Happily ever after.
Happily
Ever
After
Happily
Ever
After
Happilyhappilyhappily . . .
Everevereverev . . .

25

Koba came to, lying face down in sand that smelled strange – a mix of urine and yeast. Wrinkling her nose, she pushed herself up onto her elbows. A giant cup of tea wavered before her. A mirage. She reached for it. Hot. Scalding hot. A name materialized below the cup: MAZ-A-WA-TEE. Hot, metallic letters floated yellow and red above her eyeline. She sat up and saw she'd fallen in front of a corrugated-iron wall. It radiated afternoon heat. A billboard urged her to drink Mazawatee tea.

Drink. Her mouth felt parched, her tongue welded to her palate. When she withdrew it she felt she was ripping away a layer of membrane. Was this Tsumkwe? She didn't recall getting here. How long had she been lying against this galvanized grille?

She looked around. She saw a rutted dirt street and two concrete buildings huddled together, self-conscious of their incongruity in this impermanent landscape. Where were the people; someone she might ask about Mannie? And what was that smell?

It was coming from the crushed cartons strewn about. Chibuku. Kaffirbeer, the people at Impalala used to call it. She'd never tasted it; the smell didn't appeal, but it was liquid and she was desperate. She held her nose and lifted the carton to her lips.

Dominee Venter shook his head as he walked past. Even wild Bushmen, clearly unused to the smell of Chibuku, were now drinking it. Tragic. He folded his hands behind his back and plodded off, head down.

Koba saw a marabou stork walking ponderously away. He was narrow and stooped, white hands clasped behind him like folded wings. He seemed to be making for the building with the cross on the roof.

Mannie's dominee! She tried to stand up, but her legs gave way. 'Sir, dominee,' she called, but her voice was weak and the stork tramped on. Koba tried again: 'Dominee, verskoon my . . .'

Fanie Venter stopped and looked around. Who'd spoken to him in educated Afrikaans; surely not the Bushman woman now pushing herself drunkenly up against the trading-store wall? Reminding himself that she was God's child, he stomped back to her.

Koba preferred not to ask the marabou about Mannie. Her dealings with whites had been jinxed, and this subject was too precious. Instead she asked if she might see the body of the woman killed two days ago.

'You are family, are you?' Fanie Venter asked. Koba nodded. The stork looked as though he wanted to say more, but had decided to keep his beak closed for the moment. He indicated for her to follow him. She did, walking slowly on feet that felt swollen and sore. 'Wait here,' he said when they reached a yard outside the church building. He disappeared and Koba sank onto a low, whitewashed wall. She stared at the sunflowers drooping against the wall opposite, like spent dancers. I should gather the seed, she thought, easy food, but she was too tired to move.

A door opened and the stork returned with a chipped enamel mug and a pitcher.

'I think you need this,' he said, pouring water out for her. She grabbed the mug in both hands, banging the rim against her dusty teeth in her haste to get it to her mouth. She glugged it all down, not pausing to breathe, aware only of a delicious wetness soothing her swollen tongue, her raw throat, her rasped palate. When she felt the mug being taken from her grasp, she bobbed her thanks.

Venter poured her another mugful; then another. Koba drank until she could feel the cool liquid all the way up to her eyeballs.

'Thank you very much,' she gasped in Afrikaans.

'Gits, maar jy kan drink soos a Dorsland trekker,' he said. The reference was lost on Koba. Marta had been selective in her history lesson on the ox-waggoned exodus of Afrikaners from British-ruled South Africa in the eighteen hundreds. She hadn't mentioned that many had perished in the Thirstlands.

'Monenie worry nie,' he said, seeing her incomprehension. 'Come, I'll show you your auntie.'

There was only one small window to disperse the darkness of the storeroom, but a candle burned on a shelf above the body. It gave off a waxy smell. Koba stepped in eagerly to escape the heat outside, but immediately felt as if the walls were closing in on her.

She'd had this sensation before; she'd seen dead bodies before, those of her parents.

Mannie had told her she'd lain on her mother's bloody chest soon after she'd been shot. Koba didn't remember. She was afraid of fainting. She gripped the doorframe, fighting panic.

When her vision cleared, she saw a pallid version of N!ai's face before her, bound up in what Koba could only think of as a toothache cloth. Was it just this strange frame that made her surrogate mother look unfamiliar, she wondered, or was it the stillness, the absence of essence, of N!ai-ness? Without the upturned lips and fleeting dimple, this face was barely recognizable as N!ai's. She hoped |Asa and Zuma would take comfort from that when they saw her.

N!ai's hands were folded across her chest, her fingers like slim brown sepals at the collar of the yellow dress. To Koba's relief there were no blood stains. Silently she begged forgiveness for bequeathing her the fatal dress.

'It was yours, wasn't it?' Venter said.

Koba looked alarmed.

'Don't worry; nobody's blaming you, my girl. Your friend, the young man, told me something about your situation.'

'Oh, sir, did you see him today? Where can I find him?'

'He left just after lunch. He had a bulldozer to return.' Venter said severely.

Koba wondered if she'd understood correctly. What was Mannie doing with a piece of heavy machinery? He'd obviously displeased the marabou. He explained about the road camp about an hour to the south of Tsumkwe.

The desperation in her face made him speak kindly. 'I'd take you there, but my little Volksie won't make it with the road like it is now, even though your young man has flattened the edges. But I tell you what, we'll find you a place to sleep and in the morning you can take the donkey.'

The marabou was good-hearted, Koba thought, but there was no need to tell him that time was against her. Mannie would be heading for the Spears, but she had no idea where the rendezvous point was. She had to catch up with him well before he reached the comrades. The expedition to Angola sounded too dangerous.

They both heard the self-important rev of a powerful engine gearing down. Venter looked startled, put his fingers to his lips and moved to the window.

Koba wasn't tall enough to see out, but she heard the vehicle skid to a stop close by. Immediately two doors were flung open.

'It's the police,' Venter whispered. 'I'm sure you have nothing to hide, but maybe it's better to make yourself scarce.' He hurried out.

Koba eyed the window. She could fit through it, but she'd have to reach it first. A drum of kerosene stood in the opposite corner under an overhanging shelf. She was about to roll it towards the window when she heard voices. She dived into the dark behind the drum.

'Well-well, sooner than I expected, Officer. We've been cut off for days because of the road.' The marabou was making a poor job of hiding his surprise, Koba felt.

'Ja-no, it's still bad in places, but they've flattened the bush a bit, so . . .' she heard a familiar voice say. Then Koba heard man-talk about routes and vehicles, then, recognizably, the policeman said he'd come to investigate a hit-and-run accident. Koba knew now who he was: the honey badger who'd met her at Onderwater station, the one who cared more for handcuffs than for people. She shrank back further behind the barrel.

'Let me offer you a cup of coffee first, Sergeant Du Pree?'

'No thanks, Dominee, if you can just show me the body . . .'

'Ja-but, don't you want to examine the scene of the crime? Before it gets dark, I mean.'

'My boy will see to that – Boysie, look smart, jong.'

Two pairs of feet stepped into the room. The voices were louder now. Du Pree snickered. 'Did she die of toothache?'

Koba heard a long pause then Venter's icy tone.

'I am not a doctor, but I'd say it was the bakkie reversing deliberately over her skull that killed her. If my wife hadn't bound her up like that, I think you'd find her left eye somewhere near her ear, Sergeant.'

'Oh-ja, sorry, I didn't mean any disrespect. Ja-ja, I see. Mmm, no wait, it's a bit dark in here. Can you switch on the lights?'

'The generator hasn't kicked in yet. There's a candle, or I can fetch you a torch.'

'No-no. I've got one here . . .'

Koba heard a click and saw a beam of light.

No sound, then the police officer said: 'Hmm . . . She's older, um, a *mature* Bushman female, wouldn't you say? Non-traditional clothes; a very distinctive yellow dress.' Koba could almost hear the policeman's brain ticking over. 'Tell me, Dominee, did you know this woman?'

'Well-now, I saw her the day before. It's in the statement I gave over the telephone. She came to the door with a man who was looking for a lift.'

'A man? A kaffir, er, bantu?'

Koba heard a spike of interest in Du Pree's voice.

'Was he known to you?'

She thought she heard the shake of the marabou's head.

'So, a stranger.' A pen was scratching across paper, fast. 'And where did he say he wanted to go?'

'To the Workers' Compensation Hospital in Johannesburg. He was an amputee and his stump was giving him trouble.'

'Could *he* have been the driver of the bakkie that hit her?'

'Ag-shame no, he could hardly walk, let alone drive. Listen, son, it's in my statement, along with the fact that my wife and I both smelled alcohol on the deceased. I'm sorry to say she may have been drunk.'

'Ja. They get motherless-drunk easily, do these folk.' Du Pree's interest waned. He began to swing the beam idly around the storeroom. Koba tensed as the silence grew and the beam came closer.

'Come, let's leave the poor woman in peace,' Venter said. With more urgency than Koba thought he should have.

'Good so, Dominee.' Reluctant footsteps and, from the doorway, Koba heard Du Pree ask, 'By the way, you haven't seen any strange *white* men around lately, have you? Young men; a boy . . .'

'Oh, there you are, Fanie.'

Koba heard the bustle of a tray.

'This coffee's getting cold, so I've brought it to you.'

'Ag thanks, Elsie, we're just coming.' Koba heard the relief in the marabou's voice as they left the storeroom.

She waited five minutes then, with a last look at N!ai, Koba slipped out. She had to find Mannie before the policeman did. She had to warn him. But where did the dominee keep his tame animals?

Despite getting back from Tsumkwe late the previous night, Du Pree strode across the red-polished cement step of the Onderwater police station early the next morning. He had a plan.

The Marais boy was still in the area; he'd bet his pay packet on that. The dominee had met him and didn't want to admit it. The old bird had been in a flap about the last question, Du Pree thought.

Du Pree took off his jacket and hung it neatly on the peg behind the office door. Dominee and his missus had something to hide, make no mistake. That was why he'd left Boysie there to see what he could find out from the local kaffirs; though whether Bushmen would talk to a Damara tribesman without being forced to was another matter. Du Pree sighed.

He walked over to the high windowsill in the office and stuck his finger into each of the two flower pots standing there. African violets. He wasn't keen on pot plants himself, not on any kind of bloody plants, but these had been brought in by his superior's wife, Mrs Adelmann: 'To cheer the place up,' she'd said. Du Pree kept them fed and watered.

He heard the shuffle of slippers on the lino outside his office. Lena, another cast-off from the boss's wife, employed as the station cleaner and tea girl. Lena, the bane of his office life. The Ovambo woman neither cleaned well nor made good tea. She deserved the sack, if you asked him; plenty of hungry kaffirs out there who'd be only too glad to have the job. But Lena was one of Mrs Adelmann's good causes.

As usual, Lena's tramped-down footwear slap-slapped past his door without pause. A dozen times he'd told her she should take the drinks orders on her way in, but did she listen?

'Morning, Lena,' he sang out from behind his desk. 'Coffee, two sugars, quick-quick.' Stupid cow. He sat down and began mulling over the Tsumkwe situation.

The whole business with the run-over Bushman woman was confusing the picture. He suspected that twisted son-of-a-bitch, André Marais. The oke was stupid enough to ride down the one pedestrian in a street so empty even weeds didn't blow across it. And callous enough to reverse back over the body. And who else drove a bakkie with Firestone 125s and had an obsession with Bushman women? First the little one from the station and now this one.

Du Pree could remember neither the name nor the face of the Bushman female he'd collected from the station, but her yellow dress had stuck in his mind. The fact that another Bushman woman had turned up wearing it suggested André may not have disposed of her all those months ago, after all.

But why kill the older Bushman woman? Du Pree wondered, clasping his chin between thumb and forefinger. Mistaken identity – had to be.

The bastard hears his cousin is here, guesses the boy is going to find his kaffir sweetheart and races off to stop him – family honour, maybe? Ja-well, Marais was a proud bastard and a well-connected one, Du Pree reminded himself.

Du Pree decided his own career prospects would be best served by finding young Manfred Marais. He steepled his fingers in front of his chest as he went over his notes:

A. Counter-insurgency is the future. SWAPO and the other so-called liberation movements are going to be increasingly troublesome – obvious from the intelligence reports coming in.

B. Stationed here in Onderwater: ideally placed to monitor activity to and from the north-west and the north-east, right where the terrorists would be coming into and leaving from. Possibility of a cell of insurgents working in the area, maybe with a big cache of illegal arms or route plans for smuggling new recruits across the border for military training by the commies.

He leaned back. If he could find such a cell then that would get him noticed, that was for fokken sure. And it wasn't just instinct that led him to believe Mannie Marais was up to something illegal. There were supporting facts. He made a list of them:

1. Report received – SAP, Pretoria 23.12.64. Suspect fraternized w. known ANC members, Jeppe St Police Station, Jhbg.
2. Marta Helena Marais (née Hoffman) – suspect's mother, linked to anti-apartheid activists in SA.
3. Manfred Hoffman Marais, arrested for contravention of the Immorality Act – kaffir-lover. Prison tag: 'Hotnot Romeo'. ANC recruit? Going for MK training?

For sure! Du Pree punched his fist into the palm of his other hand. If he could find Hotnot Romeo he could follow him all the way to a rendezvous with extra pips on his shoulders.

Which was why he was in the office bright and early, he thought. Now, he had a helluva lot to organize if he was going bush-whacking for a while. Good job old Adelmann was away on holiday; he could draw what he needed from the stores without having to explain. But where was his coffee?

'Lena!'

Nothing. He flung himself up from his chair and strode to the door. 'Lena!' he bellowed down the passage, making the Governor of the Protectorate of South West Africa tremble in his frame on the wall.

He found Lena in Adelmann's office sweeping dust from one corner to another. She stared at him from under her enormous anvil-shaped headscarf, but didn't move when he demanded coffee, first in German, then in Afrikaans. Was she being insolent or was she even more stupid than he'd thought? he wondered. Either way, his caffeine craving was so great he might assault her. He went to phone André Marais instead.

'Did I get you out of bed, ou maat?'

André winced at the crackle of the phone against his ear. It had been a brandy and Coke night. He always needed a lot of doubles when his mother wanted him to play cards. Now it felt like someone was using steel wool to scour the inside of his skull.

'Er, morning, man. No-no, I'm up. Er, just going crop-spraying, so ja, what can I do for you?'

'An official enquiry, I'm afraid.'

Du Pree enjoyed hearing André swallow rapidly. 'I've just been in Tsumkwe investigating a hit-and-run case . . .' Not even the sound of the fat bastard breathing now. 'Victim was an unknown Bushman female wearing quite a distinctive yellow dress, one with a frilly business around the neck. You know the one I mean.'

'Er . . .' André cleared his throat. 'I can't say I'm one for noticing what kaffirgirls wear, ou maat.'

'Funny, I'm just the opposite. Men, women, Bantus, whites, I notice the smallest things; and I remember them, hey!' Squirm, you fat worm, Du Pree thought. 'Ja-no,' he continued, 'I've definitely seen the dress before, I could testify in court to that. Mind you, it wasn't on the victim at the time. It was on another woman, a much younger one. But to get back to the deceased – a mature female, quite different from the other one, especially with her skull all crushed. Not a pretty sight. If you can imagine someone using a fifty-pound hammer on a boiled egg . . .'

He paused to let the information sink in.

Might take a while, he thought. He heard a snort. Here it comes.

'Listen, you fok! If you're accusing me of . . .' Then André seemed to remember he was on a party line with the country's most curious operator. 'You, you' – his voice trembled – 'I'll meet you in your office, with my lawyer, then we'll hear your fokken . . .'

Du Pree sighed. The fun was over. Even if he impounded the bastard's bakkie right now and took it to forensics, he'd still have to find witnesses, build a case and then persuade the prosecutor it was worth bringing one of the region's eminent citizens to court for the sake of justice for an unknown Bushman woman whose family didn't even know they had recourse to the law.

Best to concentrate on counter-terrorism. 'I don't recall accusing you of anything, ou maat. My enquiry's about your cousin, Manfred Marais. Have you or your mother seen or heard anything from him or his family since we last spoke?'

An hour later, after he'd made his own coffee and drunk two cups in succession, Du Pree swung the fully equipped pick-up out of the police-station yard. The morning had not been unproductive. He tuned the police radio to Springbok and whistled along as the presenter announced 'Hospitaal Tyd' over the programme's catchy jingle.

26

Du Pree found Gerrit Wolfaardt in the middle of a self-made dust storm, levelling the dirt road to Tsumkwe like he bore it a deep grudge. The giant blade rammed into the earth so hard Du Pree saw the front wheels of the huge grader lift.

Du Pree soon found out why. On Boxing Day, Gerrit's girlfriend from Upington had sent him packing, for no good reason, the young man complained. Now Gerrit wanted to finish the project, take his money and get back to the city lights. He wasn't interested in availing himself of the construction industry holiday.

Staying seated high up in the yellow cab he confirmed he'd had a visitor at the camp, both before and after Christmas. 'Ja, seemed a nice enough youngster, but the nightwatchman tells me the little skelm took the bulldozer for a ride one night. Bosbefok, I suppose. You get like that out here in the sticks. Not me, no siree. I'm buggering off before it happens. Don't want to be reduced to getting my kicks from driving a 'dozer at thirty miles an hour.'

Du Pree narrowed his black eyes. 'What happened to the joyrider?'

'Nothing. He brought the bulldozer back with not a mark on it *and* he paid for the diesel, so no harm done, hey?'

'You should press charges,' Du Pree urged. 'Company property's your responsibility and you say the bulldozer was taken without permission.'

'Forget it, man. I'm not coming back to this dump if I can help it.'

To Du Pree's annoyance, the foreman wouldn't be persuaded, so all he could do was take down a description of Gerrit's visitor. As expected, it matched that of the youth he'd given a lift to; the one he had a picture of in his file; the one who'd unaccountably had charges against him dropped by the South African Police. Ja-no, Manfred Hoffman Marais is one lucky youngster, Du Pree thought. 'So when did this oke leave?' he asked.

'Sparrow's fart this morning.'

'Did he say where he was going?'

'To the Himba area, I think. Kaokoveld, isn't it?'

Du Pree drove away due west, sun directly overhead. It was hot, but if he opened the windows on both sides of the cab he'd get a through-draught, he thought. The dust wouldn't be too bad after the heavy rains. He'd drive along the dirt track in the direction of the Kaokoveld for a while and then cut through the savannah grass and head northwards, skirting the Etosha game reserve, he decided. There was no way young Marais was going to the Himba lands. That boy was headed for the border or his name wasn't Hendrik Cornelius Du Pree. Ja-no, the little commie would cross the Okavango river then disappear into Angola; ANC recruits did. But this one was in for a surprise, Du Pree thought.

Koba was already on Mannie's trail. Several hours earlier, unseen by Gerrit, she'd approached the nightwatchman and learned that Mannie had been and gone. The old man was uncommunicative until Koba explained that she knew Mannie's people. 'They raised me,' she said.

The nightwatchman looked interested and invited her to sit in one of the folding chairs he'd appropriated in Gerrit's absence.

'Grandfather will have to excuse me. The man I speak of has forgotten something and I must go after him to return it,' Koba said, trying to sound calm.

'You *met* with this white man in Tsumkwe?' the old man asked, looking surprised.

Koba nodded. It would take too long to explain the facts correctly, she thought.

The old man appraised her through narrowed eyes, then he said, 'He is not bad for a white man, that boy. We had some sport.' He pointed to a bulldozer parked near by and winked. 'But you will find trouble if you mix yourself with him, daughter.'

Koba didn't understand the wink, but felt the old man could be right about trouble ahead. She had a faint tapping sensation in her chest she suspected had nothing to do with the exertion of kicking hard at the ribs of the horse all the way here. But she was going to ignore her tappings, just as she planned never to rely on oracle discs again. It was time to follow her heart and only the old man knew which way that had gone. She beseeched him for information.

'Aie, you like him too much,' the old man said, shaking his head. 'Well, you will soon catch him, on your animal. He walks.'

Koba explained that the horse wasn't hers and begged the nightwatchman to return it to Tsumkwe when he could.

'You borrowed the animal?' he asked.

Koba nodded, looking uncomfortable. She was baffled when he burst into laughter. His dangling earlobes danced with glee.

I have no time to be this man's entertainment, she thought. 'Please, grandfather.'

The nightwatchman said with a sigh, 'He walked away with the sun shining on his fighting arm, early, early this morning.'

In grey calcrete dust Koba found Mannie's trail. He walked like a white man, trudging so heavily it was as if he'd ploughed a furrow with his feet. She'd catch up with him soon enough.

The thing I never dared look for is just beyond the rim of the horizon. Hnn, hnnn, hnnnn – ya, ya, yaay!

She gave a little skip and began to loosen her hair ornaments. First the three at the back, then the white-beaded triangular one that hung over her forehead. She tossed them into a bush and started on the next one, all the time keeping up a chant and a mile-crunching pace.

This world had different colours from the one she'd left, different too from Impalala – grey here, and lilac, with blue in the stones, fine yellow grass and gliding green birds with blushing faces. She stopped briefly to watch these parrot-like side-steppers screech at one another as they competed for grass seed.

She was determined to find Mannie and stop him joining the Spears. Together they could go anywhere. If Mannie said Botswana, she would follow him there, no matter what the discs had predicted.

How will the colours and the birds look in Botswana? she wondered.

And my house? It must have thick brick walls for coolness, a tin roof for the rain to bounce off; a safe nest for our baby. I will cook that white food he likes. What-they-call-it, looks like termites' eggs, doesn't taste as good . . . *rice*, that's the name. I will cook it on the stove.

You don't know how to use a stove, Bushgirl.

She hesitated mid-stride.

You don't know how to cook /Ton things, or clean them.

I will learn. My Frog-boy will teach me.

Your neighbours will laugh at your Ju/'hoan ways. You know black people call us Masarwa and think we are animals.

Hold your tongue, Cricket. They will not laugh if I am the wife of a white man. They will not laugh at my big husband with his golden hair.

She tossed her unadorned head and walked with lifted chin.

A few miles further on and Koba's unease got the better of her excitement. Aside from the soft drumming in her chest, the skin of her back prickled, as if someone was watching her. She whipped round and looked. Nothing to see but sere grass, bending under a breeze. She listened, buck-alert, and heard the krik-krak of insects, the hot hum of earth baked by the afternoon sun and a faint rattle from the north – palm leaves clattered by wind on the Okavango riverbank, far, far away.

I wish the passing wind would double-back and whisper what it sees down the track, she thought. But the breeze continued on its way and so did she, gaining on Mannie with every step. He seemed to be walking towards the spreading acacia whose dark umbrella punctuated the lake-bed flatness of the landscape. A too-obvious landmark, she sighed to herself.

A few more sweating miles and she caught snatches of sound on the hot wind. Men, not too far ahead; perhaps right under the acacia. Its base was hidden from her view by a thicket of lacy grey thornscrub. She crept towards it, silently as a civet. She heard Mannie's voice.

'Better late than never, hey?'

Her cracked lips split into a grin. Two other voices, men speaking township English.

'Ha-ha-ha, Hotnot Romeo! We have been sitting here long time waiting for you. "Moses," I said, "he will not keep a date with *us*; with a little brown maid, sure thing, but with his comrades? Aikona!"'

'Howzit, bra,' said Moses. 'Glad to see you got balls to come back, man. We thought you were a lover not a fighter. Heh-heh.'

Koba peered through the lattice of leaves. Mannie was shaking hands with two young black men whose accoutrements puzzled her. Both wore army boots, but the uniformity stopped there. The smaller – Moses, she thought – had a white helmet on. It was daubed with tufts of rabbit fur and some guinea fowl feathers. Across his chest he'd draped an ammunition belt. Cigarettes stuck out of the cartridge compartments. He had a knobkierie shoved into his belt and a machete hung down his back.

His taller companion – Jabu? – had wrapped strips of animal skin, hard to see what kind, around his red-trousered legs. Over one shoulder hung a mangy-looking leopard skin. Koba imagined it had served many years underfoot. Jabu wore it like the mantle of a Zulu warrior, along with the horns he'd attached to his red beret. Cow horns.

Koba wanted to laugh. The skinny young men reminded her of the thorn tree saplings Marta used to decorate with bright baubles for Christmas. But she didn't like the look of the machetes both boys had. Jabu's weapon protruded from the scuffed brown school satchel at his feet.

Their camping spot was littered with spent cartridges and crushed beer cans. Koba noted the shattered bones of a large bird amid a pile of feathers with large gobs of flesh still stuck to them. Hnnpff, to shoot a bird and then not eat it all, she thought.

More dismaying was Mannie's diffident attitude towards the pair.

These must-be the comrades he met in prison. But they are children! They should be playing in their mothers' yards with stick guns. They pronk-pronk like a pair of baby springbok in borrowed horns. A big bull will make them tuck their flashing tails between their legs and run away. I must take Mannie from them.

Koba rose to leave her hiding place, but found that her thighs trembled so violently she didn't trust them to support her. She told herself it was from all the running she'd done in the last two days.

No, is because you feel shame for the way you are dressed, Bushgirl.

Why should I feel ashamed in front of boys dressed from a rubbish heap?

Their bodies have /Ton clothes; you have only animal skins to cover your nakedness.

Noiselessly she wriggled further into her kaross. She did care what Mannie's companions would think of her, and of him, once they realized who she was. She would wait until he was alone. Then she could explain about the shoes. She would tell him she wanted to go to Botswana. They should go soon.

Ten minutes later, the men were still teasing Mannie as they leaned against the tree, smoking. Moses pulled a carton of Chibuku from his bundle. They passed it between them. She smiled sympathetically when she saw Mannie grimace as he took a swig, but she hoped he'd have more. It would bring on a need to urinate and then he'd separate from the clowns and walk into the bush.

Minutes passed and, though her legs felt stronger, her unease grew. Presentiment of danger or a longing to be with Mannie, it didn't matter what the cause was, she decided, but she couldn't bear to remain hidden any longer. Holding her kaross tightly across her chest she burst out of the scrub.

'Huw-ah!' Moses gasped, spilling the contents of the Chibuku carton down his front. The beer soaked the cigarettes in his bandolier. Jabu, with his back to her, spun round. He had a revolver in his hand and it was aimed at her.

'Wait!' Mannie screamed. He threw himself between her and the gun. 'Koba! What are you doing here?'

Koba's throat tightened. She found she couldn't tell Mannie she'd come to be with him, to walk to Botswana with him as his future wife. She could barely look at him. She was shaking and her fear came not from the weapon pointed at her, but from the derision she'd seen replace alarm on the faces of the black men.

'Who is she?' Jabu demanded.

'It's Koba, my, my . . . girlfriend,' Mannie spluttered, spreading out his arms the better to shield her from the wavering firearm.

'She shouldn't be here! Indaba yamadoda lena,' Jabu fumed, lowering the gun but keeping it unholstered.

Moses began to laugh. 'Heh-heh, so this is Hotnot Juliet. I thought it was a tokoloshe!' He doubled over, slapping his knee with mirth as he pointed at Koba.

Mannie threw himself at Moses, knocking him to the ground. The pith helmet rolled away, a hollow egg half. The boys wrestled in the dirt as Mannie tried to get a punch past Moses' defences.

'Hold this!' Jabu thrust his revolver at Koba, took off his horned beret and tried to pull them apart. He was soon drawn into the fray. To Koba it looked like a heaving, hissing, multi-limbed dust devil. She felt afraid for them all. For all their teasing and horseplay, she'd never seen Jul'hoan youth fight seriously – purposely injuring another was unheard of among her people.

'Stop, stop,' she pleaded, but the flailing dustball rolled on. The tapping in her chest had turned into a violent tattoo. She suddenly realized Mannie was fighting for his life, not just for her honour – she saw Moses reaching for the machete on his back.

Two-handed, Koba pointed the revolver skywards and fired. The scuffling men froze like leverets caught in lights.

Jabu was first on his feet. 'Give me the gun,' he demanded.

'It's all right, Kobatjie.'

Mannie's voice behind her, then she felt his arm encircle her and gently remove the weapon from her shaking grip. She turned and crumpled against his chest. She wasn't aware she was sobbing until she heard him say, 'Hush, liebchen,' the words Marta used to comfort him as a crying boy. She felt him cup the nape of her neck with his palm, his thumb stroked her, her tappings lessened. She burrowed into his warm chest, smelling salt and dust and his musky man-boyishness. She was where she belonged. She was home. 'True n!ore,' she murmured, lifting her face to gaze up at him through tears of joy. She saw that buttons had been torn from his shirt, that he had twigs in his hair, but he was smiling broadly. He would know she had no other boyfriend, never would have.

She remembered a scrap she'd got into with Mannie when they were children. They'd rolled in the dirt, tumbling down a riverbank into the water. Marta had been furious – crocodiles, she'd yelled – but they'd sat in the shallows, covered in mud and grinned at each other for the first time. Koba relaxed. Children fought, and these pretend soldiers were just that.

Then she heard it: the unmistakable drone of an engine, an engine whose voice she knew. It was the self-important truck she'd heard pull up outside the church storeroom in Tsumkwe. An image of the policeman's badger-face sprang into her mind's eye. Had he come for Mannie with some biting handcuffs? Had he led André here? Now she understood the reason for her palpitations. The man must have followed Mannie's spoor, as she had, but much faster. And he must have heard the gunshot.

Jabu thought so too. 'You brought someone here, you brought the pol-is,' he shouted, springing towards her with bunched fists.

'Now wait a minute.' Mannie squared up to him. 'Koba would never have . . .'

Standing next to the arguing men, Koba had the feeling that she wasn't there. She heard Mannie's spirited defence of her as he gave the agitated black man a potted history of what she had suffered, much of it at the hands of the police, he claimed. Koba kept her eyes down, for once glad of being spoken of as if she wasn't there.

Yet it wasn't the conversation that was making her absent herself. It was something to do with her tappings. Like bony knuckles, they rapped insistently at the hatches she'd battened down against them. She felt too weak from lack of food and rest to resist. She closed her eyes momentarily and immediately felt herself and her child being lifted up. A lullaby sounded in the sky; she hummed along, rocked by the wind and cradled by the clouds. She opened dreamy eyes and looked down on Etosha. There were four giraffes, drinking splay-legged from a waterhole, and a herd of twitching springbok, two hundred strong, that filled her hunter's heart with hope. She could also see people, herself included, the small, still one, watching Jabu and Mannie snarling at each other like dogs and Moses, the meerkat, dashing, bustling, bundling up scattered belongings as if they were stray pups.

And the police van, there it was, bumping and bucking across the yellow-grey land, still far off, but heading inexorably towards the acacia tree. She wanted to swoop down and whisper in Mannie's ear that she could lead him out of danger. She could show him how to hide in this empty land.

Like a honey guide I would flit before you, show you where to walk, my love. I will lead you to the sunrise, far-far from these dangerous boys, away from the pol-is who want to send you back to prison, away from the Unknowable that stalks us somewhere out here.

She tried to concentrate her mind on the immediate danger. Getting Mannie safely away would mean leaving the comrades to their own devices – no time to hide Christmas trees in the grass, she thought. They must fight, or flee. She was sure they'd be caught or killed.

I don't care. They think I'm a tokoloshe.

They cannot be bad boys – only stupid ones. They are going to fight for justice for black people. This will help the Real People too, in the end.

Insect was right, Koba thought, but she didn't want to listen.

Despite Marta's best efforts, Koba didn't care for politics. She was too busy trying to balance on the narrow ledge of her own existence, a place outside both the white and the Jul'hoan worlds. She resented being shunted forwards and backwards across the subcontinent on the whim of first one group and then another. But with the insistence of her tappings came the thought that her own dislocation was why there needed to be a fight.

But I am not a fighter. I am just trying to stay alive, to live and live my own life with my Frog-boy. We are too young to do big things.

That is not the thing you said to !Asa. You said people should get up off the sand and do things for themselves.

Heavy people, yes, not small ones like me.

Jabu's shouts intruded on her thoughts. 'Why she come here, hey? She could be a sellout, spying for the pol-is. Why I must not think that, hey-hey?' Jabu's neck muscles were roped with rage.

In that instant Koba felt herself fall back to earth. She was not nothing; she'd stood by long enough. 'Am I an ant?' she asked Jabu.

'Eh?' he said, blinking.

She put her hand on her hip. Her kaross opened, baring one breast. 'You talk about me like I am a thing of the ground, a thing you walk over. You are not the only one who has reason to fight the pol-is. *My* reasons would make a stone weep, but *you* do not need to know them.' She yanked her kaross closed. She didn't want him to see her heart thumping. 'Only one thing you must know: I came here for *this* man. I love him and I want to be with him.' She heard a yell from Mannie. 'Is not possible to hide my man now that he stands among people with no bush-sense, so I will help you all . . .'

Mannie could wait no more. He lifted Koba clean off the ground and hugged her hard, then he danced her around the acacia tree, not letting her feet touch the ground. 'She loves me, she loves me, she *loves me*!' he shouted.

Jabu and Moses stared at him open-mouthed. 'He dances in the face of danger!' Jabu shook his head.

'A lover not a fighter, I told you, bra,' Moses said. Then all three began to laugh – too long, too loud, Koba thought, hearing the hysterical tone of condemned men making jokes.

Jabu sobered up soonest. 'You say you can help us, little sister. How?'

Mannie put her down, but kept his arm around her.

'First, you must make this look like a poacher's camp.'

Mannie laughed. 'Ja-jong. You two are a real pair of baaries when it comes to the bush, hey?' He kicked at a discarded tin can. 'Tomato pilchards! What big game hunter's gonna eat tinned fish, hey?'

Koba cut in. 'No time for games. You men must pick up your rubbish and run.'

'Hey? Wait now, where will you be?' Mannie asked.

'Doing women's work. Sweeping you-all away.'

Moses and Jabu laughed, but Mannie's face crashed. He alone grasped what she had in mind. 'No,' he protested, '*no!* You can't sit here and wait for them to find you. They'll arrest you.'

She needed to look him in the eye to convince him. She slipped out of his embrace and explained the only way all three of them could escape was for her to be the decoy.

'No! You'll go back to jail. They arrest poachers in game reserve areas.'

'What they will arrest me for? *I* am not shooting animals. They will think I am the maid for this camp.'

Mannie would not be mollified. 'If it's the oke who collected you from the station he'll recognize you!'

'No. I was Yellow Dress last time the pol-isman saw me. Now, like this.' She indicated her skins.

Jabu was rooting around in his satchel. 'Look.' He pulled out a square of pink cotton cloth and hurried over to tie it around her head in the style of a domestic servant's scarf.

'Wear it like so and he will not know you. Honkies think all "meide" look the same.'

Mannie ripped it off Koba's head. 'Don't touch her,' he snapped.

Jabu backed off, hands up, showing the pale of his palms. 'Sorry, buti, sorry, sisi, no disrespect, okay?'

Mannie ignored him. He wanted no more to do with these men, especially Jabu. Out of his element, a police cell, the young Zulu didn't seem so fly. And Moses was pathetic. A court jester for Prince Jabu. Who did he think he was, ordering Koba around?

But Mannie saw, too, how childish he'd been, trying to impress the MK boys with his liberal-white credentials. Their war wasn't his war and all he wanted to do now was put as much distance as possible between his girlfriend and these men. He'd fight apartheid, but in his own way. After all, as Moses had said, he was a lover, not a fighter.

He turned to Koba. She was gazing at him with a look he'd never seen before. What was it? he wondered.

In the old days, not long ago, he'd known all the expressions of her beautiful face. When she was happy she blazed a burnished gold.

When she laughed hard everything turned up – her toes, her nose, her mouth, even her eyelashes seemed to curl more. When she was sad she was still as water in a secret pool.

He put his arm under her elbow and hurried her away from the men, who were scrabbling in the sand to collect the telltale AK47 bullet casings. 'You don't have to play decoy for them, Koba. Me and you can still go to Botswana. I've got a compass. I know the bearings. You find a place for us to hide, and when the danger's passed, I'll get us there.' She tried to shake him off. He held her by the triceps and forced her to look at him. 'Jissus, Koba! We've been through *so much* to be together – you and me both. Don't we deserve a chance now? Please, man, let's not part again, not even for five minutes.'

A tear slid from the corner of her eye and down her cheek. 'I came here to tell you we should go to Botswana. I was ready. And to tell you something else . . .' She smeared the wet away. 'Now, with the pol-is coming, we must make another plan. I have to hide our paths. Can you not see there is no time to sweep two trails? Must we leave them' – she jerked her head towards the two boys – 'to be hunted and shot?'

She didn't need to say any more. Mannie had a vivid image of being in a truck chasing fleeing black figures. On troubled nights he heard again the shots that had killed Koba's mother and father. He dropped his hands to his sides, ashamed of his selfishness. If Koba could do this for a pair of strangers who'd insulted her, going along with the plan was the least he could do.

Mannie took a deep breath. 'Okay. What do you want us to do?'

Koba issued instructions to the young men and they set about following them.

They relit the fire using damp wood. A very visible column of black smoke rose into the air. Koba nodded and set to sweeping the ground where it was obvious there were four sets of prints. She found missed bullet shells, a Johannesburg bus ticket, pages from *Drum* used as toilet paper. Moses burned them while Jabu hid the blasted bird carcass along with the pilchard can. All the while Mannie hovered, standing so close to Koba she bumped into him twice when she turned around unexpectedly. Another time she would have laughed, told him to step off her shadow. It struck her now that she had none.

Finally, she pronounced the camp convincing enough as a poacher's hideaway.

'Come on, come on,' Jabu shouted.

An open, sandy expanse to cross before they could hide themselves in the long grass. Koba hesitated; they'd be vulnerable out there, meerkats for a buzzard to swoop on, she thought. Mannie grabbed her hand, dragging her along while the comrades raced ahead. 'Stay on the clumps, grass hop, you moegoes!' Mannie shouted at their fleeing backs. 'You're giving Koba too much work.' As they approached a thorn thicket she glimpsed a tiny buck backing into it. It had enormous white-ringed eyes, which gazed out sorrowfully as she passed.

Too soon for Mannie, they reached the long, tawny grass. He felt Koba pull her hand from his. The foursome looked back towards the camp. A dust cloud barrelled towards it.

'Go!' Koba said.

Moses addressed himself to Mannie's heaving chest. 'That is a *very* big woman . . . that one.' He saluted Koba. 'I am sorry of the disrespect.'

'Thank you, Comrade Koba,' Jabu panted, then with a clenched fist salute and 'Amandla!' he was gone.

'Go well,' Koba said softly, watching them winnow away.

As soon as they were out of earshot Mannie spoke. 'Okay. I'm gonna go with them as far as the river and then I'm coming back.'

Koba snapped to attention. '*No!* Mannie, I'm not doing this for them only. I've got a bad-bad feeling inside. If you don't go you will *die*. There is something, something . . .' She gestured vaguely. 'I can feel it here!' She slapped her chest. 'You must go where pol-is can't follow. I need you to live, for, for . . .' It wasn't the time. '*Go*. You must!'

'Jis, okay, okay. I promise.' He was taken aback by the force of Koba's fear. He'd never seen her so distressed. He bent down, put his arms around her. 'You come to *me* then, okay? Soon as it's safe for you, you hear? I'll wait, Koba. I'll wait for as long as it takes. And I'll get word to the dominee at Tsumkwe. Okay?'

She nodded against his chest then eased herself from him. He felt it as a rip, as if his skin had been peeled off and his heart exposed.

'You must go.' She gave him a light push on his chest. It felt like a blow.

'Ja.'

'Now!' She took a step away from him.

'We won't kiss?'

'No.' She took another. She was no longer hidden in the grass.

'W-wait . . . how will you find me?'

She tapped her chest. 'True n!ore,' she said, smiling.

Mannie began to back away. Twenty paces from her he called out: 'Do you remember those cowboy fillums? Walking apart like this makes me feel like we're in one.' He quick-drew an imaginary gun. She laughed and raised her hands in surrender, a small brown figure on an open white plain. 'You are my honey.'

'You, my salt.'

Finally he turned and began wading away, breasting through the high grass. The stems sprang back behind him and soon he was lost to her, submerged in a savannah sea. She wrapped her arms around her middle then and began to weep, crouching down and rocking herself and her unborn child. Tears fell into the dust. They looked like the rain-splatter markings on the coat of the dik-dik. Angrily she swept them away with a bushel of grass and set to work eradicating the footprints. One print, then another, then another. His, hers, his, hers.

It was hopeless. The history of their journey stretched out too far behind her. She couldn't wipe it all away. She sat back on her heels, dreading what she had to do. The vehicle closed in; she felt its horse-power charge through the soles of her feet.

And then nothing. The white earth stilled. No engine sound, no bird calls, no wind; the Kalahari had paused, mid-stalk.

The silence was shocking; it rang in Koba's ears. She trembled, but knew she had to stand, be seen; she'd promised to be the decoy. Very slowly she drew the pink scarf from her kaross and tied it around her head. Very slowly she rose.

Her head appeared unexpectedly in that empty landscape, like a pink impala lily thrusting up from the desert floor. To her right a disturbance in the grass, something coming, creeping, leaving seed heads shuddering in its wake. The Unknowable, Koba thought. A shot rang out and she pitched forward, falling face first into the golden grass.

Hours later she would be roused by a flutter inside her womb, a tiny fist unfurling to explore the walls of its cocoon. Koba would open her eyes to see the hunting star dragging itself across the vastness of the Kalahari night sky and know that her journey was far from over.

Glossary

afkak	(literally: shit off) extreme physical exertion
!aia	a state of transcendence
aikona	'no way!' (an informal word expressing strong negation)
amandla	power (a Xhosa and Zulu word used as a rallying cry against apartheid)
baaries	fool
bakgat	marvellous, great
barra	bounty
basie	little boss
blerry	bloody (used as a swear word)
bliksem	(literally: 'lightning') a term of personal abuse, such as swine, bastard
Boesman	(literally: 'Bushman') a word used to describe those who are part of the Khoisan group of the indigenous people of southern Africa. A term with a problematic history, now considered by many to be offensive, with San preferred in official contexts
boet	a brother
boetie	diminutive of a brother
bosbefok	'bush crazy'; to be sent crazy by time spent in the bush
bra	(township-speak for 'brother') a form of address for a male friend; 'dude'
buti	a form of address for a male friend; 'brother'

dusties	the pilots of crop-duster aircraft
fillum	a film or movie
finished and klaar	'and that's that'
gifbakkie	a truck used to carry drums of pesticide used for crop-spraying
gits, maar jy kan drink soos a Dorsland trekker	'God, but you can drink like a Dorsland trekker'
gogga	a creeping thing, a bug
Hotnot	(abbreviation of Hottentot) an offensive term for a Khoisan person
hxaro	the San custom of creating partnerships between people, cemented by the reciprocal act of giving gifts
jislaaik	'good grief' (an expression of astonishment)
jôl	a party, a date
jong	a cub, a child, a puppy (a patronizing form of address)
Jul'hoan	the name of Koba's group (plural: Jul'hoansi)
jy	you
kaalgat	(literally: 'bare-arsed') stark naked
kaffirboetie	(literally: 'kaffir brother') a very offensive term for a white person sympathetic to black people
kak	crap
kaross	a cloak made of animal hide
khakibos	a plant originally grown as horse fodder, named after the khaki-clad British soldiers who first grew it
knobkierie	a round-headed stick used as a club
koeksister	a syrup-coated doughnut in the shape of a plait
kugel	a sphere or ball (German)
lekker-cracker	'sweet!' (an exclamation of delight)
liebchen	darling, sweetheart (German)
liewe Jissus	dear Jesus (used as an exclamation)
liewe magies	good heavens, goodness gracious
lightie	a young boy

mamparra	an idiot
mapuza	the police
Masarwa	a pejorative term for the San/Khoisan people
meid	(plural: meide) a derogatory term for a black woman, from the Dutch for 'girl'
melktert	a traditional Dutch milk tart
mielie	an ear of corn
mi !xa xobo	an expression used when one sees a dearly-loved person who has been away a long time
Mma	a polite form of address to a woman
moegoe	an idiot
moffie	'namby-pamby'
monenie worry nie	don't worry
mos	in fact, actually
n!a'an	a form of respectful address
nogal	'of all things'(an expression of some surprise)
nǀom	a spiritual energy harnessed for healing
nǀomkxao	(plural: nǀomkxaosi) an owner of medicine
n!ore	(literally: 'tree-water'), territory
n!ow	a spiritual energy
oke	a person
ou maat	an old mate, as in 'my old mate'
ouseun	an older son; old boy, as in 'my old boy'
ousus	an older sister; old girl, as in 'my old girl'
poefter	(derogatory slang) a male homosexual
poes	(obscene slang) the female genitalia
posie	home
rondavel	a circular hut with a conical thatched roof
sies-man	an expression of disgust, annoyance and disapproval
sisi	a form of address for a black woman; 'sister'
suid-wester	a settler in the former German colony of South-West Africa, now Namibia
sit die deksel op	put the lid on
seun	a son

thasi nǀa'ang	(literally: 'wearing only your penis'), naked
tjerrie	a slang term for girlfriend
tjoepstil	absolutely silent
tjom	a friend or 'buddy'
ǀTon	a white person
toppies	timers, as in 'old timers'
toyi-toyi	protest dancing
troepies	troops
tsamma	the citron melon, a fruit native to the Kalahari
tsotsi	a gangster, a layabout, a good-for-nothing
twak	nonsense
Umkhonto we Sizwe	Spear of the Nation (MK), the armed wing of the African National Congress
umfaan	a boy (Zulu)
vasbyt	determination
verneuking	cheating
verskoon	excuse, as in 'please excuse my'
vry	to make out or court, to 'snog' or 'neck'
yebo	yes (Zulu)

Note on the Juǀ'hoan People and Language

From the evidence of palaeontological finds and scenes depicted in ancient rock art, experts believe that groups of hunter-gatherers have inhabited parts of southern Africa for 40,000 years or more. The San people of Namibia, Botswana and Angola are thought to be descendants of the stone-age artists. They have been labelled Bushmen, Hottentots, Masarwa, Khoisan and San by westerners and other Africans. However, these people have no collective name for themselves. The particular group in this book have always referred to themselves as Juǀ'hoansi, translating as 'real' or 'ordinary people'.

From their perspective, the world outside their camps was a hostile place. Water and food were scarce, they faced natural predators, such as lion and hyena, and they were persecuted by invading pastoralists, both black and white, for centuries. The San (as some anthropologists now refer to Bushmen) were not blameless, however, sometimes provoking attack from the settler pastoralists by poaching their livestock and stealing the goods of returning migrant workers. It became common practice to shoot 'Bushmen', abduct their children and use them as indentured labourers on settler farms in what was then German South West Africa. Modern times have seen no let-up in the problems faced by these formerly nomadic people, and nowadays the Juǀ'hoansi are unable to live solely by hunting and gathering.

To this day, the Jul'hoansi use a trance dance ceremony for community healing purposes. Jul'hoan shamans claim to derive their healing power from spirit guides, usually antelope, whom they meet in a mystical world when they trance. Some shamans say they have an ear for the voices of their ancestors, who might make their presence felt in the form of mini dust tornadoes, or 'dust devils'. Some members of the Jul'hoansi are able to heal certain physical ailments using their knowledge of medicinal plants.

San languages and dialects are unique in containing the largest inventory of consonants found in any known language. They also have a particularly complex phonology of implosive consonants or 'clicks', which westerners have historically struggled to master. However, the sophisticated verbal arts of click-language-speaking peoples are recognized today as among the most intricate and beautiful in the world.

Only in recent years have linguists developed orthographies – ways to write San languages. These languages have clicks, made when the tongue is drawn sharply away from various points on the roof of the mouth. The main examples found in this novel are:

ǀ	**Dental click**, as in ǀTon, white person. (Sounds like the reproach: 'tsk'). Place the tip of the tongue immediately behind the top front teeth and pull gently away.
ǂ	**Palatal click**, as in Nǂaisa. Similar to above, but made by pressing the front of the tongue to the roof of the mouth (on the ridge just behind top front teeth). The tongue is then withdrawn quickly from the ridge.
!	**Guttural click**, as in Chu!ko. A popping noise made at the back of the mouth, by drawing the end of the tongue away from the curve where the alveolar ridge meets the hard palate.
ǁ	**Lateral click**, as in Gǁaoan. (Similar to the sound one uses to urge a horse forward.) Suck one side of the tongue sharply away from the alveolar ridge.

The language is rich in wordplay, metaphors and euphemism. Conversation is entertainment for the San; they are skilled storytellers and mimics.

Acknowledgements

Thank you to my n!a'an for sharing her Jul'hoan wisdom with me, and to my early readers, Jackie Pieterick, Louka, Xanthe and Yiannis, for their insight and encouragement.

The patience and perspicacity of my editor, Alan Mahar, and copy editor, Emma Hargrave, are greatly appreciated. And thanks to Penny Rendall for pointing me in the right direction.

In Chapter 21 I have used the lyrics of a Jul'hoan children's song, as translated by Dr Megan Biesele, in *Healing Makes Our Hearts Happy*. In the same chapter I have used the words of a healer called Khall'an, which were reported in the same book.

About the Author

Candi Miller, born in Zambia and brought up in South Africa, has been a journalist and advertising copywriter, and now lives in Staffordshire where she teaches Creative Writing. Her first novel in the Koba series is *Salt and Honey*.